An alibi too soon

By the same author

A Death to Remember
Still Life with Pistol
Dead Ringer
Seeing Red
The Hanging Doll Murder

An Alibi Too Soon

by
Roger Ormerod

Charles Scribner's Sons
New York

Charles Scribner's Sons
Macmillan Publishing Company
866 Third Avenue, New York, NY 10022

This is a work of fiction. Names, characters, places, and
incidents either are the product of the author's imagination or are
used fictitiously. Any resemblance to actual events or persons,
living or dead, is entirely coincidental.

Library of Congress Cataloging-in-Publication Data

Ormerod, Roger.
    An alibi too soon / by Roger Ormerod.—1st American ed.
      p.   cm.
    ISBN 0-684-18930-5
    I. Title.
    PR6065.R688A79   1987
    823'.914—dc19   87-37457
                                      CIP

10 9 8 7 6 5 4 3 2 1

I

It seemed a good idea to take a break at Welshpool, as it was quite obvious we would be very late home if I drove straight through. Amelia was excited about the place we'd found – a converted water-mill – and was chattering away like mad as I hunted out a hotel, but I didn't need persuading. I loved it too. As we were unpacking we decided to stay on a couple of days, and take another look at that mill.

'When it's raining,' I said.

'Sometimes I can't understand a word . . .'

'We'd see it at its worst.'

'It's a water-mill, Richard. They're at their best with the millrace full.'

'And their noisiest.'

'You're not turning against it!' she cried.

I laughed. 'I love it. Besides,' I told her, 'I've got an old friend living not so far away. It would be grand to see him again.'

Detective Chief Superintendent Llewellyn Hughes, that was. He'd been an inspector to my sergeant, and had climbed on from there rapidly. It was on his final promotion that he'd managed to transfer to his beloved Wales, and to there he'd retired.

'It's something like our mill,' I said. 'A converted barn, or something like that. I'll have to look him up in the book and give him a ring.'

'After dinner, Richard, please. I'm starving.'

It was a fine August evening, and from our corner table in the dining room we could watch the sun going down over the mountains, and somewhere out there over our mill, which was on a tributary of the River Vyrnwy. I was probably a little unresponsive over the meal. My mind had turned to Llew Hughes.

It's a mistake, you know, to go back and see old friends. They're always recalled as they were, and at their best of what they were. Never their ill humours and bitternesses, but their laughter and fellowship, their strength. We hadn't really kept in touch, Llew and I, just the odd letter detailing any high spots. Llew was retired, as I was. But he was writing his memoirs, and I wasn't. I wondered whether I'd be in them, and smiled at the memory of what he might write of those times, what he might dare to.

'What's funny?' Amelia asked, raising her eyebrows in appreciation of the tropical fruit sorbet.

'He'll have changed,' I said, not really a reply, but she nodded, seeing beyond the words. 'It must be eighteen years since I saw him last.'

'Your friend Llewellyn?'

I nodded. 'I bet he's almost forgotten me. Won't even recognise me now.'

But would I recognise him? I could see him in my memory clearly enough, a tall, gangling man with a gloomy face, behind which there had lurked a quiet, sardonic humour and a keen wit. Even then he hadn't owned much hair, and was probably bald now. I gave him a bald head, and looked at him afresh, but what came through most clearly was his voice, an actor's voice, deep and resonant. He could do wonderful things with that voice during interrogation, his tone winkling out admissions, however firmly desperation had hidden them.

'I'll phone him now,' I said, and left her to her coffee. Amelia didn't mind. She loves sitting quietly, wrapped in her own personal contentment.

I looked him up. Llewellyn Hughes. There were eight of them, but only one with the address: Ewr Felen. Welsh for yellow acres, he'd written, though he hadn't got an acre, and it was yellow only when the broom was in flower.

He answered only with his number, an old habit. I said: 'Llew, it's me. Richard.'

The delight in his voice was so intense that it bordered on relief. 'Richard! You old reprobate! You must be psychic.'

'What?'

'I was just thinking about you. Wondering why you haven't been in touch. I've been writing . . . Richard, I must see you.'

'Hold it.' I laughed, hoping it sounded real. But in truth I was disturbed. His voice did not contain the old confidence. There was a waver to it, an uncertainty. He couldn't be that old! 'I'm here, Llew. Welshpool. A few miles from you . . .'

'Coming to see me?' he asked, all eager hope.

'I had that intention. I'm at a hotel, with my wife.'

'Your wife? You'll bring her along. There's a bed . . .'

'You didn't hear what I said, Llew. We're booked in. Welshpool. I thought . . . perhaps tomorrow . . .'

'No.' There was a click. His teeth? He was fighting for self-possession. I felt cold, dreading what he might have become, mystified by his attitude. There was a slight pause, and when he went on he was in

6

control, his voice firm. 'Come this evening, Richard. Please. Bring your wife, but come as soon as possible. I have to see you. There's something . . . something in my memoirs . . .'

He stopped. I waited a second, but he didn't go on.

'I heard you were working on them.'

'It's driving me crazy. Tonight, Richard. If you can possibly manage it.'

Amelia was at my elbow in the lobby, frowning, plucking at my sleeve. I bent, holding the phone away from my ear.

'But if you've spotted it . . . no vast hurry, surely.'

His voice was very quiet and distant. 'I saw this . . . oh, three months ago. I've been trying to make sense of it. I tell you, Richard, a most important case, and I think . . . I feel . . . I believe we were wrong.'

I was sure of one thing: Llew Hughes had never submitted a case for prosecution unless he'd been a hundred per cent certain. He sounded stricken, bemused. I glanced at Amelia. She pouted, reading my concern, and she nodded.

'I'll be right there, Llew,' I said. 'Give me half an hour.'

I hung up. Amelia simply looked at me. I said, 'He sounds ill.'

She smiled. 'I'll pop up for something warmer. You know how cold it gets, up in them thar hills.'

That was Amelia, trying to draw a smile from me. I went out to my Triumph Stag, and put up the hood. It would have taken too long to explain to her the true extent of my concern. Llew had sounded senile, his brain no longer coping with intricacies. But he would not have embarked on his memoirs without preparation. He'd always been meticulous on detail, and would have taken with him into retirement photocopies of relevant documents of all his most interesting cases. He would have collected together spare photographs of scene-of-crime details, all his own personal notebooks, everything necessary to prompt even a failing memory. Yet he'd spotted something wrong. Some detail missed? Such a thing would certainly have worried him, the Llew Hughes I'd known, with such a finely tuned sense of rightness. But he'd agonised over it for three months . . . and he still could not see the truth! No wonder he was shaken.

I felt a sudden urgency to get going, and was irritated at the delay. But then Amelia came running across the hotel car-park, having found time to slip on low heels and slacks, with a little jacket over her jumper.

North out of Welshpool, the road soon becomes more narrow and begins to wind. I was heading for Pentrebeirdd, through which I'd driven only that afternoon. Our mill was a mile from there, farther up the river. My mind was hunting around for his full address, as Ewr Felen wasn't much to go on amongst the tangled lanes I knew I was heading for. Stupid of me, I should have asked for directions before ringing off. But I knew it was somewhere the other side of the A495. I hadn't reckoned on the apparent lack of hamlets and villages, on the rare signposts bearing Welsh names, none of which I recognised. There was probably no urgency, but I couldn't persuade myself of that.

The light had gone from the sky, the shadows dipping into the valley and lying like heavy fog. My headlights flickered over sparse hedges and stone walls, and occasional sheep blinked into the lights and scrambled into the banks. I was getting nowhere, and becoming annoyed with myself.

The telephone kiosk was actually lit, and unvandalised. It stood at a crossing of lanes in a vast expanse of rolling hills, their peaks dark against the sky.

'I'll have to phone him,' I said, and pulled in beside it.

I was standing at its door, searching out change, when Amelia nudged me for attention.

'Richard!'

There was something urgent in her voice. I turned to her. She simply pointed beyond my shoulder.

The two peaks framed the steeper rise ahead. Unless my sense of direction had gone completely haywire, we were looking north. The red glow could not have been the sun setting. I ran back to the car, knowing we'd found him, my heart racing.

As I reached over and watched Amelia into her seat, gear already in and my foot playing on the clutch, a car came fast down the road we were facing. I had only my parking lights on, and before I could snap on the heads he was past. So I couldn't be sure of a thing. Its undipped lights blinded me, then it was past, and all I could have said was that it was a hatchback. I let in the clutch, spun the wheels, and slammed the box into second as I took the rise.

The lane narrowed. Grey walls flung themselves back into the lights, and the wheels scrabbled on loose slate chips. I had no time to glance towards the red glow, but Amelia's grip on my knee told me the story. Gradually, as the glow increased, so did the pressure of her fingers, until the fire was at my right shoulder and she screamed: 'Right here, Richard. Right!'

The entrance through which we turned was a gap in the wall, and led directly into the open, the track now being part of a naked, rocky field. Ahead of us the building blazed. I took the car as far as I could, but the heat was already reaching out. It hit my face as soon as I got out of the car.

It had been a long barn, wooden, and defenceless against fire. Somebody had split it into two floors. In the windows of the upper floor the panes had already gone. Flames were beginning to play through the roof, and the black smoke was shot through with red.

I had on my anorak and a cap, which I pulled down over my eyes. My driving gloves would supply a small protection against the heat. Amelia saw my intention.

'Richard, you can't . . .'

'I've got to try.'

We were having to shout, the roar of the fire was so loud. Beside the building I could see, from the flicks of reflected red catching its surface, that there was a mountain stream. Amelia followed my eyes and thoughts, and ran to it, whipping off her jacket. She plunged it into the water and came running back with it dripping. She didn't have to say anything. She knew there'd be no unnecessary heroics from me.

We were standing as close to the main door as the heat would allow. She had her arm over her eyes. I was considering the door, hoping it was as flimsy as it looked, as I wasn't going to be able to make more than one attack on it.

Through the roar and the crackle there was coming an intermittent sound I'd been unable to identify. Now I realised it was a dog barking. On and on, close to hysteria.

I clamped the soaking jacket over my face, gasping at the unexpected chill of it, and charged at the door. The best way is with your foot, but that gives you no impetus. What I needed was a good run at it, because I knew I would not be able to force myself very far against the heat.

The door collapsed to my shoulder and I ran in over it as it threw up sparks and ashes. The hall was a tumbling chaos of smoke, through which the flames were reaching. I saw nothing of walls or floor, could feel nothing but the heat that clamped on to me, seeming to throw me back. I could not have gone on, no more than the three stumbling steps my entrance had initiated. Then I was aware of dragging at the cuff of my slacks, and looked down. It was a small terrier, still doing his guarding act, so I knew Llew couldn't be far away.

The fire drew in a gasp of fresh air from the gap behind me, seized on it, and the roar became close to an explosion. Woodwork was collapsing beside me, but as the fire gulped at the air it withdrew for a second the roiling smoke, and I saw Llew lying at my feet.

He was face down, his arms spread forward, and, like the dog, he'd been existing on the thin layer of air there would be down there. I could spare only one hand, the other still clutching Amelia's jacket to my face. I grabbed hold of the neck of his jacket and began to drag him towards the open doorway.

The dog hung on to my cuff. For this I was glad. I knew I could not have returned for him, and would have hated that.

We got out into the open air, and my anorak was smoking. It smelt like hell. The dog still hung on, but he was limp, lying on his side as I dragged him, teeth locked in the trousers.

Amelia came rushing up, much too soon. The heat gusted out behind me. I gasped for her to get back, and she snatched at my arm, withdrawing her hand quickly.

'Get it off!' she gasped.

My anorak had a foam plastic interlining. I pulled Llew a few more yards and tossed Amelia's jacket into her arms. Then I could release him and tear off the anorak. The dog lay at my feet.

'There was a phone box . . .' I began, the smoke rasping in my chest.

'I know.' She turned away towards the car.

'Ambulance. Fire service.'

'I know.'

I bent down. The dog was stirring. His first thought was for my fingers, but for that he had to release my trouser cuff, so I was free to kneel beside Llew.

He was breathing. I could hear it rather than detect it. The back of his jacket was gone and I tore off the smouldering remains. The dog gave up trying to bite me and just lay there, whimpering. For a moment I turned aside, picked him up, and took him over to the stream. What had been white was now a shrunken brown. I dumped him in the stream and lifted him out, laying him on the bank, and returned my attention to Llew.

Amelia came running back from the car, shouting, 'Somebody's coming, Richard.'

I spared a glance behind me. Sirens in those empty lanes and the blue winking of lights.

'How is he?' she asked.

'He's alive,' I meant Llew.

'There's something in his hand.'

I'd noticed. It was an A4 manilla envelope, scorched across one corner. He had it gripped in his right hand. His precious memoirs? No, too thin for that. I detached it gently and turned it over. In the red, turbulent light I could just detect the printed words across its face: EDWIN CARTER.

'Have a look at the dog,' I suggested.

She said nothing, crouching beside him. I turned Llew on his side. One cheek was burned raw, one eye was closed. The other, naked of eyebrows and lashes, glared at me redly.

'Richard . . .'

Then it closed.

At that point the professionals arrived, and I got to my feet. The fire must have been visible for miles, and someone had put in a call.

The chief fire officer was brisk and urgent. 'Anybody else?'

'He was living alone.'

He was relieved, and turned away to direct his men. There was plenty of water available in the stream. The two men from the ambulance thrust me aside and bent over Llew.

'It was you got him out?' asked one of them.

'He'd almost reached the door. How is he?'

'Alive.'

But they were so gentle with him that I felt they weren't sure how long that would continue. In the back of my mind was a memory of Llew's words on the phone. He'd been writing to me, and all the while, this past two weeks, I hadn't been home at the cottage on the south coast, I'd been within a few miles of him, admiring a water-mill.

I stood and watched them easing him into the ambulance. Amelia stood beside me. When I turned to her she had the dog in her arms, tears running down her smoke-brushed cheeks. She wept for the dog, not Llew, yet the dog lived and seemed to be recovering. I suppose it was because the dog was there, a tangible symbol.

'There's some stuff in the car,' she whispered, and she wandered away. I walked over to the ambulance.

'How bad is it?'

They're always reluctant to commit themselves. 'We'll see.' He stared at me silently for a moment, then conceded. 'I'm sorry. I can't see much hope.' He told me the number to phone later.

I watched them drive away until the tail-lights disappeared. No siren now, just the winking lights. The hurry is always towards the incident. On the trip to the hospital, care and concern put a light foot on the pedal.

When I turned back the flames were dying. The building was simply gutted, with very little left to burn. I strolled over to the fire officer. He glanced at me.

'Hang around,' he suggested.

I nodded. 'Any idea how it started?'

'You got here – I suppose . . .'

'Coming to visit.'

'And it was well alight?'

'Yes.'

'You shouldn't have gone in. I suppose you realise that.'

I grimaced at him, but he didn't notice. 'Oh, I do.'

'But having done that . . . then you should be able to tell me how it started.'

'Should I? I'm afraid I don't know. I was asking.'

'You didn't smell petrol?'

'All I could smell was my smouldering anorak. You mean you smelt it?'

He scratched his chin. The dying red glow carved his features into angles. 'Funny how the smell lingers, but it always does. Round at the side I got a whiff. Somebody lobbed in a petrol bomb.' He grunted. 'Perhaps.'

'His car . . .'

'It's in that shed over there, and quite safe.'

I said nothing else for a while. Sometimes you have to take a firm hold on your emotions, otherwise they can lead you into trouble. At last I said:

'This isn't exactly in the centre of a riot area.'

'Hardly.' Then he said something in Welsh that was probably very profane, ducking his head. 'That's why I've radioed the police. So if you wouldn't mind hanging on . . .'

'My wife is upset.'

'I'm sorry.' His voice was hard and inflexible. He too was upset.

'We'll wait,' I assured him.

I went to sit with Amelia in the car. She'd managed to dry the dog with the blanket from the back seat, and she'd found some sort of soothing cream in her handbag. She was applying it to the dog's ears, which seemed to have caught the worst of it.

'How's he doing?' I asked.

'He,' she said, 'is a she, and she's quite exhausted, and in shock I think.'

'Where's that damned policeman?'

'Police?'

'That fire was probably deliberate. A smell of petrol. Oh hell, hell and damnation!'

We were silent. They were damping down the remains. After a few moments Amelia spoke softly.

'This alters things, doesn't it, Richard?'

'I'm afraid so.' But I couldn't at that stage say how.

A minute or two later a small police van arrived, manned by a very young policeman with a strangely mature air of authority. I got out to have a word with him. He was brisk, was willing to listen, and got rid of me with efficiency. I told him about the hatchback I'd seen, driving away from the scene, who we were and where we were staying, and who the occupant of the house had been.

'I know, sir,' he said, his voice even. 'I was proud to have the Chief Super on my patch.'

'Can still be proud, surely. He'll be back. Rebuild. Start again.'

'One hopes so, sir.'

His name was Davies. He asked politely that I would wait at the hotel to see him again in the morning. I told him I had no intention of leaving. He went to have a word with the fire officer, and we were free to go.

The dog was asleep, Amelia nearly so. Reaction usually produces exhaustion. I started the car and drove away, she opening her eyes for a moment, giving me a weak smile, then dozing off again.

It was late. We had to ring for the night porter. He allowed us into the lobby, not pleased with our appearance, but he got the key for us.

'About the dog, sir. I'm sorry, it's a hotel rule . . .'

I glanced at Amelia, knowing what I would see. There was a sudden spark in her eye, a tenseness about her. I was tired, suddenly cripplingly tired. One more push, and my temper would go. I produced a crisp fiver and gave him no time to argue, slapped it into his hand, and led the way firmly for the stairs.

Say this for him, he read my mood more accurately than I'd read him. Fifteen minutes later, when we'd had time to clean up a little, and while I was contacting the hospital, he appeared at the door with a large tray. He'd done it himself, a pot of tea and biscuits, a dish of scraps from the kitchen for the dog, and a bowl of water. He put it down on a side-table and stood back, made a tiny bow and said something in Welsh. *'Croeso Y Gymru.'*

From beneath the teapot peeped the fiver.

My call came through. The man spoke softly for a few moments. I hung up, and turned to Amelia, sitting there on the edge of the bed.

'I'm afraid', I said, 'that we've just acquired a dog.'

Late as it was, I knew I wasn't going to get any sleep until I'd had a quick look through that manilla envelope. Amelia made no comment, but simply requisitioned more than half the bed and went straight to sleep.

A quick look, did I say? What I found myself looking at was Llew's notes for his chapter on the case of Edwin Carter, for whose murder his nephew, Duncan Carter, had been sentenced to fifteen years' imprisonment. Also included were a dozen scene-of-crime photographs, and copies of statements from that time.

His recent notes disturbed me. They started off in a logical manner, with his plan for the chapter, almost as we'd been taught at school, for essays.

> Apparent suicide. All the elements. Manic-depressive. Witnesses to this — everybody involved agreed. Grounds for assuming murder: money. (As usual! By heaven... the number of times...) Reminds me of Simpson

That page ended there, as though his mind had drifted off the subject and he'd been unable to recapture his concentration.

Another page (there was no sign of the one that must have preceded it):

> Lucky the inspector spotted it. Richard Patton that was... no, Victor Grayson, Patton... whoever it was, he spotted it. The case hadn't come to me at that time, being a simple suicide. It was the wrong garage that did it. The car in that garage not having the radio to close

that door. So how did he shut himself in? Even the button outside – that didn't work. So what was he supposed to do? Dash outside and operate the radio in the other car, and run back under the door as it came down? It was just not on.

So it came to me. A murder investigation, and of course, with the timing

Nothing more on that page. I couldn't make head or tail of it, but I'd noticed he hadn't been sure of the investigating officer involved. With a sinking feeling I realised that poor Llew's mind must have been going. But he'd been insistent and excited when he'd spoken to me on the phone, and he'd admitted to believing he'd been in error. Or someone else had .

I read on. A page of indecision.

So tried it with an official driver. Fourteen miles each way to the nearest. Nothing remembered there. Best time: twenty-seven minutes. Those lanes! Tried it at night. Better, said driver – no approaching headlights. This time twenty-four minutes. Say forty-eight, there & back, at best. Add time for buying. Near as damn it an hour. But... oh hell, if not there – where?

Where booze from!!!

How the hell could he have – can't get it out of my mind. His eyes. Swore he was innocent.

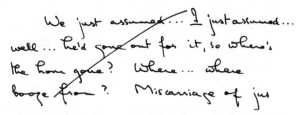

We just assumed... I just assumed...
well... he'd gone out for it, so where's
the home gone? Where... where
booze from? Miscarriage of jus

The page ended there. I turned to the next one quickly, not wanting to pry into his disturbed mind. This was a photocopy of the long statement made by Duncan Carter, in his own hand. I skipped rapidly through it, a plain and categorical denial of his guilt, followed by a statement of what he had done that specific evening. In the margin Llew Hughes had scribbled: 'Must see him about this'.

About what? The comment was opposite the paragraph that read:

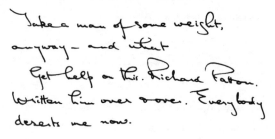

I had used the car that
day, and driven it
back into the garage.
I was aware that this
Must see was the wrong garage,
him about and I did not use the
this hand radio to try the
door. Why should I?
It was a fine day, so
there was no reason to
close the door.

Gradually, as I leafed through them, Llew's notes became more disordered, until I could hardly make sense of them.

Take a man of some weight,
anyway - and what
Get help on this. Richard Patton.
Written him over + over. Everybody
deserts me now.

*Another attempt on my life. Or
maybe not. Grayson not sympathetic.
Must concentrate. If not from
there ... timing later. Even more
blasted alibis.*

I threw it away from me, and glanced briefly at the photographs: a man belted into a driving seat, head down on the steering wheel; a garage, its door up, a car inside; a close-up of the car, a crate of beer on the back seat, bottles of spirits lying against it; a more distant view of the car in the garage, which showed it to be the left one of a pair, with another car parked outside the right-hand one.

By that time I was too tired to go on. The dog was asleep in the patch Amelia had left me, so I simply put my head back and slept in the chair.

I say slept, but you know what it's like. You're restless, and if your mind's subconsciously pounding away in the background you can expect a thick head in the morning. This I got. Also an aching back, one foot that had to be stamped awake, and a hot forehead.

Amelia made coffee with the equipment the hotel had laid on in our room, and I sipped at it, staring at the dog. She was livelier that morning, but you had to search well down through the fur to find the original white. All was singed brown, except her ears, which had lost all hair and were a violent red. I matched them with my forehead and the backs of my hands, so I could feel sympathy with her. I lit my pipe, and we named her. Cindy. Short for Cinders, that was. Not very subtle, is it? I had a quick bath and a shave, and took Cindy out for a walk, while Amelia prepared herself for breakfast.

It was necessary to sneak out through the kitchen, where the chef intercepted me, having heard about the fire, and offered a bowl of milk. For the record, during the whole time we were there the staff, up to and including the manager, turned a blind eye to Cindy's presence.

We strolled the town. Why do big men with small dogs look so stupid? I imagined this to be so, anyway. I returned, with a lead and a dog basket and bedding from the pet shop, and installed Cindy in the car. I left her there, and went on up.

'Guess what?' I said.

Amelia turned from the window. 'She's barking.' This accusingly.

'Look.' I opened my palm to show her the small medallion. 'This was attached to her collar. It says: "My name is Cindy, and I live at Ewr Felen."'

'Coincidence,' she said.

'Yes. Not the only one, is it?'

She didn't take me up on that, so we went down to breakfast, where Constable Davies joined us for a cup of tea. He was wearing slacks and a short, zipped jacket, so didn't attract undue attention.

I hadn't got a good look at him the previous evening, and my memory was only of his abrupt and seemingly unemotional approach. Now I was facing him, and could watch the play of feeling on his face. It was a sharp face, clean-shaven with a pointed chin, the dark hair abundant. His eyes were brown and intelligent, his voice still unemotional. But its flatness of tone was, I began to realise, due to control. His eyes flashed, but his voice remained quiet. The questions he put to me were unaggressive, but he pursued the answers stubbornly.

'Glad I caught you,' he said, risking a tiny smile. 'I suppose you've heard about Mr Hughes?'

I inclined my head.

'I hope you folk weren't intending to dash away.'

I glanced at Amelia. She shook her head. 'No specific plans at the moment,' I said.

'Though I suppose – you being a friend of Mr Hughes – you'll have been connected with the police ...' He left it hanging, one raised eyebrow making it into a question.

'Ex-Detective Inspector,' I told him. 'I worked as a sergeant with Llew Hughes, when he was an inspector. That makes it clear, does it?'

'Very clear, sir.'

'Ex,' I said. 'You don't have to call me sir.'

There was not a hint of a smile when he stared at me. 'If you don't mind, I'll make up my own mind about that.'

Like that, was it? To Davies, the title of sir was not a simple measure of rank or title, it was either a keep-your-distance formality, as used to a member of the public, or a mark of respect.

I sat back, one elbow over the back of the chair. 'You mean you don't trust me?'

'I don't have to ... need to. All that's necessary is to make sure you're still around when the Chief Inspector gets here.'

'Without levelling any charges?'

'I can hardly imagine any charge I could make,' he said blandly. Then he leaned forward. 'And I don't intend to be pressured into a position where I might be prejudicing any future action, Mr Patton.'

Behind her hand, but nevertheless undisputably, Amelia giggled. The amusement was aimed at me, but Davies sat there, not allowing himself to glance towards her, and two pink patches bloomed on his cheeks. I stuck my pipe in my teeth to disguise the grin I felt to be on its way.

'Put you in an awkward position, haven't they, lad?'

'The situation here . . .'

'But you're doing fine.'

His mouth twitched. 'And if you're going to patronise me . . .'

'Sorry. Did it sound like that? No – I meant it. Short-handed at the station, I bet.' He nodded. 'And you've been left to stall things along.'

'That's about the size of it.'

'No need to worry, you know. We shan't be leaving in a hurry. Would you, with an old friend dead, and probably killed? Go on, you can agree, you won't be committing yourself.'

'I wouldn't be leaving.' Then he shook his head angrily, at himself, I suppose, and his face relaxed. He even managed a smile, but it was hesitant. He didn't know how far he dared to go, and didn't trust his own discretion. Yet he was talking to somebody who would at least appreciate his dilemma. Suddenly it burst from him.

'Well, look at it. Just take a good look at how it was last night. Mr Hughes, up at his place, quiet and isolated. Somebody wanted him dead, or at least silent, and set fire to his house. Oh, don't worry, there's not much doubt about that. It was deliberate.'

I nodded. 'That seems certain. Go on.'

'But it didn't happen two nights ago, a week ago . . . *next* week. It happened last night, and just after you people arrived here and decided to drive up there and visit. What a coincidence!'

'They happen.'

'But . . . just at that time!'

'Let me tell you about the dog's name,' I said gently.

'Who but you could possibly be number one suspect?' he demanded.

I considered him carefully. It was now a matter of whether I could trust *him*. He could have been instructed to throw out the suggestion. I said:

'My wife and I were talking unguardedly in the dining room – in here. I'm already fairly certain that Llew Hughes was in the process of querying the result of one of his past cases. I phoned him to say I'd be right along. All this could have been overheard, so anyone wanting to put a stop to Llew's activities – and incidentally destroy all his notes and what not – could have driven off ahead of us. There'd have been time. I got myself lost.'

I stopped. It was strange to be on the wrong end of an interrogation, even though this one was informal. I was over-elaborating. I could see that Davies realised this, too. He was shaking his head.

'Even so . . .'

'And that's why your Chief wants to see me?'

'I reckon. Guess.'

Did I detect a lack of confidence in his superior?

'Then he should have come here himself.'

'He's up at Ewr Felen. What's left of it. He simply told me to make sure you'd be available.'

'Ah!' I set to on the task of filling my pipe, to give my eyes something to concentrate on.

I glanced up, surprising his look of expectation.

'The best thing', I suggested, 'is to pretend this discussion never happened. That'll leave us both with a clean sheet.'

'I shall report exactly what was said.' He frowned.

'Don't be a young fool. Tell him what's been said, and he'll skin you alive. We forget it. Let him make his own points, and I'll give him the same replies.' He was jutting his lower lip with uncertainty. I leaned forward and changed the subject while he hesitated. 'Now . . . I'll need to get in touch with an inspector, one Llew Hughes worked with at one time. It could well have been after he came to Wales. A man called Grayson. Ever heard of him?'

His mouth twisted. 'It's Detective Chief Inspector Grayson who's coming to see you.' It spread into a grin. 'Sir,' he added.

I slapped my palm on the table with delight. Cups jumped in their saucers. 'Coincidence!' I cried. 'How's that for you?'

'They happen.'

'Between us, we're going to get this fire-bug.'

'You and me, sir?' he asked hopefully.

'I meant Grayson and me, laddie.'

'You obviously haven't met him.'

I glanced at Amelia. I'd sprung it on her, this intention to become involved, but she must have guessed. Her eyes were grave. She was remembering how I'd been so firmly discouraged from interfering, once before.* I returned my attention to Davies.

'Tell me about him,' I suggested.

'Not much to tell, really. You can imagine, we don't get much top-rank CID work around here. They usually send us a sergeant. But

* *Still Life with Pistol.*

Mr Grayson . . . he's got a reputation. He succeeds, you see. But he doesn't stand for anybody sharing things. Not even the rough stuff, when it happens. He handles that himself, too. They say he's clever. I don't know. Never met him, until today, but you hear things. He's not going to be friendly, Mr Patton. Not one little bit.' No doubt he'd offered his own suggestions. He was shaking his head.

Davies hadn't been long in the force, and he'd been working a country beat, where he'd achieve more by open friendliness than by suspicion. He was young and eager, and certainly too outgoing. He'd got a lot to learn. It wasn't his lack of experience that had led him into undiplomatic disclosures. I realised he'd done it deliberately. He had wanted to warn me.

I said evenly: 'I shall bear in mind what you've told me, Constable.'

He took that as a signal that the meeting was ended, and got to his feet. To indicate that it was he who had ended it, he said: 'Then you'll be here, Mr Patton? The hotel.'

'Here, or around. I *want* to meet your Chief Inspector.'

We watched him walk away. I hardly dared to look at Amelia, fearing her disapproval.

'I might have guessed,' she said.

'Llew wanted my help. He's written to me . . . he says. More than once. You can't expect me to walk away from it.' And he'd written: 'Everybody deserts me now'.

'Letters?' she said. 'What letters?'

'I was looking through that envelope, and he mentions having written to me. I really must see what he wrote. Oh damn it, and I'm going to have to see this Grayson . . .'

She tapped my knuckles with a teaspoon. 'I can get your letters, Richard.'

'How do you mean?'

'Why are you always so self-centred! What am I supposed to do, sit back and watch you get yourself into another mess? This Grayson won't want to see me, will he?'

'If he does, it can wait.'

'There you are then. I'll drive home to the cottage and fetch them for you.'

'But it's two hundred miles away.'

She lifted her chin. 'You'll just have to be patient, Richard. I wasn't proposing to do the double run in one day.'

'Heavens no. Of course not.'

'But I could if I wanted to.'

'I'm sure you could.'

'Then don't say it in your doubtful voice, or I'll have to prove it.'

'I don't doubt you for one moment, my dear. But you know you don't like driving the Stag.'

'You'll be needing that,' she told me, looking past me vaguely as she planned everything. 'I'll hire something. We shall be needing a change of clothes, if we're going to be stuck here.'

'Me, anyway.'

'So while you take Cindy to the vet, I'll see about a car.'

'You can do that by phone.'

'So I can,' she agreed. 'Clever Richard. So while I do that, you just trot along to the vet's, and if that horrible-sounding Grayson turns up while you're away, I'll keep him talking.' She nodded, satisfied she had everything covered.

I couldn't remember arranging any of this, or agreeing to it, but that's how Amelia is. We could have used her in the force. She'd have had all our tough customers in tears inside five minutes.

'Right,' I said. 'Fine.' I couldn't decide whether to thank her or compliment her. 'I'll do that, then.'

And that was how it was. I took the new lead out to the car-park and rescued Cindy, and we walked along to the vet's together. I wasn't feeling quite so ridiculous. It was a lady vet, who said, 'She's from Ewr Felen, isn't she?' And was very sympathetic. We left with a pot of ointment and an assurance that Cindy would be just fine.

Before I'd even crossed the lobby I could tell there was somebody special around. Cindy nearly vibrated her tail loose, and made yipping sounds. The voices were from Amelia and a tall, hefty man, who were sitting on one of the corner bench seats in the lounge.

'Here he is now,' she said.

When I released the lead, Cindy was off and bounding into his lap. He ducked his head as she nibbled his ear, then he got to his feet, Cindy beneath his left arm, his right hand thrust out.

'This is Chief Inspector Grayson,' said Amelia. 'My husband.'

He was an inch taller than me, an inch or two wider at the shoulders, but slim at the hips, a solid, wind-hewn man with a low brow and a broad forehead and bushy eyebrows. He looked as though he'd be difficult to knock over. Half laughing at Cindy's excitement, he took my hand and mangled it a little, then he put her down and said:

'What's that stuff on her ears?'

'For the burns.'

'It stinks.'

'She doesn't seem to mind.'

And so we met, me completely wrong-footed because I'd been planning my approach to a stolid toughie, and had met a softie head-on.

Amelia gave me time to recover, explaining that Reception had been a great help, that the red Fiesta out front was a hire car and that the keys in her hand fitted it, and that the overnight bag at her feet was in case anything happened. She generally covers all contingencies.

Grayson, his head inclined forward courteously and his eyes glowing, said he hoped to see her again, and took her hand in something closer to a caress than a shake. I kissed her, and she promised to phone.

'The minute you get there,' I said.

She flicked me a smile, and then the door was swinging shut behind her.

Grayson turned back to me. The change in his face was minimal, but the expression was completely altered. This was the Grayson about whom Davies had spoken, the inflexible Grayson, who would stand no nonsense. His eyes told me that, the set of his jaw.

'And now, Mr Patton . . .' he said, flicking those bushy eyebrows at me.

3

I had taken him up to our room and ordered a pot of tea. He'd commandeered the only easy chair, so that Cindy could go to sleep on his lap, and it was a matter of the upright chair or the bed for me. I sat on the edge of the bed and filled my pipe.

'She was glad to see you,' I said, pointing the pipe stem at Cindy.

'We're old friends.'

'So you kept in touch – with Llew, I mean.'

'Heavens yes. We worked together very closely, before he retired. Friends, you might say, he a widower and me a bachelor.'

'You surprise me.'

He looked at me through cigarette smoke. 'That we were friends?'

'That you're not married.'

He showed me a few teeth, all of them very white. 'Not much in it for a woman, is there? I mean – wife of a chief inspector! All that overtime!'

'Ah!' I said. 'Yes.' I poured tea, and pushed it over to him. We had run through the preliminaries, and I had an idea he'd already embarked on something he wanted to pursue. I led him in. 'And recently? You've kept in touch, you say.'

He shrugged, his shoulders moving ponderously. 'You know how it is with a lot of people. They make their job their whole life, and when they retire it's as though something gets switched off. Llew was like that. Not having to flex his brains any more . . . well, it just seemed to flag. That was why he started on his memoirs. My suggestion, it was, to keep his brain active . . .'

'Your suggestion?' I interrupted. 'But didn't he take with him lots of copies and notes and things like that? He must have had it in mind.'

He nodded. A concession. Good point, feller. 'But I had to push him into starting. Once he'd begun, then it was fine. For a year or so, when he was writing about his earlier cases. I know a lot about you, Richard Patton.'

'I'm not sure I like that.'

'Mostly complimentary.' But I'd meant it gave him an advantage. I smiled. 'Then his memory was all right.'

He didn't see that as a joke, just grimaced. 'Don't you find it's like that?' he asked. 'As people grow older, they remember things very clearly from the distant past, but not so well from recently.'

I nodded. 'It's like a computer, I suppose. In the old days the cells were young and retained the memory. But the cells become older, and more recent stuff isn't locked away so well.'

'Exactly.'

Oh, we were doing fine, like two old chums chatting away, though one of us seemed to have forgotten that the subject of our conversation had died in a fire the night before.

'But you encouraged him,' I said, seeing that he wasn't going to go on.

'Well . . . you have to. He consulted me, you see.'

'The Edwin Carter case?'

'How did you guess that?'

'Llew mentioned it. He was worried . . .'

'Exactly. On that one, he went completely overboard.'

'We're still talking about his brain?'

'Frankly,' he said, 'I just didn't know how to handle it. The damned case became a kind of obsession with him, this feeling he said he had that something was wrong.' His voice had taken on a crisper tone. 'And it was *my* case,' he claimed firmly. 'He hardly came into it at all. The facts were down there on paper, on his desk, and he'd hardly taken a good look at the scene of the crime. But all the same, he's been worrying that something was wrong.'

I pretended not to be watching him. His vehemence might not have been genuine.

'Did he say what?'

He relaxed, waving a hand and making smoke patterns. 'Everything was vague. Damn it all . . .' He laughed lightly. 'D'you know what he wanted me to do? He wanted me to trace where Edwin Carter had got the booze. I ask you. After ten years! It could've been dozens of pubs.'

'Hopeless,' I agreed. 'Did you try?'

'No, of course not.'

'So it was all in the timing, this murder of yours?'

'Not even that. You can see why I couldn't take Llew seriously.'

We weren't talking about Llew's death, so maybe he wasn't taking that seriously, either. I wondered whether he was working round to an oblique apology, that he hadn't kept a sufficiently close eye on his friend. Testing that out, I reached behind me for the manilla envelope and tossed it on to his lap.

'That was in his hand when I got him out. The case was certainly an obsession with him.'

He raised his eyebrows at me, and for one moment there was anger in his eyes. But after all, I'd been suppressing evidence, though only overnight. Yet his anger could have been because I'd rescued it at all.

I watched him as he went through it, his eyes moving fast over what must have been familiar to him, even though ten years old. I saw that his knuckles were white. He thrust each successive sheet or photograph beneath the sheaf of paper with decisive rejection. He would not have liked the fact that the cases in Llew's memoirs which had involved Richard Patton had been kind to him, whereas this one – this specific one that Grayson claimed as his own – stood a chance of being admitted as an error, a miscarriage.

In fact (and the thought clicked in the back of my mind almost as a physical blow), Grayson would hate the thought. One of his cases shot down in flames! Heavens, it could well affect his career, if it went as far as producing a pardon for the man who'd been sentenced.

I did not want to consider the possibility that Grayson might have found it necessary to prevent Llew Hughes from continuing with it. Not in that way – his friend, and the dog he now cradled in his lap whilst his free hand played in her fur.

He slid it all back into the envelope and tossed it on to the carpet.

'Well . . . that gives you a rough idea,' he said in dismissal.

'You mean, he'd reached the stage where he was incompetent? You think the fire was an accident?'

He was playing with an unlit cigarette between his fingers. 'I'm not sure what I mean . . . yet.'

'There was a smell of petrol.'

'Means nothing. The idiot kept a spare can of petrol in the outhouse attached to the building.' The word 'idiot' had been said with affection.

I pushed him a little, wondering whether he would resist me. 'But he writes – in there – about doing some re-investigation on the case. Do you know anything about that?'

'He'd been trying to contact the people involved at the time.'

'With success?'

He flexed his lips. The teeth showed again. 'Success in so far as he did contact some of them, I understand. But he got no new information.'

'Did he go to the prison and see the chap you arrested? Duncan Carter, wasn't it?'

He gave me a wry look. 'Duncan Carter came out on parole a few months ago. Yes, he saw him. I can't say I approved. He could've been raising false hopes, to suggest there might've been something in doubt about the original case.'

'Yes. But if he raised false hopes in Duncan Carter, he might have raised a little apprehension in somebody else.'

'What somebody else, for God's sake?' he demanded, so violently that I knew it wasn't a new idea to him.

'If Duncan Carter didn't do it, then somebody else did.'

'No,' he said. 'I'm not having that. Carter did it. The thing was open-and-shut.'

'All the same . . . not long after Llew Hughes started feeling around, there were attempts on his life.'

'Nonsense.'

'Llew said that – wrote it.'

'Haven't I been trying to tell you, his brain was going.'

'You don't have to persuade me,' I said quietly. 'It's Llew's death you're investigating.'

He seemed to shake himself internally, and take a grip on his anger. To hide it all from me he got to his feet, turning to place Cindy on the warm chair, easing his shoulders. I thought for a moment that he intended to leave, but no, it was only a refresher.

'The fire could have been an accident,' he said with calm decision. 'Or he could've got on the wrong side of somebody local. I'm not even going to consider that his death could relate to the Carter case.'

He wouldn't want to, of course. 'Then you won't mind if I think along the same lines as Llew?'

'I bloody well would, you know. In fact, I'd put a stop to it.'

I grinned at him. 'I'm not going to ask you how. There's nothing illegal in asking people questions. I was just wondering whether I could expect any co-operation.'

'You must be crazy.'

'Never mind then. But I did think you'd prefer me to start off on the right foot . . . or perhaps, if you could satisfy my curiosity, not start off at all.'

He eyed me cautiously. I took a few seconds to light my pipe, then went on: 'As you say, it'd be a bad thing to suggest to Duncan Carter that there could be a chance of a pardon anywhere.'

'Don't you dare!'

'Particularly as I'm not too keen on this idea of raking over past cases. There's too much . . .'

'You're not?' he pounced in.

'Are you?' I pointed the stem at him. 'Impersonally, mind you. As a general principle.'

That got him. He'd been staring out of the window, but now he returned to his chair, scooping up Cindy and replacing her on his lap with one smooth movement. He leaned forward eagerly, his face glowing.

'What I think . . . it's easy to go back and get somebody talking their heads off – investigative journalism they call it. The idea's to produce something – anything – that's in favour of the sentenced person. You know how it is. The thing goes through, up and up, to the Home Secretary, who has to think if there might've been a miscarriage of justice. But by that time there's been so much publicity that he hasn't got much choice. Play safe, and hand out a pardon.'

His cheeks were flushed with emphasis. There was anger in the bite of his words. This was a man who hated the thought of his own decisions being questioned.

'Not as simple as that, surely.' I watched as he shook his head stubbornly. 'And in any event, didn't somebody once say, better a hundred guilty persons on the streets than one innocent in prison?'

'Innocent!' he said in disgust. 'Does it make 'em innocent because there's a doubt? Some past witness pressured by a reporter . . .'

'Facts that might have produced a verdict of not guilty, if they'd been heard at the trial.'

'Ah!' I'd said what he'd been waiting for. 'But this isn't the trial we're talking about. This is the present, looking back at it. This is a re-trial, only now there's only one judge, who's the jury and the prosecution and the defence. Something is put before him in favour of the accused – but where's the prosecution, who might well have shot it to shreds if they only had the chance? *That* would be a miscarriage of justice, freeing a person just because there's a doubt.'

I looked away from him, this man who never had doubts and refused to accept their validity in any context. 'The law states that the accused must have the benefit of any doubt. Surely it's better, even at a later date – *this* later date – to investigate the possibility of any doubt in the Carter case.'

'There *is* no doubt.'

'Then suppose you tell me.' I suggested quietly. 'Tell me your case, about which you have no doubt.'

I watched the light die from his eyes, the muscles round his jaw relax, and slowly a smile gathered round his mouth.

'Got me going there, didn't you!'

'Got yourself going. The snag is that I know nothing about the Carter case. You're the expert. So . . . what d'you say? Hmm?'

His was a forceful personality. He could have told me to go to hell, and left me to fumble along with it. But he also possessed supreme confidence in himself and his abilities. He would display his accomplishments without shame, as a challenge. Nevertheless, he eyed me for a few moments critically. He might well decide he dared not trust me, and with reason. But would he dare to allow me to wonder whether his lack of trust might cover a secret doubt within himself? I thought not. I was right.

'Very well,' he said. 'How much do you know?'

'Assume nothing, and give me the lot.'

'Right. Now . . . this was north of here, but still in the county of Powys, and ten or more miles from the border with England. That matters, as you'll see. A large house. It'd been bought a few years earlier by this Edwin Carter, who was around fifty-five at the time, as a weekend retreat. He had the money at that time, when he bought it. You'll know the name, perhaps. Edwin Carter. Playwright. Started on the television and graduated to the stage, the West End, and made a great success of it.'

'Can't say it means anything,' I told him, 'but I was never one for the stage.'

'Take my word for it, then, he'd made a lot of money. These were social-comment comedies, and he'd got a bit too big for his own good. He decided to do his own directing. You know the type, big-headed and think they can do the lot. Anyway, he failed as a director, and the last two plays he did were flops. He was broke.'

'This is relevant?'

'Kind of. It comes into the motive bit. All right? Well, he was throwing a party . . .'

'When he'd failed?'

'That was the type of man he was, and *that's* relevant, too. It was a kind of wake. Eat, drink and be merry, tomorrow we sign on the dole. Edwin Carter was a manic-depressive. Way up one minute, way down the next, and like a kid on a swing in the park, the higher he went one way, the higher he went the other.' He frowned. It didn't sound quite right, but I got the point. 'So there he was with his party at the big house. It was a Sunday. At the house were six or so people from the stage and that sort of thing, and his nephew Duncan, who wasn't from the stage – he was an organist, in fact – but he'd associated in a minor way with his uncle in the writing of the plays.'

'I'm with you.'

'Now you'll realise this was 1976. At that time, though it's eased off now, you couldn't find a pub open in Wales on a Sunday. Edwin Carter got himself tanked up into a fine state of roaring ecstasy and decided they needed more drinks. This was around ten in the evening. August. A fine night. He said he was going to drive out and get a fresh supply of booze. People tried to restrain him, but it was more of a good laugh than anything else. So off he went. Ten o'clock. He'd have nigh on fifteen miles to drive to any pub that'd be open. You could say a good hour and a half on the trip.'

'There was mention of this', I said, 'in that envelope. Llew timed it.'

He nodded. 'On that case, it was about the only thing he did do that took him away from his desk. He seemed to think the time was critical, but I couldn't see it. I'll tell you . . . this house. A large place with its own drive, its own lane really, and a wide parking space at the front of the house, and two garages at the side. Those were a hundred yards from the house and just off the drive. Two garages, and two house cars, you might call 'em. One was Edwin's, the other belonged to his secretary, a niece of his called Rosemary Trew. She lived at the house. That evening, all the visitors had their own cars parked out at the front. They'd come for the party and were staying the night. Duncan, the nephew, had been staying there for the past few days. He'd borrowed Rosemary Trew's car that day, but when he'd brought it back he'd put it in the wrong garage. This was because his uncle had driven up to London that day to see if there was any chance of saving the last play.'

'On a Sunday?'

'This is show business, friend. They work funny hours, when they work at all.'

'Righto,' I agreed. 'So Uncle Edwin drove back from London for his party and to welcome his guests, and found the other car in *his* garage. Did it matter?'

'Not to you it wouldn't. Not to me. But to Edwin Carter it mattered. He played hell, but not enough hell to trouble to get 'em switched over. The point was, you see, that they were up-and-over doors, and radio operated. So . . . for the system to work, they had to keep to the correct garage for the correct car.'

He seemed to be making a big point of this, but I wasn't really with him on it.

'It meant the doors stayed open,' I commented. 'So what?'

'So you can't get yourself poisoned with car fumes when the garage doors are open.'

'And that was how it was? Carbon monoxide poisoning?'

He seemed irritated. 'Yes. Will you let me tell this in its proper sequence!'

Did he allow his suspects to do that? You can bet he didn't. I grinned at him and he managed a small smile in return.

'Your own time,' I said.

'Where was I? Any more tea?'

'It's cold. I'll send down for some beer if you like.'

'Not on duty.'

'You're on duty? Oh heavens, and what have I been saying?'

'If you don't want to hear . . .' He shrugged. 'You're trying to distract me, but you won't succeed. This party. Around ten, Edwin Carter went down to the two garages – the shortest way was by way of the terrace, outside that big dining hall they were using. His niece, Miss Trew, went with him. Did I mention her?'

'You did.'

'She was trying to persuade him not to go, but there was no stopping him. He was going to use his own car, but it wouldn't start. You can imagine his language. But he wouldn't quit, and said he'd use the other car, which was hers, a Triumph Dolomite with an automatic box, which he didn't like, which didn't improve things. But she hadn't got the keys because Duncan still had 'em in his pocket, so she want back to the house for them, and when she got back and handed them to him he said something unpleasant, so she marched away and left him to it, and it was about five past ten when he finally got away.'

'You've got a good memory for detail.'

He grimaced. 'I read it up before I came out.'

'So you thought Llew's death *did* have something to do with Edwin Carter's?'

'Not really. But I thought you might.'

I nodded, tapping my teeth with the pipe stem. He was a complex person. I now realised he *expected* me to look into his old case. He'd warned me off. Perhaps he'd already known that wouldn't have any effect.

He stared at me blandly as he went on. 'Five past ten, and Edwin drove away. By ten-fifteen they'd organised party games in that dining hall. All the guests were involved. But the fact is that Duncan was the only one not joining in. He wanted a word with his uncle, so he was restless. At a quarter to eleven he went down to the garages. Again at eleven, then eleven-twenty. And there he was, standing and looking into the distance for headlights – this is *his* story – when he realised he'd heard a humming noise stop. If you can make sense of that.'

'Maybe I can.' I wasn't going to stop him now.

'And he realised that the door of the garage in which he'd left Rosemary Trew's Dolomite was down, and he said he suddenly felt that his uncle was inside there with the car, and he'd just heard the engine stop. He said he couldn't get the door to go up, and he ran for help, and somebody else managed it, and there was Edwin inside, dead.'

He stopped. A flair for the dramatic, Grayson had. He put Cindy on the chair again and took a few paces round the room, gesturing as he continued with his story.

'When I got there they said they'd touched nothing, just put on the light in the garage then stood around outside. The assumption was suicide, *their* assumption. They said it was typical, that he'd obviously had a swing into deep depression, with that long drive. The beer and the rest were there on the back seat. He was belted in, and there was a bruise on his forehead. As though he'd driven in fast and braked hard. The petrol tank was empty. They said there was plenty of reason for the depression, and later I found he'd had those two successive flops with his plays. So fine. But I didn't like that bump on his forehead. If he'd knocked himself out, how had the gearbox got into parking position? And how had that blasted door got itself shut?'

I realised that we'd at last reached what he was aiming for. His dark eyes gleamed and his head came up. This was a matter for pride.

'These radios,' he said. 'One in each car, hand-held things. But they were tuned differently. The one in the Dolomite would've closed the *other* garage door. So . . . if it'd been suicide . . . well, look at it. He'd have had to stop the car, leave the engine running, operate the radio in the *other* car – that was his own – which was parked outside, then dash back before the closing door cut him off, get back in the driving seat, and belt himself in. I ask you! And the car lights were off. What suicide would choose to go out in the dark? I just couldn't accept it.'

'Llew said something on those lines.'

'But it was *my* thinking.'

'Granted. But there has to be more.'

'It was all a matter of how that door was closed. There was a button beside the doorway in the wall, for manual operation outside, but that wasn't working. So that left the radio in the other car. You can see, I was thinking about murder at that time.'

'Naturally.'

'And the only one – the *only* one, because all the others were with each other in that dining room – who could've been down there when Edwin returned was his nephew Duncan. And Duncan had a motive. His uncle used to pay him for work Duncan did on those plays. Fancied himself as a playwright did Duncan. And Edwin hadn't paid him anything for a year. Duncan was the primary beneficiary under Edwin's will. And guess whose fingerprints were on the only thing that would've closed that door, which was the radio in Edwin's own car. Duncan's. And nobody else's.'

'Could he explain that?'

'He said that when he realised the Dolomite was inside the garage, he ran to the other car and tried the radio, but it didn't work.'

'And I suppose you tried it?'

'It worked for me. At least, the mechanism hummed when I switched it on, but when they lifted the door they'd had to do it by force, and they'd broken the linkage.'

I thought about that. 'It sounds a bit slim. And they convicted him on that?'

'Motive – he thought he'd inherit. Means – the car in the garage and the radio in the other car. Opportunity – he was *there*, at the right time, and the rest had positive alibis for each other.'

'But you never got him to admit it?'

He laughed, a mirthless sound, I thought, directed at himself, at his only failure in the case.

'Give me a tough villain any time. You can break them down. But that Duncan Carter! He was broken down before I could say a thing, dithering and nervous, contradicting himself every other word. Not living in this world. An organist, he said he was. Deputy organist and choirmaster at Lichfield Cathedral. Get him talking about music, and all of a sudden the words poured out. Apart from that, he didn't know a thing. Didn't even own a car himself. You'd never believe – when we came to take a statement, we couldn't get a word down. In the end he wrote it himself.'

'I know.'

'You'll just *have* to meet him.'

'I look forward to it.'

He was abruptly serious, staring at me with suspicion. 'You're not convinced, then?'

'Llew wasn't. I'd like to think he'd still got a bit of brain left.'

'When all he could think about was how far Edwin had to go for the booze? What could it matter? He got back with it in time to die.'

'You've got a point.'

'Well . . .' He pulled an ear lobe. 'I'll be in touch. You'll be wanted for the inquest, of course.' He walked back to his chair and swept up Cindy into his arms. 'Come along, old girl.'

'Heh!' I said.

'Might be able to find her a good home.'

I could feel the chill in my throat. 'And if not?' The words matched.

'She'll have to be put down, won't she.'

'Yes, she'll have to be put down, right on that chair. And now.'

'Oh . . . oh!' he said, grinning at me. 'You're keeping her?'

'Yes. Away from you.'

He tipped a cold cigarette in his lips, walked to the door, looked round, and said: 'Nice meeting you.'

Then we had the room to ourselves. 'Did you hear what he said?' I asked Cindy. Then, a late reaction, I was laughing. It'd been Grayson's method of checking that we wanted Cindy. He was a man who enjoyed risk.

4

From the window I watched him walk across the street to where he'd parked his white Volkswagen Golf. The fact that it was a hatchback meant nothing. There are thousands of them. I reckoned it would be a GTI. Grayson was the type who'd relish the tearing acceleration and the unattainable top speed.

I was far from certain about him, but I had to assume he'd given me the go-ahead to take a fresh look at the death of Edwin Carter.

My watch told me it was five minutes past eleven. Amelia had left a little before ten, and it was unlikely she would complete the journey in under six hours. So I had time on my hands, time to take a look at the scene of Edwin Carter's death.

Grayson had been persuasive about his logic in assuming murder, but the basic reason for suicide had been there, and I'd not been fully convinced. I rescued the manilla envelope from the carpet and looked for clues as to where to begin. The house was called Plâs Ceiriog. My map of Wales showed a place called Glyn Ceiriog around twenty miles north, so the odds were that the house was in the area. I dumped Cindy on the passenger's seat, and we got going.

The hood was still in place from the night before, and I left it like that, in case Cindy had a dislike of driving and made a sudden dive for freedom. But she was car-trained, and settled down at once.

The main road north from Wellington to Oswestry was a trunk road, which I took at a fair speed, then on to Chirk. There I turned west, straight for the mountains. Ceiriog turned out to be a river, and the lesser road followed it faithfully, climbing steadily towards its source. Very soon I was due to run out of roads, and I was only eight miles from the border. But probably I was ten or more from an English pub.

Having had experience of the confusion the lanes could produce, I stopped often and asked for information. The Welsh accents became more difficult to untangle, and there didn't appear to be much interest in the difficulties of a lone Englishman. All I could see was mountains all round me, and the occasional buildings were distant farms.

I found it by accident, drawing up to ask at what I thought to be a farm, and discovering it to be a deserted hutment, then noticing a very indistinct sign directing me up a lane beside it: 'Plâs Ceiriog'. It seemed a remote location for anything but a farm. Even the sheep would feel lonely.

Mountains crowded me, thrusting and elbowing the lane into contortions. At one point the sparse pines marched down the slopes from either side, and I was surprised to round a bluff and discover that the lane drove through them, at that stage resembling a maintained drive. Beyond the trees it opened out again, and there was the house, nestling on the south-facing slope, with more trees beyond it but with the view open across the valley, where twin streams met to urge the water onwards to become the River Ceiriog, with beyond the valley the peak of the Berwyns.

Plâs Ceiriog. Surely a rich man's folly from the Victorian age, built to accommodate oil lamps and natural water from the mountains, their fuel from their own pines. How had they lived through the winters?

I drew the car in and got out to have a look. The building had matured into its enfolding hills and become part of the landscape. The red brick was dulled from exposure to the west winds, the walls clad with rampant creepers. The gardens, evident as such only from the slightly different green against the grey sparseness of the hillsides, had been allowed to slumber on to return to the mountain. I could see the terrace, itself a flat plate of green from that distance. It ran along the whole length of the house. The tall windows caught a reflection of the blue sky. This would be the rear of the house. The drive curved out of sight beyond it. I could not make out the two garages, which, as Grayson had explained it, should have been on this side of the house.

I climbed back into the car and drove on slowly.

A fold in the land had hidden them. As I rounded a crop of meagre thorn, there were the garages, just off the drive and below the house on the terrace side, hidden from it by the determined planting of a row of rhododendrons. I pulled off the drive on to the grass-strewn patch of hardcore that fronted the garages, and stopped.

Cindy jumped out after me. I took the lead in my left hand. We stood and contemplated the garages.

Both doors were now closed, and gave the appearance of having been so for a number of years. I walked up to them. The foot of wall between the doors had a plate inset in it, with two buttons side by side, one for each door. I assumed that, when operating, a single button would actuate its door with a push. Door closed; one touch opened it. Door open; one touch closed it. It would probably have been the same on the radio transmitters; one push of the button would make the door do the opposite to what it was.

I touched one of the buttons. There was a hum, and slowly the left-hand door began to rise. It took about twenty seconds, then was fully slid away beneath the roof. Inside, facing me, was a gleaming black BMW, one of the 500 series. I stared at it for a moment, then touched the button again. The door hummed down in quiet obedience.

I stood back, a little disconcerted. Where had I got the impression that the house was uninhabited?

There was a soft chuckle behind me. As there'd been no menace in it – in fact, more a luscious delight – I turned slowly.

'A big man', she said, one finger poised in front of her lips in case an outright laugh should need suppressing, 'ought to have a big dog.'

'I'm having enough trouble handling this monster,' I told her. 'I'm sorry. I assumed there was nobody living here.'

'You're quite a distance out of your way, on that assumption.'

'I'm not out of my way. I wanted to look at the house.'

'And at my car?'

'I didn't know there was a car inside.'

She smiled. 'But of course you didn't – you told me you assumed the house was empty. Did you plan to break in?' Then, with no pause for a reply, she went down on one knee to Cindy. 'Whatever's happened to the poor thing? And . . . what is it?'

'I didn't plan to break in, she's been in a fire, and I think, when she's white again, she'll be a Westie.'

'The little darling!' She straightened, Cindy in her arms and loving it. 'What fire?'

'Last night,' I explained, 'about twenty miles south of here. Cindy, there, came out of it alive.'

She was now staring at me with grave, brown eyes. Her face was expressive, alive, her brow high and her dark hair drawn back, caught in what looked like a green rubber band. The effect was one of angles, a sharp jaw and high cheekbones, ears displayed, with a ring in one and a sleeper in the other. Her mouth was wide, flexible, seeming always to be poised indecisively between humour and solemnity. In tailored beige slacks, she was slim, the whole effect accentuating her height. She was tall, five feet eight or nine, and carried herself with an easy grace. She could have been knocking on fifty, could well have opened the door. There was a confidence about her, an assuredness of her place in the world. I found myself wondering whether I should know her, and realised I'd subconsciously linked her with previous mentions of the world of the stage.

I had been staring at her too long. She moistened her lips and glanced away.

'This stuff on her ears smells awful.'

'It seems to help.'

'And who', she asked, realising I wasn't going to offer it, 'failed to come out alive?'

'A former friend of mine. A man called Llewellyn Hughes. Ex-Detective Chief Superintendent.'

'Ah!' she said, nodding. She used ten seconds to unclip the lead from Cindy's collar, hand me the lead, and bend to put her down, then she had worked out the connection. 'And you're also police?'

'Also Ex. I worked with him as a sergeant, years ago.'

'You're not the one ... but of course not. He was so brisk and humourless.'

'I'm not the one. Richard Patton, if we're to get on to names.'

'And I'm Rosemary Trew.'

We formally shook hands. Her fingers were long and slim, the nails short and uncoloured. She turned away and began to stroll back towards the house, and I was forced to follow. She was leading me away from the garages. We circled the rhododendrons and headed up a gentle slope towards the terrace.

'I remembered the name, you see,' she explained. 'Your friend was in charge when my Uncle Edwin died. Now the Chief Superintendent dies, and the following day you wish to look at the house. Would you mind explaining the connection?'

Her attitude had changed completely. Her formality was cold, even biting.

'I would, as a matter of fact. Mind, I mean.'

She stopped dead, and turned to face me. The little bob of hair at the back swung out, then returned to disciplined position. Her lips were in a firm straight line.

'Then I suggest that you return to your car and drive away again.'

'Which I would have done, if you hadn't started to walk me up to the house.'

'I can easily walk you back.'

'Thank you. That would be most pleasurable. I did hope you'd explain to me about the garage doors. But . . .' I shrugged. 'I can call again.'

'You're just as unfeeling as the other one was,' she declared, sounding disappointed.

'Who? Grayson?'

'*That* was his name.'

'Unfeeling, perhaps, but efficient. Grayson I mean, not me.'

'Efficient my . . . What is it you want? Why have you come here?'

'Perhaps a little water for Cindy. I think she's dehydrated. The fire, you know.' I was stalling, not wanting to discuss any aspect of Edwin Carter's death with one of the people involved, before I'd read more carefully through Llew's notes. But there was an air of brisk intelligence about this woman that convinced me that she would not leap clumsily to conclusions, and a naked honesty that I knew I had to test.

'Llew Hughes was writing his memoirs,' I told her.

'And you're intending to finish them for him?' she asked, her right hand flicking past my face, dismissing both the memoirs and my ability. 'If that's the case, you'll need to get your facts straight.'

'What I had in mind.' I meant the facts.

'Then get one thing firmly in your head before you put pen to paper: dear Duncan did not kill my uncle.'

'Did he not?'

'Of course not.' She was relaxed again, and was once more walking towards the house, her steps positive and her chin high. 'If anyone did, it was me.'

'I suspected you from the start.'

'And if you can't be serious . . .' She glanced darkly at me. 'You're smiling, ' she told me severely.

'One minute you're sending me packing, the next you're accusing yourself . . . what can I do but smile?'

'You can take more notice of what people say than the other one did.'

'Grayson?'

'Once he'd got one idea in his head, nothing would budge him.'

We had reached the terrace. The flags were uneven and covered with the green stain of algae. She was leading me towards the far window, which stood open as a door.

'What idea was that?'

'He said it was murder, when obviously poor Uncle Edwin committed suicide.'

So she had nothing new to offer. A pity. But I couldn't turn away now, particularly as she said, as a directive: 'You're staying to lunch, of course. I have some friends here . . .'

And I had thought the house to be empty! There were seven people in that room. They sat to one side on folding chairs at card tables, lounged against the wall chatting, peered suspiciously at the buffet table against the far wall, four men, three women. This would have been the dining room mentioned by Grayson, the one used for party games after Edwin Carter had driven off into the night looking for fresh supplies of liquor. But at that time it would surely have looked different. There would have been pictures breaking up the naked expanses of oak panelling. The two chandeliers, now looking decidedly dusty and dejected, would have been lit and sparkling. Heavy Victorian furniture would have been thrust back against the walls, along with the dining table.

Now the oak block floor was a large, cleared space, broken only by strips of wide, white tape, affixed in squares and oblongs and large enclosing blocks. The lighting – not switched on – was from standard lamps of the studio variety, very functional.

I'd seen something like it before, when I'd visited a television studio to interview one of the executives, whom we later arrested. They were rehearsing a play.

Rosemary cast her eyes around. Then she brought her hands together into the praying position in a small, undemonstrative slap.

'Everybody. Please. This is a friend who's come to meet us. You'll be interested, Drew. He's a policeman.'

Nobody cheered. Nobody clapped their hands in delight and said, 'Oooh!' They looked at me with indifference, and returned to their Scrabble and their prawn cocktails.

'And this is Cindy,' said Rosemary, with a noticeable increase of enthusiasm, holding her up. 'Wouldn't she be ideal in act two, Mildred, you on the settee . . .'

'No you don't,' I said, before I realised she was ribbing me.

'She's brown,' said Mildred plaintively, 'and you know I'll be wearing blue.'

'Of course you will, dear. Don't worry about it.' Rosemary turned to me. 'Mildred thinks blue's her lucky colour,' she whispered. 'But of course, quite out of the question.'

I agreed. Mildred Niven. I knew her face from the television screen, knew her name from the list of guests on the night Edwin died. But Miss Niven – sorry, Dame Mildred – was in her eighties, surely, a tremendously overpowering lady when she got into her part, and not, I'd have thought, at seventy on that night, a potential murderess. Nor, come to think of it, a likely participant in party games.

Rosemary took me round for formal introductions. Most of the people were of no interest to me, apart from the fact that I knew their names and faces. Yet they looked strangely different in their jeans and blousons, their caftans, their jumpsuits, and without television make-up. They nodded. They smiled. But I was just an outsider, not in the business.

Only Drew Pierson showed any interest, as Rosemary seemed to expect. He was due to appear on the honours list any time, surely, one of those actors I'd watched grow old, first as the young hopeful in films of the forties, graduating by way of the Royal Shakespeare and the National Theatre to character parts in television, when his face had grown old enough to display character, to the supreme accolade of being permitted to advertise somebody's butter in a commercial.

Drew Pierson was playing the part of the police inspector. Any tips would be appreciated and ignored.

'We're doing a revival of Uncle Edwin's *Fair's Fair*, opening at

Coventry in six weeks,' Rosemary told me. 'Drew's the policeman. He's very good at it, aren't you, Drew?'

Drew Pierson inclined his head, and produced his famous smile of bemused self-depreciation.

'And you,' I asked her, 'what part are you playing?'

'I'm directing,' she told me, her expression indicating I was a bit slow, not realising. Then she touched my arm, forgiving me, and turned to Pierson again.

'Drew. You were here, the night Uncle Edwin died. You tell him.'

'Tell him what, darling?'

'How he died. Why he died. Oh . . . you know.'

I had recognised Drew Pierson's name, too, from the guest list for that night. But Pierson didn't know anything. He'd been acting for so long that he didn't know anything that wasn't down on paper as a speech. Or so I at first believed.

Rosemary whipped up a script from the buffet table and walked away to have words with a young couple who'd been practising their kissing scene in the corner. Pierson suggested I should try the salad with a little of the pâté. I slipped some of the pâté to Cindy on a paper plate and dug into a prawn cocktail, while Pierson poured me a glass of white wine. My lunch, that was.

He asked me: 'What do *I* know about it? Tell me that.'

That shock of white hair had been with him as long as I could remember. His face was severely lined, and his mouth was loose enough to retain crumbs in the corners. He was dressed in a formal three-piece suit with an open-necked shirt, revealing a chain disappearing into a hairy chest. He blinked at me mildly.

'Go on, interrogate me,' he invited. 'Break down my resistance. I want to see how you do it.'

'I don't want to interrogate you. I'd need a closed room and a rubber hose. But you can tell me – why was Rosemary so certain he committed suicide?'

'Who? Edwin? I suppose he did. Try the red, it goes better with prawns. Oh yes, it was on the cards. If he hadn't, I think I'd have killed him myself. Dear Edwin. Give him a sheet of paper and he'd write the most divine dialogue. I was with him for years, you know. Six of his plays. Success after success. And none of your tantrums with him, you understand. Playwrights are so touchy. Every word a jewel, and nobody must change it. But not Edwin. Tell him it didn't speak right, and he'd alter it. Divine.'

'But not at the end?' I asked, slipping Cindy a prawn.

'They'd call for him at the final curtain, you know. Author, author. He loved it. But it wasn't enough. Greenslade used to direct for him, before he went on to films. Clyde Greenslade.' He raised his glass, peered through it, then downed it in one gulp. 'A very unsympathetic director, Clyde. Mark my words. But Edwin . . . Author, author wasn't enough for Edwin. It had to be producer, producer . . . Oh yes, he financed the last two himself, and directed them. Wanted the lot. Greedy Edwin. The little sausage rolls are rather nice.'

'So . . . as a director he failed?'

'A complete flop, dear boy. You'd have thought he didn't really understand his own plays. Two in a row, complete flops. And I was the lead in both. Almost wrecked my career. I could cheerfully have killed him myself.'

'But all the same, you came to his party.'

'Of course. He was my friend. I think your dog's going to be sick, you know.'

I got her out on to the terrace in time. Clearly, I had a lot to learn about dogs, so I apologised to Cindy, and we went back inside.

Rosemary had the two youngsters in the middle of the room, reading to them from the script, with wide sweeps of her expressive fingers. Drew Pierson was now sitting at a card table by the side wall, facing Mildred Niven, a glass of red wine close to his hand. I rescued half a dozen of the sausage rolls, and went to join them.

Dame Mildred glanced at me, then down at her knitting again. The needles flashed, as did her eyes.

'You didn't tell me', I reminded Pierson, 'why you're so certain Edwin committed suicide.' I was not, at that stage, probing the physical problems involved, but the emotional ones. It was all very well dumping Edwin into a psychological bracket: manic-depressive. But it was not enough. And these people had known him, and worked with him.

But had they? My impression was that the miserable author was expected to disappear into the background, once rehearsals began, so that he'd not protest at the mangling of his play.

'The man was unstable,' Pierson stated complacently.

'Now Drew,' said Mildred severely, 'that will not do, and you know it.' For one smallest part of a second the needles had paused whilst one of them pointed at him accusingly. Pierson grunted, and peered into his glass. 'You must not give our friend the wrong impression.'

She turned and smiled at me. That smile! In repose, her face assumed a somewhat grim expression, accentuated by a wide mouth that drooped at the corners and a square, firm chin. She rationed the smile, which illuminated her face. 'Drew', she explained, 'has always been rather superficial, I've noticed. Edwin Carter was simply a dear man who tried to please, and tried too hard. He was a brilliant playwright, but didn't realise it himself.'

Pierson cleared his throat. He had the natural authority that converted it into a momentous event, and I automatically awaited a deep pronouncement.

'Edwin', he said, 'was a fool to himself. He wrote wonderful dialogue. But he had no self-confidence. If I asked him to change my words, he would.'

'And no doubt. . .' Mildred nodded. '. . . for the worse, knowing you.'

'I was going to ask about that,' I said. 'I thought authors were encouraged to keep out of the way.'

Mildred chuckled. 'Just try it with Edwin. He clucked around like an anxious hen.'

'But not sufficiently anxious to refuse amendments?'

'I never asked him,' she said. 'My lines were me, my dear. I spoke them, and they were true. And it was tight dialogue. Do you know what tight dialogue is, Mr . . . er?'

'Patton,' I said. 'And I don't.'

'It's dialogue that follows on itself, each speech naturally luring on the next, all linked together as far as three or four speeches further on, and all flowing smoothly. Edwin Carter was a wonderful playwright. It's a pity he'd never accept it.'

'Surely, the evidence of success . . .'

'There are people who will never accept they are succeeding in what they can do well, serious authors who feel they must write comedy, and vice versa. Pianists who must be conductors. And footballers who must be cricketers. Oh, you could go on . . .'

'I heard', I observed, biting into another sausage roll, 'somebody describe him as big-headed.'

Drew Pierson laughed, that rumble of his that shakes the gods. 'Edwin! It was painful to watch.'

'He blushed,' Mildred explained.

'Yes?'

'When anybody praised him,' Pierson explained.

'And he was desperate,' Mildred amplified. 'You could see it in his eyes. Desperate for some sort of success he could recognise himself.'

'You're telling me why you believe he committed suicide.'

Click, click went the needles. Something bulky and blue was growing as I watched.

'We knew, you see,' she said. 'Edwin tried to be a director, and he slaughtered his own plays. Nobody could convince him that he was a success as a writer. And nobody needed to tell him that he'd failed as a director. We *knew* he was near breaking point. That night . . . his party. Just the sort of thing he'd arrange, of course, celebrating his failure. It was as good as saying out loud: I always told you I was no good, now I've proved it. We came, his friends, to hold his hands. It was all building up, his wild and enthusiastic mood, like a volcano waiting to blow its top. We knew that if we didn't keep an eye on him, anything could happen.'

'And yet you didn't,' I reminded her gently. 'You all let him drive away into the night, with the obvious expectation that his mood would switch to black depression.'

She flicked that smile at me again, but now it held a tang of contempt.

'A critic once wrote about a play I was in: "I did not enjoy so-and-so's play because I didn't go to it. I couldn't stand his previous one." That's you. You were not here. You do not know these people.' A movement of the needles encompassed the room. 'The show must go on. You know. A good example was that evening. We went on. Party games. We wanted him to return to happiness. On the surface, we were happy. We are actors, young man. Actors.'

'And you were here?' I asked, not distracted by being called a young man. 'In this room. Yourself. All the time.'

'I was here, keeping a quiet eye on the proceedings.'

'In case the jollity flagged?'

'Naughty,' she said. 'But yes, I was here.'

'And nobody left the room, for one moment . . .'

'I would not be prepared to swear to that. But for moments only. Except for Duncan, of course.'

'Not being an actor, he couldn't pretend to be happy?'

'He had said he wanted to see his uncle privately, and he was in here and out again, back again, like a restless waif.'

'Waif?'

'Waif was what he was. Lost. Unhappy.'

'He was not', put in Pierson, 'in the business. Of course he was lost, amongst a crowd of extroverts.'

Once again I was aware that Drew Pierson saw more and understood more than he pretended.

'So Duncan was sort of elected to be there when his uncle returned?' I persisted.

'He elected himself,' Mildred said. 'The danger point – that was how I thought of it myself – would be when Edwin returned. Of course, it was realised that Edwin might not have gone all the way to the nearest pub across the border. He could quite easily have abandoned such a stupid idea . . .'

'He was insistent,' Drew reminded her.

'. . . and returned early without the stuff he'd gone for. But Duncan, I'm sure, went down to the garages several times, just in case.'

'Including the time when Edwin *did* return,' I commented.

'But no,' she corrected me firmly. 'He was obviously not there when Edwin actually arrived, because Edwin had time to get himself shut inside that garage with his engine going. Hasn't anybody told you that?'

I glanced at my watch. Time was running away. 'But that's the point, you see. If Edwin committed suicide, he must have gone to extreme lengths to bring it about. And shown determination.'

'That', she nodded, 'was Edwin all over. Determined. Particularly when he was doing the wrong thing.'

There seemed nothing more to say. I got to my feet and said goodbye, and hoped I'd be able to get to the opening at Coventry, and very nearly found myself bowing. That was the effect Mildred Niven had on people. Drew Pierson caught my eye, and winked.

I picked up Cindy, and moved to the open door on to the terrace. The two young actors were standing side by side in a rectangle of white tape, which I assumed to represent a settee on which they would be seated, rehearsing their small scene.

She: I'm sure father's getting to like you.
He: Then why does he ignore me?
She: It's because he loves me.
He: He glares.
She: I told you, he loves me.
He: I don't glare, and I love you.
She: You're glaring now.
He: But not so expertly as he does it.

Rosemary, facing them, raised her eyes from the script. 'No dear,' she said. 'A tiny pause before the word "expertly", as though you're not sure which word to use. You'll see. It's a laugh line. And Marj, a toss of the head when he says it. Hmm?'

So that was directing. It seemed to matter. They ran through it again, and darn it, the lad made the line amusing.

I thought I'd have to leave before catching her eye, but it seemed I already had. Rosemary raised her arm and wiggled her fingers at me. It did not mean goodbye, it meant I'll be seeing you.

Cindy and I went down to the garages, where I stood again and contemplated them. Infuriatingly, I could not see what Llew had been worried about. I could not understand his comment: where booze from? Whether early or late, Edwin Carter had returned with drinks on the rear seat of his car. He must have arrived during one of Duncan's restless returns to the dining room, if Duncan was to be believed. Or he'd returned to be welcomed with a blow on his forehead, if Grayson was to be believed. The exact time of his return seemed hardly relevant, if Duncan had been the only one free from party games for the whole period between Edwin's known departure and his known death.

Once again I pressed the button. Up went the door. I tried the other button. Up went that door, too. In the one garage was the BMW, in the other nothing. My curiosity overcame me. I went in beside the car and tried its door. It was unlocked. Wondering whether the radio was still used, I hunted around and found a small black box, about the size of a transistor radio, in the glove compartment. It had a short aerial, an on-off switch, and in the centre of one side a single red button. The radio looked old enough and sufficiently used to be the original.

I took it outside and stood back, switched it on, and pressed the red button. Sedately, the door hummed down to hide the car. The door of the other garage remained open. I pressed the button again, and up went the door. Great fun. Then I had an idea. I moved back a few yards, and tried it again. The door closed. A few more yards. Nothing. So the range was limited to about thirty yards, I reckoned. I moved two paces closer and up went the door.

A bright idea gone up the spout. I'd been wondering whether it could have been possible to close that door from the house, by radio. It did not seem so.

So . . . for Edwin Carter to have committed suicide, what would he have required to do?

First, we'd have to assume he drove in fast and braked hard, to get that bang on his forehead. Steering wheel? But surely that assumed he wasn't wearing his seat belt. Was it compulsory at that time? No? But he'd had one fitted, because Grayson had mentioned it. And anyway, I suddenly thought, if he'd braked that hard, surely all that expensive booze would have shot off the back seat. Or some of it. I made a mental note to check the photographs for any confirmation of that point.

Second, we'd have to assume his lights were on, and he left his engine running when he got out of the car. (Always assuming the bump on the

45

head had left him conscious, he having raced into the garage in such a hurry to put an end to his own life.)

Third, he had to close the door. I'd been told the button on the wall wasn't working at that time. He would know that. He would know the radio in the car he'd just driven home would not operate *that* door, so the only thing left was to use the radio in his own car, parked outside the other garage. So . . . did he go out to that car and take the hand radio from it back into the garage, and operate it from there? He did not, because it was still in his own car afterwards. Therefore, he would have had to operate the radio from outside, put it back inside his own car, and run back before the door closed on him.

Fourth, he would have to sit again in the driver's seat, fasten the seat belt (which probably hadn't been fastened when he arrived) and switch off the lights. Why switch off the lights? To prevent any small line of light from edging past the door and alerting rescue? They had been off, though, the car's lights.

I tried the red button again. The door slowly closed, and this time I compared it with my watch. Nineteen seconds, I made it, though it was half-way down in five seconds, no doubt because of the levers involved. It would have meant a mad scramble to get beneath that lowering door before it was too late.

Thoughtfully, I raised the door again, switched off the radio, and returned it to where I'd found it. I closed both doors with the external buttons.

I now had complete sympathy with Grayson's reasoning, and could not believe that Edwin Carter had committed suicide. So what the devil had been worrying Llew Hughes?

When I got in the Stag and started the engine I realised that I'd spent far too much time on it. Amelia would phone, and I wouldn't be there.

'Fasten your belt,' I said to Cindy. 'We're in a hurry.'

5

The trip back to Welshpool was nerve-racking, not simply because I had to go easy on the brakes, otherwise Cindy would've spent all her time climbing back on to the seat, but mainly because I knew my Amelia. I'd been anxious to see my letters from Llew, and she'd realised it, had offered, and dashed off to ensure my continuing happiness. How would it seem, then, if I was not there when she phoned?

The Stag was pulling to the left on braking (one of the reasons she didn't like driving it), and needed double de-clutching to ease the box from third to second (another), so that I was not really equipped for taking winding lanes at speed. Once on the main road from Chirk, I managed to make up a little time, but it was ten minutes to four when I drew into the hotel car-park. I'd calculated that she would possibly reach the cottage by four. I grabbed up Cindy and rushed inside, stopping only at Reception for the key.

'Any messages?'

'No, sir. Sorry.'

I took the stairs two at a time. No need for apologies, it suited me fine.

The phone began ringing as I slipped the key into its slot. I left the door swinging for Cindy to follow, and pounded over to it.

'Amelia?'

'Richard! Oh . . . I'm glad you're there.'

The tone of her voice alerted me. 'What is it?'

'I'm . . . well, I'm at Tewkesbury. Richard, I've had a bit of an accident.' There was a forced chuckle, to reassure me. 'More haste, less . . .'

'Are you all right?'

'Yes, of course.'

'There's no of course about it,' I said severely. 'What happened?'

'It's raining here. What's it doing there, Richard?'

I glanced out of the window. 'It's dull. Amelia, what on earth does the weather matter?'

She drew in her breath deeply, let it out with a sigh. 'The roads . . . the sudden rain . . . well, it was slippy, and I took a corner too fast. It's all right, just a skid into the ditch, but there's been all the fuss, police and what-not, and phoning the hire people.'

'To hell with the car,' I said heavily. 'What about you?'

'Not a scratch.'

'Now tell the truth.'

'Just a little sprain of my left wrist. Nothing more.'

'You've seen a doctor . . .'

'It's nothing. Don't fuss.'

'Shock, you know. You should rest.'

Another sigh. 'I'm calling you from a hotel room. I planned to stay the night . . .'

'I'll be right there.'

'Nonsense,' she said firmly, with a touch of annoyance. 'I'm staying because I've got to get another car . . .'

'I said I'll come.'

'. . . and they're taking some time to find me a car with an automatic drive.'

I was silent. My admiration for Amelia kept receiving little jolts, every time it showed a tendency to doze off.

'So that I shan't need to keep using my left hand,' she explained.

'I did get the point,' I assured her. 'I just couldn't think what to say.'

'Well, you might say the letters could wait until tomorrow. You could lift *that* bit of worry from my mind – that there's no panic for them.'

The manilla envelope was close to my right hand on the low table. I knew I now had to probe it inside out for clues as to what Llew had meant. There could be important clues in his letters. I ached to read them, or have her read them to me.

'Now you get some rest,' I said cheerfully, 'and if you feel like it in the morning – and only if you do – drive on to Devon. But no hurry, Amelia. Really. I haven't been sitting in the bar all this time, you know. I've been up to the house.'

'Which house?'

'Where it happened. There's lots to tell you, but for now I'll just say there's no possibility it could have been suicide.'

'So your friend Llew was all wrong, and there's nothing . . .'

'Not necessarily wrong. I've still got to comb through this envelope. But it was definitely murder.'

'Then you need the letters. If the car's delivered in time, I can still . . .'

'No!' I lowered my voice. 'No, my dear, there's not a bit of hurry. Years have gone by – what's another day! I'll dig into this, and you get your rest . . .'

I still wasn't used to having a dog around. Cindy's low growl I took to mean she objected to my talking to nobody. My reaction was too slow. I half turned, and there was an impression of something moving fast towards my right ear. Then agony shot around my brain, and only stabilised when I opened my eyes and realised I was lying on the carpet.

It settled into a throb that blurred my vision, then died down as I groped for reality. In my fall I'd knocked over the table. The phone lay squeaking at my feet, but not within my grasp when I tried to reach for it. I levered myself into a sitting position, and my hand touched something that rolled. I grabbed for it, and discovered it to be a bottle of brown ale. Full. With the cap intact.

Cindy was staring at me with mute query from a yard away.

I managed to reach the phone. Amelia was saying over and over, in rising panic: 'Richard, Richard!'

' 'Elia,' I mumbled. 'S 'all right.'

'What's happened? I didn't know. Oh Lord!' She was close to tears.

'Bottle,' I said. 'Lef' door open. Some . . . body came in. Belted me wiss a bottle.'

'Your voice is funny.'

'It'll come ba . . .'

My eyes scanned the floor. There seemed no sign of the manilla envelope. I realised I still held the beer bottle in my left hand.

'Give me a sec,' I pleaded. 'Goin' to swill my face.'

I weaved over to the bathroom and put the cold tap on full, splashed my face and dried it, felt behind my right ear, winced, but discovered no blood on my fingers.

'Are you there, Richard?' she was demanding when I got back.

'Two invalids,' I told her. 'One at each end.'

'Your voice is stronger, anyway.'

'I've been knocked out before,' I boasted. 'I left the door open, and somebody must've been following me. Heard what I was saying. They hit me with . . .' I held it up and blinked it into focus. '. . . a bottle of Wem brown ale.'

'How you can joke . . .'

And indeed, I realised through the pain and the persisting confusion, I was feeling lighthearted. I'd been getting nowhere, and gradually realising that there could well be nowhere to go. Or so it had begun to seem. Therefore it was encouraging to receive a belt on the head. It meant there was something to hide.

'Amelia, love, listen carefully. Five minutes ago I'd have said there wasn't much to investigate. Now . . . I know there's something.'

'Your voice is back to normal.'

'Yes. But I don't understand what's going on, who's involved, what they know. D'you see what I'm getting at?'

'Are you sure your brain's back to normal?'

'Listen then, and tell me whether this is logical. I'm now known to be asking awkward questions. Other things could be known. Our place in Devon . . . that could be known.'

'Surely not.'

'But we can't be certain. The person who knocked me out could be heading there right now.'

'You're stretching things, Richard.'

'Trying to get his hands on those letters.'

'Really, I hardly think that's likely.'

'All the same . . . suppose you go down there alone, suppose *they* are there at the time . . .'

'Oh . . . come on!'

'I'd rather lose the letters than have you involved. I'll tell you what to do. Cancel that hire car and stay where you are, and I'll drive to Tewkesbury. Ask the hotel to switch you to a double room . . .'

'Richard . . .' she was saying. 'Richard . . . please. I'm grown up, you know. There can be no danger. I will do what I planned to do, and phone you again. Tomorrow.'

'Don't you understand . . .'

'And do look after yourself. You should see a doctor.'

She hung up on me. And she hadn't told me where she was staying. My fault. You can't be high-handed with someone like Amelia, and really, I *had* been exaggerating the likelihood of anyone driving all that way for my letters, even of there being much chance they would know where to go. Nevertheless, I did feel I should play safe, and try to reach the cottage in Devon before she did. Even if it meant grabbing a sandwich and starting as soon as possible.

Worrying about this, indecisive, I walked over to the door to close it. The brown envelope was lying just outside in the corridor. When I picked it up I saw that there were teeth marks in one corner. Teeth marks, and what looked like a single spot of blood.

She was eyeing me with her head on one side, still concerned. What do you get a dog for a special treat – which doesn't make it sick, of course? How do you tell them? I picked her up and she licked my nose, and that was all she required. I rang down and asked them to send up sandwiches and a bottle opener and a glass, and when they came I drank the brown ale and ate the sandwiches, with Cindy's help.

I had the contents of the brown envelope spread on the bed, wondering where to start and not really concentrating. I was still worrying about Amelia. Shouldn't I be packing – or would we be returning here? Nothing would settle in my brain and become an intention. I took up the photographs, and the phone rang again.

My hand swooped for it. 'You've changed your mind . . .'

The calm voice cut in. 'Mr Patton? This is Rosemary Trew.'

'Yes,' I stammered. 'Well yes. Hello.'

'I'll ring off if you like.'

'No . . . don't.'

'The lack of enthusiasm in your voice, my friend . . .'

'You caught me by surprise. And I was expecting somebody else.'

'A woman?' Said with a laugh on her breath.

'Yes, as a matter of fact.'

'I do admire honesty.'

I took a deep intake of air. 'And what can I do for you, Miss Trew?'

'Rosemary, please. You left very abruptly, Mr . . .'

'Richard,' I said, trying to mimic her tone, not too pleased. 'Please.'

'Well, Richard, as I was saying, you left abruptly. Our little chat – surely we'd barely scraped the surface.'

Hmm! I thought. I certainly had stirred up something. 'I'd really come along to get a general idea of the setting.'

'And the garages. You were interested in the operation of the doors.'

'I found time to check on that, before I left.'

'I wondered why it took you so long.'

She said that with calm serenity, allowing me to realise that she'd been interested in my movements, in me.

'There were other things,' I admitted cautiously. 'Details I would have liked to check. Perhaps I can call again.'

Silence.

'When it's more convenient,' I amplified.

'It's convenient now. If you'd waited another five minutes, you'd have seen that we broke up rehearsals for the weekend. But you had to rush off . . .'

The strange thing was that I didn't think her tone was assumed. So the warmth in her voice could well have been genuine, even though the necessity to see me again would not be personal. She needed to discover what I was doing, why, and how well I was succeeding. That meant I had to seize the opportunity.

'If it's convenient now,' I said, 'perhaps . . .' Caution prevented me from total commitment.

'Perhaps what?'

'We could meet . . . a meal . . . this evening.'

'I could give you a meal here.'

'Well . . . no. I mean, couldn't we meet at Oswestry, say?'

'Neutral ground?' A lilt in her voice, a challenge.

'Half-way, I'd rather put it.'

'I know a little place,' she told me. Of course she would. She'd know all the little places for miles. 'The Rendezvous. Shall I book a table? Say yes.'

'Very well.'

'You might try to sound more gracious.'

I could imagine her lips pouting. 'I shall be delighted.'

'Eight o'clock suit you? I'll book. See you there.'

She rang off.

I stared at the dead phone in my hand, not sure who'd propositioned whom, and completely confused as to my own motivation. Certainly, in view of her interest in my movements and actions, I had to see her while I had the opportunity. But if her interest included something personal, would I be able to resist the temptation to reciprocate? And I didn't know, damn it.

My plan to leave for the south coast was now jeopardised. If I was going to meet Rosemary at eight, I could reach the cottage before Amelia only if I drove through the night. With a sinking feeling I realised that I'd made a mistake. I fumbled in the drawer of the dressing table, where I'd seen the phone book, actually had it open to T for Trew. R., before I stopped myself.

There was a mental image of Rosemary Trew standing watching her phone, waiting for me to call and cancel, and I knew I couldn't do it. Blast the woman, I thought, and the image smiled in triumph and walked away.

And yet, had she been calling from Plâs Ceiriog? The call could well have been intended to place her there, in my mind, if in fact she was still in Welshpool, having only recently bopped me on the head with a bottle of beer. But if that were so . . . surely she'd not have gone to the lengths of justifying the call by virtually insisting on our meeting that evening.

Confused, then, I tried to work out how much time I could spare to go through the envelope. I could not deny a stir of pleasure at the thought of the evening to come, and had to persuade myself it would be a working engagement. Consequently, I had to comb Llew's notes, to decide whether there was anything useful to be extracted from Rosemary later.

There seemed to be nothing. I read her statement, which repeated what I already knew, plus the details of her own movements during the critical time.

She had been her uncle's secretary and virtually his housekeeper for the last three years before his death. She, more than anyone, knew him and his mental condition. She could see a plummet into depression on its way. So she'd been worried for him. She had gone with him down to the garages, whilst the others were trying to get together for party games. There, she had watched as he tried to start his own car, and failed. But he'd been so determined to go on his booze-hunting trip that he'd insisted on using the other car, Rosemary's Dolomite, even though it had an automatic gearbox, which he detested. She had returned to the house for the keys, which Duncan had in his pocket, had met Duncan on the terrace, had told him the situation, and then gone back with the keys. There, her uncle had taken them from her ungraciously, and in a bit of a huff she'd left him to it. She was telling all this to Duncan, on the terrace, when they heard the engine start, and fade away as he drove off. Then she'd left Duncan and gone inside to join the others. Duncan had refused to do the same, and strolled around until his uncle returned.

This was all stated in official language, but I've tarted it up a little, reading between the lines. But even with the emotional background, what was there? Nothing.

I had a bath and decided on the blue suit, not certain whether the Rendezvous would be jeans and sweat shirts or black jackets and bow ties. So I aimed for in-between. Cindy clearly knew we were going out and looked expectant. As I didn't know when she would feed again, I went down to my friend the chef, who supplied a dish of the soup of the day and some more scraps. This inside her, Cindy looked sleepy enough, so I took her outside to the car. It was ten minutes past seven. Just right.

The Rendezvous didn't look much from outside, and the parking patch was a stretch of waste ground. Normally, I don't like leaving a virtually open car in such places after dark, as I guessed it would be when I came out, but this time I was confident. Nobody was going to get into our car with Cindy there.

I took her for a little walk round, to make sure the seat remained dry, then tucked her away, and was just straightening when the BMW drew in beside me.

'Richard!' she said, locking the door and turning to me. 'This is very pleasant.'

She took my hovering right hand in her left and gave it a tug. As I was standing firm, it drew her closer to me, and she gave me a quick kiss on the cheek.

'I do like a man who's there on cue,' she told me, and linked her arm in mine.

6

It was better inside, with a bar on your right as you went in, and the dining area farther back. The lighting beyond the bar was very dim and intimate, and in consequence, presumably because you wouldn't be able to read them at the table, the menus were displayed at the bar.

53

She slipped easily on to the bar stool. She was wearing a loose, floppy long-sleeved blouse with a tie neck, and coolie trousers tight at the ankles. There was still not much evidence of make-up or jewellery, though her nails and lips were now pink, and the ear-rings sparkled as they danced.

To my raised eyebrows she responded: 'A gin and tonic, I think.'

This I ordered, along with a brown ale. 'In the bottle, please.'

She gave a delighted laugh. 'I'd heard that policemen always drink beer, but I never guessed it was true.'

'That's not the reason.'

I allowed the suspense to build up until the drinks arrived. Then I showed her the bottle. Wem.

'I wanted to check,' I told her. 'It's the same, the very same bottle. I was knocked out this evening by this one's brother.'

'Oh!' she said, her eyes wide above the rim of her glass. 'Is that true?'

I turned my head and showed her the bump. She reached out a hand to confirm it, but withdrew it before the fingers touched. Perhaps it would have been too intimate a contact. 'Oh . . . poor you.'

'I wonder why,' I said, holding up my glass. 'Cheers.'

She sipped, eyeing me gravely. I'd have sworn my news had surprised her, she took so long in deciding what to say. Finally:

'So that's why you came.'

'Because I was assaulted?'

'To question me, pump me, as they say. Try to get a clue . . . not simply to meet me again.'

'That too.'

'Oh Lord, it's going to be hard work, I can see. You're so . . . cold.'

'The evening's young.' Doesn't one say stupid things, just to keep the conversation going! 'Suppose we get it out of the way?'

'If you wish.' She avoided my eyes, hiding her disappointment in me by making a point of it.

'I was quite a while checking on the operation of those garage doors. You said you packed in almost at once. Now . . .'

'I am not stupid, Richard. Let me say it for you. Yes, they all dashed away. Their free weekend. The rest of the week they live in. Yes, they could have been either ahead of you or behind you. Yes, they *could* have been there . . . wherever it was . . . and knocked you out.' She took up her glass and sipped it again. It seemed she'd finished, but I said nothing. She tossed her head, the hair being loose around her ears at that time, and swirling into place obediently. 'Me too, if you want to hear that. Depending where you *went* when you drove away.'

'Welshpool,' I said. 'You phoned me there. Remember?'

'Oh!' she said, dipping a finger in her drink and sucking it, a casual gesture to cover her confusion. 'But surely you'd said . . . mentioned Welshpool.'

'I'm quite certain I didn't.'

'Oh damn you.'

I nodded agreement, and waited. She pouted at me, and sighed deeply.

'You're so blasted persistent! I found out. Does that satisfy you? No, I see it doesn't. You spoke about your friend who died in a fire. I phoned the local newspaper and discovered his address, which was near Welshpool, so the odds were that you were staying in Welshpool . . . heavens, I simply phoned around.'

She'd over-elaborated. Was she *that* nervous? I helped her out, giving an easy laugh to smooth the way. 'Was it so very important?'

'Do you want me to strip and dance a fandango? Really, Richard, you can't be that naïve! A woman doesn't care to display her thoughts and emotions, not at a very first meeting. All right. So now you know. Yes, it *was* important. I like you, Richard. Does it have to take hours? Damn you, say something.'

My, how they can deflate you! I looked very solemn, and said: 'Shall we look at the menu?'

At last I'd said the correct thing. She laughed, and the awkward moment was gone. Also gone, I could see, was any chance I might have had of getting down to serious business. Strangely, that seemed a relief. We consulted the menu together, and the head waiter was at once at our elbow.

We decided on the pâté, with duck à l'orange to follow, and he led us through to our table. It was a matter of leading. After the bar, the ill-lit interior was treacherous. Our table was in a corner, intimate and, I guessed, carefully specified. He said he would send over the wine list.

I asked for fresh drinks, a sherry for me this time, and, my infallible method, told the wine waiter we were having the duck and what did he recommend? He suggested a burgundy. It didn't matter to me whether the wine was red or white, as they would look exactly the same in that light.

'You come here often?' I asked.

'You should', said Rosemary, 'have opened with that, and not started in on your interrogation.'

'I'm a clumsy fool.'

'Tell me about yourself.' An attacking move. 'Apart from that.'

I told her. A retired detective inspector . . .

'Retired early?'

'As a matter of fact, yes. Does it show?'

'Not in this light.' Which was just good enough to show me the flash of her teeth.

'I wasn't working with Llew Hughes at that time,' I explained. 'That's my friend who died . . . you know.'

'At Ewr Felen.' It indicated that she *had* enquired, and discovered his address. She nodded. I said yes, there.

I was realising that I was still examining every word she said for cracks and flaws. With an effort I pulled myself together, and, understanding, I was certain, she gave me a moment by sipping her drink and examining the décor.

'It wasn't my case,' I explained. 'I'm sorry to keep coming back to it, but I want you to be clear on that. I was working in the Midlands at the time your uncle died. But I know that Llew wasn't happy about the outcome.'

The entrée arrived. It gave me a small break, but as soon as the waiter had left she leaned forward.

'But surely . . . on just that . . . you wouldn't go to all this trouble.'

'It was his death, you see.'

She shook her head. 'I don't see.'

'Someone perhaps not wanting the original verdict to be upset.'

'But all the same . . .'

'The coincidence. Me having arrived on the scene.'

'His death could have been . . . for some other reason.'

'Well . . . you see, I was just about to decide that myself. The original case seemed tight. Then somebody had to go and bash me on the head.'

She chose her words very carefully. 'From what I know of you, I don't find that strange. You make a lot of enemies, I expect.'

'I'm not usually so awkward.'

'Except with women?'

'I go to pieces. I don't get the practice, you see.' She laughed delightedly, flatteringly. A man likes his pleasantries appreciated, I thought. You see, there I go again.

'The snag is', I told her, 'that an attempt was made to steal Llew's notes on the case.'

She nodded, nodded, then parted her lips daintily to insert the last portion of her pâté. 'I see, I see.'

'Which means I have to go on with it.'

'Of course.'

56

'But not now. Tell me about yourself, Rosemary. All of it.'

'I'm so glad you didn't shorten it to Rosie.'

'From the time you went to live at Plâs Ceiriog.'

The waiter again gave us time for a breather by bringing the main course; but when she began talking there was no hesitation, nothing held back, I thought.

'Now . . . let's see,' she said, chin on her hand, fork poised. 'I'll go right back to college, if you like. I'd got my degree, and no doubts at all on what I wanted to do. Act. I was going to conquer the world, and only one thing got in my way – I was lousy.'

'Never.'

She was dissecting the duck, and glanced up. 'It's true. Mind you, I was lucky. I'd been for an audition, and instead of the usual dismissal I got a few extra words. I can remember them now. "Give the acting profession a break, darling, and try to get on the buses." I wept for a week, then I tried to write a play. No good. I just couldn't do dialogue.'

'Not tight enough?'

'At that time I didn't know what that was. So I started a novel. Oh Lord, how terrible it was! And then . . .' She fluttered her fingers. 'I won't tell you about the misery in between . . . then Uncle Edwin asked me to be his secretary. I'd taken a secretarial course . . .'

'You'd found the time?'

'They call it resting, Richard, when you're not actually acting, which for me had been all the time. I'd had literally dozens of jobs to keep me going. Then along came Uncle Edwin. This would be . . . oh, three years before he died. The secretary bit was me sitting there and taking down what he read out from his notes, but really he'd already written his play, only he said I'd never be able to read it, so he read it all out to me. A secretary, that's what I was, and his housekeeper, and his nanny.'

'I gathered he was rather forceful.'

She went on, disregarding the interruption. 'He took me everywhere with him, the theatres, the hotels. All I was there for, really, was to encourage him. Richard, you've never known anyone so . . . For such a clever man – and really, he was quite brilliant – for such a man to be so inadequate! Can you imagine . . .'

'I'm finding it difficult,' I admitted, topping up her glass.

'And his tantrums! Of course, that was his natural safety-valve. Every now and then, realising his inadequacy . . . no, that's wrong, I mean *convinced* of his inadequacy, he'd get the idea that everybody was sneering at him, and we had to have one of his turns.'

'Psychology as well. Had time for a course on that, too?'

'I'm going to assume you're joking.'

'Of course I'm joking, Rosie.'

'Rosemary.'

'Sorry.'

'Now you've broken the thread . . .'

'You were talking about his inadequacy. You used the word a number of times.'

She put her knife and fork carefully side by side on her plate and leaned forward.

'You're not trying to be funny, Richard, you're trying to antagonise me.'

'No. It wasn't that. I was – sort of disappointed. You were enjoying it, cutting him down to size. And I didn't think that was you, not the Rosemary I was getting to know.'

'I was smiling because I loved him for it. No false modesty with my Uncle Edwin, he really believed he was a failure. Nothing would shift that idea from his mind, and I loved him.'

'So he tried directing.'

'He had to prove something to himself. He never married, you know.'

I thought about that, staring down at my plate, deciding I'd had enough. To eat, I mean.

'What's that got to do with it?'

'No children. He had to prove he could achieve. Get it?'

'I've got no children.'

'Then you ought to understand. Success, that's the objective with you, I bet. All the time – no possibility of failure.'

I tried to grin at her, but it wasn't very convincing and got lost in the gloom. 'I'm stubborn,' I admitted. 'People have said that.'

'Then you'll understand about Uncle Edwin. Imagine how you'd feel if you *did* fail twice, disastrously.'

'I can imagine. That, you're telling me, is why he committed suicide? Or so you believe.'

'Yes.' Softly.

'Which was what you meant when you told me you were to blame?'

'Yes.' A mere whisper.

The light, as I've made a point in mentioning, wasn't good. But now I could catch the wink of tears in the corners of her eyes. Was this why she'd wanted to see me, for encouragement on her own behalf? Nobody to hold *her* hand, nobody to shame her hidden fears to flight.

'How could you be so foolish, Rosemary – to cling to that idea all these years! That you might have saved him . . .' I raised my hand, as she'd been about to interrupt. 'Even if, at that time . . . even if you'd prevented him from driving away – well, he'd have managed it some time or other.'

'If he'd got past that hurdle . . .' I barely caught the words.

'Stubborn,' I said, 'you are. Like me. You get an idea, and nothing will budge it. In court, they showed it was murder, the jury brought in a verdict, your cousin was sentenced . . . and still you believe it was suicide, and one you could have prevented.'

The waiter hovered for our plates. I'd have killed him if he'd interrupted, but he melted away at my gesture.

'Utter nonsense, my dear,' I said softly. 'Your uncle was murdered.'

Her head began to shake like a mechanical doll. 'Suicide,' she whispered.

'No!' I waited for her eyes to meet mine again. 'He could not have closed the garage door.'

'Richard,' she whispered, 'I know about the radios. He must have taken the one from his own car into the garage with him.'

'No!' I said again, equally emphatically. 'The one still in his own car operated *its own* door, which was the one behind which your uncle died.'

'Somebody changed them over.'

'After his death?'

She nodded, lips tightly compressed.

'In order to do what?' I asked gently. 'To make an apparent suicide, as it would have been accepted, look like a murder – as it *was* accepted? The only way that could matter would have involved an insurance on his life with a suicide clause. Was there such a thing?'

'No,' she murmured.

'Well then.'

'But you see . . .' She reached out and touched my hand, giving it the seal of truth. 'Duncan can never have done it.'

'The way things were, it could hardly have been anybody else.'

'You've never met him, obviously.'

'Inadequate?'

'Now you're teasing me.'

'Trying to lure that smile back.'

She laughed. 'But he couldn't, you know. Not Duncan. The poor man didn't even live in this world.'

'But he was the one to gain.'

'Gain? You're joking again . . . surely. I see you're not, but Richard, Uncle Edwin had spent all his money – and there'd been quite a lot – on those last two plays. Nobody else would finance him when they heard he intended to direct them himself. So there was nothing left. The house –

it was on a mortgage, and with Capital Gains Tax . . . heavens, it was a liability, not an asset. All that was left was the plays. All.'

'And Duncan knew that?'

'Better than anybody. Why d'you think he was hanging around to try to catch Uncle Edwin when he got back? Money, Richard. Uncle Edwin owed him money, and Duncan knew that if he didn't get it straightaway, he'd finish up as one on a long list of creditors.'

'Hmm!' I said. 'And that's what you inherited?'

'There was some legal point, about a convicted man not being able to gain by his crime. That put Duncan out of the running, and left me with a lot of trouble and an old house. He'd have been welcome to it, I can tell you.'

She leaned back, hands on the table, then thrust herself forward.

'Now *there's* a motive for you, Richard. Somebody stands to inherit a pain in the neck, and he can see a suicide about to come off. It terrifies him, all that responsibility. So he gets in first and makes it murder – or makes a suicide look like murder.'

She grinned. I grinned back at her clever use of what I'd said.

'So that he's unable to inherit,' she declared.

'I can't see much gain there, if it meant him going to prison.'

'Ah yes, but he gets an ex-policeman interested, so that it can be proved he didn't do it, then he gets a pardon, and oodles and oodles of money in damages.'

We laughed freely together about that, and the waiter seized the opportunity to ask whether we'd like to order a sweet or would care to see the cheese board.

Over the chocolate mousse and then the liqueurs and the coffee we got to know each other. She told me how she'd tackled her sudden inheritance.

'I loved that house, Richard. Still love it. I managed to hold on to it, just, but it's only more recently that I've had any money to spare. But at first . . . oh heavens, the despair. And out there – nobody to share it with. Then I sat back and told myself off and tried to decide what assets I'd got and what to do about them. There were only the plays, of course.'

'You mean, there were unproduced plays?'

'Unfortunately, no. But I went round everywhere, making a thorough nuisance of myself. A revival, I thought. The early plays, given a new identity. But they all wanted to know how. I had to think about that, so that I could give an answer. Then the chance came. One man – just the one – said he'd put the money up, but only if I'd direct it myself. It completely stunned me. There I'd been, two hours – three perhaps –

round at his flat, pounding his floor with the script in my hand, explaining how it could be done . . . and he just laughed and said I *had* been directing it.'

'Amazing.' I meant she was.

'So there it was – after years of trying everything – all of a sudden I discovered something I could do. You can't imagine how exciting that can be, Richard.'

'Yes I can.' I had my pipe going, she a cigarette. 'Somebody should have told you, years before.'

'How could anybody know?'

'Don't you think that ought to be one of the essentials in education, whittling out the potentials and encouraging them?'

'I wish somebody had whittled me. I got tossed in at the deep end. Terrifying, Richard. But I'd had a bit of grounding, going round with Uncle Edwin, so I wasn't too ignorant. I knew flies weren't things you zipped. But to tell an experienced actor how to act! Of course, you don't tell them *that*. You tell them how it comes over, and suggest. Oh, I soon learned.'

'I bet you did.'

'And it's gone on from there. Now there's barely a break, one revival after the other . . . and now the house comes in useful. For rehearsals, the early ones, I can have the whole cast living in.'

'Apart from weekends.'

'They like to tear off home and check on the pet canary, or whatever.'

'And chase after poor old ex-coppers, to belt 'em on the head.'

'Now I thought . . .'

'Sorry. Couldn't resist it.'

'You could if you tried. The whole evening, you've been resisting like mad.'

I quickly changed the subject. 'And this backer of yours . . .'

'We now share the financial aspects, fifty-fifty. The only condition is that he's in every play. You've met him. Dear Drew.'

'Drew Pierson?'

She smiled at me. 'Fooled you, didn't he? But he's really very shrewd. Take my word for it.'

I had no difficulty in doing that. Shrewd. A man can be shrewd in business matters and a complete idiot in personal relationships.

We sat on. The waiter did not hover suggestively. Very discreet they were, at the Rendezvous, or perhaps a little short of business. I told her about the mill at Tyn-y-bont, and so it went on, until I reverted to business.

61

'Has he been to see you?' I asked. Then, at her look of blank incomprehension: 'Your cousin, Duncan.'

'No.'

'He's been out of prison two or three months now. And you haven't visited him?'

Her eyes watched her fingers pressing out a cigarette. She simply shook her head. She had spoken about him kindly, even in eager support.

'Perhaps you don't know where he is,' I suggested.

Her eyes came up to meet mine. 'I believe he's gone back to Lichfield.'

I smiled at her, waiting.

'So I heard,' she said. 'Somebody told me. Duncan was an organist, so it's reasonable . . .'

'Somebody?'

'Please don't interrogate me, Richard,' she appealed.

'Sorry, but you seem to be reluctant. I can't understand why.'

'Your friend came, Mr Hughes – oh, two months ago. Enquiring, just as you have been. It seemed he'd been asking around – all the people who were here that night.'

'You see,' I said, patting her hand. 'That wasn't very difficult, was it?'

'Yes, if you want to know. It's another connection, and I can just see you grabbing at it. And I don't want you to . . . I don't know.'

'Don't want me digging?'

'If you want to put it like that.'

'In case you find it places us on different sides? But . . . it wouldn't be like that, would it? The only person on the other side is the person who killed your Uncle Edwin, and killed my friend Llew Hughes, and bashed me on the head with a bottle. And that couldn't be you, Rosemary. Now could it?'

She held my gaze for a few seconds before shaking her head.

'It's late,' she said, probably to prevent me from pursuing it further.

'Yes.' I'd had the bill for so long it was curling at the edges. I put money on the plate, and we left. The head waiter wished us good-night, thankfully I thought.

Two lone cars in the car-park. She opened her door.

'Thank you, Richard,' she said. 'I've enjoyed it. Really I have.'

'Me too. We'll have to do it again.'

She pouted at me, and I thought her head shook in disbelief. 'I have my loyalties, that's the trouble,' she said. Then, so as not to waste the pout, she planted it on my lips, got in the car, and drove away without even a wave.

Oswestry to Welshpool – twenty miles. It was ten-forty-five. Say forty minutes to the hotel, perhaps less, a quick change into something looser, and I could do the run to Devon in five to five and a half hours. Say five in the morning when I got there. Time for a nap, and be up and about getting lunch by the time Amelia arrived, assuming she got going after breakfast, at around ten.

By the time I'd sorted that out in my mind we were on the fast road with my foot hard down. I walked into the hotel at eleven-twenty-seven. The night porter produced my key, and a message from the slot.

'Please phone your home urgently.'

For a moment my mind went blank. Then I managed to say:

'What time was this?'

He pointed to the notation at the foot of it. 22.19. That's continental, and I had to explain to myself that it meant ten-nineteen p.m. An hour ago.

I ran up the stairs, once more bursting into the room – but this time pausing to close the door behind me, pressed the button that gave me an outside line, and dialled my own number.

It rang twice. She must have been sitting by it, waiting.

'I'm here, Richard,' said Amelia, in those three words conveying exhaustion, disillusionment, and worry.

7

'You drove on,' I said accusingly, annoyed because of my own embarrassment.

'The car arrived ten minutes after I called you, so I thought it would be silly to hang around.'

'But there was no need . . .'

'I've discovered that for myself. I've read the letters from your friend, and there's nothing in them you don't already know.'

'Never mind that. How are *you*? You sound tired.'

'It's quite a while since I did such a long run in one day. Where *were* you, Richard?' she asked wearily.

'I had to go out. Something I wanted to follow up.' My mouth was dry.

I was not telling a falsehood, but neither was I telling the truth. I was feeling wretched. 'Did you get something to eat – on the journey?'

'I take it you did.'

'I've eaten. Yes. But Amelia . . .'

'Richard, I'm very tired. Just let me read you these letters, then I can get to bed.'

I took a deep breath. 'Never mind the letters. I was just about to change, and drive down myself.'

'Now that', she said positively, 'would have been very foolish. Change? What are you wearing?'

'My blue suit.'

'Formal, then? You dined out?'

I cleared my throat. 'Yes.'

'You must tell me. Some other time. Just let me read you these letters. There are three.'

'I don't want to hear the damned letters.'

A pause. I was just about to apologise for my anger, when she said, very coolly: 'But you see, Richard, you won't be able to rest until you know I'm safe, with all these people waiting to attack me to get the letters . . .'

'Amelia!'

'. . . so if I read them now, I shall be able to place them on the front step with a stone on and a little note: "I've read these to my husband, and you're welcome to them." Don't you see – then we'll both be able to get some sleep.'

'Yes.'

'Unless you've got to go out again.'

'No.'

'Then listen.'

As you can imagine, I listened.

The first one was dated ten days before.

Dear Richard,

I have not heard from you recently, and hesitate to approach you when you could be very busy. As you know, I have been working on my memoirs, and I seem to have come across a discrepancy in one of my cases. The Inspector involved does not appear sympathetic, which is only to be expected, as he was responsible for most of the brain work. But I hope that you, coming to it with an open mind, will see the disturbing detail in the photographs without any prompting.

I hope you can come and visit me. I have a bed for you and your wife. But please, have a drink at the last pub before you cross the border into Wales. Yours,

Llew.

Nothing irrational in that, except the peculiar reference to having a drink. The next one was dated three days later.

Dear Richard,
I have not heard from you. There's nobody else and I hoped – I didn't tell you that there has been more than one attempt on my life in the past few weeks. I didn't wish to pressure you, but now I feel there is some urgency.
    For your information, I have given no hint to Duncan Carter.
    Phone me, please.

Llew.

That one was a little worrying. He'd felt his danger. The third was dated two days later.

Richard,
If I do not hear from you, and anything has happened to me, ask yourself where the beer came from. I am faced . . . (scribble-scribble, not readable) . . . blank impossibility. A completely new interpretation.
    Phone me. Please.

Llew.

'And that's all?' I asked gruffly.
'Yes. And it doesn't help a bit, does it?'
'I don't know. Now . . . Amelia . . . please get some rest. And thank you.'
'For reading them so prettily?'
She'd never have used such a word, except in sarcasm. She was clearly exhausted, and I was to blame, and I couldn't take her in my arms.
'Just for being you, my love.'
Her voice held a smile. 'Good-night, Richard. Sleep well.'
'And you.'
We hung up. Sleep well, she'd said. Not much chance of that. Llew had given me a couple of clues, that it was in the photographs, and that it related to beer.

I slipped them out of the envelope. These would not be the best of the pictures that the technical section had obtained. The good ones would have gone with the main file to the Director of Public Prosecutions. One or two were slightly out of focus. The one with the beer crate and the bottles of spirit on the rear seat was not clear at all. It was possible to detect that the loose bottles were gin and whisky, and four or five small ones of tonic water, a couple of ginger ale. But the bottled beer was in a crate, which almost obscured the bottles themselves. Another detail was that none had slipped out of place, indicating that Edwin's braking had not been fierce.

One thing caught my eye. There was something about the colour of the labels. I rescued the empty brown ale bottle from the flowered waste bin and held it up. A brown label, with yellow lettering. The labels – the top edges of them – of the bottles in the crate were yellow.

It's likely that yellow and brown would be the most-used colours for beer bottle labels. Green and blue would clash with the contents. Feeling a stir of interest, I looked closer at the photograph. The name on the label was obscured by the top edge of the crate. But on the side of the crate, as raised letters on the brown plastic, I could just detect the word: BURTON.

I went out and down to the lobby, where the night porter was dozing. I rubbed two pound coins together between my fingers, and he woke at once.

'Not retired, sir?'

I was sliding the coins along the surface of the desk.

'You're a drinking man,' I said.

'You want me to get you something?'

'No. It was a question. Are you a drinking man?'

'It's been known.'

'So you'll know the beer of the district.'

He eyed the coins, looked up at me. 'Intimately, sir.'

'And if you were drinking beer, what would be most likely?'

'Draught bitter.'

'Whose?'

'Evan Thomas's at the Sheep's Head.'

'What brewery?'

'Oh . . . I see. It'd be Wem, I suppose.'

'We're in Wales, here. Oswestry's in England.'

'Until we take over.'

'Would it be Wem there?' I knew the answer, I'd tried it.

'Oh yes. Indeed it would. Wem for miles around. The brewery's only fifteen or so miles away.'

'Ah!' I said. 'There wouldn't be any from Burton, perhaps?'

'Burton? Never heard of it. No such brewery around here.'

'Then I suppose', I said, turning away and leaving the coins behind, 'you'll have to do with Wem. Good-night.'

'Good-night, sir.' He sounded as though he thought me to be quite mad. As I suppose I was, mad to make assumptions on one word. But I'd worked for years in the Midlands, where Burton wasn't simply a brewery, it was a town full of breweries. Burton upon Trent. The whole town smells of the fermentation. Rumour has it that, pound for pound, the Burtonites are heavier than their fellow Britons. It's the smell.

All right. I paced the room and tried to reason myself out of it. An empty crate from Burton upon Trent could well have found its way as far as Oswestry, and there been filled with Wem ale. Possible. They get mixed up. But . . . from a hundred miles or so? That seemed unlikely. And the beer bottles in the crate had labels on them that did not look like Wem's. Suppose they were from Burton. What could I make of that?

The basic assumption was that Edwin Carter, on the night he died, had not gone out and bought that beer at the nearest pub across the border, nor the spirits and the rest. Yet it *had* been there, on the back seat, visible, crying out its message for all to see. The message was that he'd gone for drinks and returned with them. But . . . it now appeared that this was not so, and that message was therefore false. But it had been such a definite message, so I had to assume it had a purpose. Therefore its message had to be inverted.

So Edwin Carter had not gone out at all. He had not even driven away from that garage. It had been said – by Rosemary – that she *heard* him drive away. What she must have heard was the sound of the engine dying as the door slowly closed, imprisoning him with the car.

That meant he had died earlier than had been assumed, before the party games began. At *that* time, nobody had had alibis. They were round and about, not yet having gathered in the dining room. The only people who now had alibis for the time Edwin left – or was thought to have done – were Rosemary and Duncan, who had been within sight of each other as the engine sound died away.

It meant that Duncan could not have performed the necessary actions required to kill his uncle. He had *not* killed him, unless the alibi Rosemary had given him was false.

No wonder Llew Hughes had been disturbed. And yet . . . he had also been uncertain.

But of course he would, if it all rested on a single word on the side of a beer crate.

Having settled this neatly in my mind, I climbed into bed, switched off the light, and composed myself to the night's sleep I'd not expected to get.

I still didn't get it. For hours I tossed and turned. There were snags. I hadn't even started. You can see the difficulties, I'm sure. If not, get out a map and have a look at it. Lichfield is only twelve miles from Burton upon Trent, and Duncan Carter was now the only one *with* an alibi.

I was the first in the dining room for breakfast. There was a razor nick in my chin, and my hair, what there is of it, was untidy. I wasn't pleased to glance up and find Grayson looking at me dispassionately.

'Join me,' I said, in a tone indicating I didn't want him to.

'For coffee, perhaps,' he agreed, and I looked round and caught the waitress's eye. He took the seat opposite me and picked up the menu. 'I'd try the kipper. They're good round here.'

I waited. When he had his coffee and was stirring in sugar he said: 'Been busy?'

'Here and there.'

'You're not convinced?'

'That Edwin Carter was murdered? Oh yes, I'm quite convinced of that.'

'But you've spotted something?' For all his elaborate casualness, he was uneasy.

I had not the slightest intention of telling him what I'd spotted. I bypassed the question. 'Any progress on the death of our mutual friend?' I asked. Then, at his lifted eyebrow, I amplified: 'Llew Hughes.'

His slight smile acknowledged my move. 'Not much. There'd been trouble between Llew and a local farmer. Sheep wandering on Llew's land, and whose responsibility it was to maintain the fence. Not enough to justify burning his house down.'

'With Llew in it. No. So you're going for accident?'

'It seems the most likely. The inquest's on Thursday, and we'll ask for an adjournment if anything else comes to light. From you, for instance.'

I grinned at him. 'You're pinning your hopes on me? I wouldn't do that, if I were you.'

'Oh?' He looked down at his cup. 'If you're heading for home, don't forget the inquest.'

'You misunderstand,' I told him. 'I meant, I might come up with something you didn't hope for.'

68

He flushed slightly, but his voice remained under control. 'Are you setting out to prove me a fool, Mr Patton?'

'If I come across that sort of evidence, I'll let you know first.'

His fist closed on the table surface. I said quietly: 'I believe I can show that Duncan Carter didn't kill his uncle.'

He breathed out slowly, a quiet hiss between his teeth. 'Believe?' he asked. 'Show?'

'No proof, to be sure. But evidence.'

'What evidence?'

'I don't intend to tell you.'

'Are you telling me you're deliberately obstructing me in the course . . .'

'Don't be a fool. This isn't your case. You closed it, successfully, with a conviction. Ten years ago. I'm obstructing nothing. And if, by chance, I discover who *did* kill Edwin Carter, then I'll be assisting you in the case you're at present working on – the death of Llew Hughes.'

'I tell you, Patton . . .'

'You tell me nothing,' I said. I looked up at the waitress, who'd appeared at my elbow. 'I'll try the kipper, I think. Join me, Mr Grayson?'

'Thank you – no.'

'Kippers for one,' I said. 'That's plural, my dear.'

Grayson had been sitting tensely, but now he seemed to relax. 'You're a very difficult man to deal with,' he said. 'I told you, I read Llew's early chapters. He seemed to admire you. I can't see why.'

'We change,' I told him. 'All of us. We get older and less patient. There's less time left, you see, so you can't afford to waste it. I'm sorry if I seemed a little short.'

'Forget it.'

'But you can help me, if you will.'

'So that's why you've changed your tune.'

'Buttering you up? True. I want information. That garage and the radio.'

'So *that's* it.'

'No. I can't argue with your deductions there. But . . . you said you checked the radio that was in his car, the one parked outside, and it operated the door of the garage he died in.'

'The mechanism. It operated that, not the door. They'd had to break the linkage to lever the door up.'

'Yes. It was the range I wanted to ask about. I tried it, yesterday, and the range was about thirty yards. Did *you* try for range?'

'Thought of it,' he said complacently. 'Thirty yards was about it. If you're thinking it could've been done from a distance, that's out.'

'Just checking.' She brought me my kippers. Plural. I eyed them with pleasure.

'So,' he said, pushing back his chair, 'how do we keep in touch?'

'For the inquest?' I asked, teasing him.

He straightened to his full height. 'Progress. I'm interested, Mr Patton. Intimately.'

'Of course. I was forgetting. I can't tell you my plans, except that they involve Lichfield.'

A slow smile spread all over his face. 'You're going to see Duncan. Then you're in for a surprise.'

On that cheerful note, he left. I tried the kippers. Not as good as we got on the coast, certainly not smoked. I ate the lot, nevertheless.

I phoned Amelia the moment I got up to our room.

'Sleep well?' I asked.

'Terrible.' I could picture her, sitting at the kitchen table with tousled hair and a cradled cup of coffee. But of course, the phone was in the hall!

'How's the wrist?'

'What? Oh! I haven't given it a thought.'

'Good. Now listen. I wanted you to know that your journey wasn't wasted.'

'I'm pleased about that. Now Richard . . .'

'The essential clue was in the letters. I had another look at the photos, and the whole thing is turned on its head.'

'You don't have to sound so excited.'

'It means I'll have to see a number of people, but just at this moment I can only locate one. Duncan Carter. He's at Lichfield.'

'What you should be doing, Richard . . .'

'So that gives us three alternatives.'

'You can't have more than two alternatives, Richard.'

The fact that she was picking me up on semantics, and kept using my name, meant she wasn't feeling sympathetic towards my intentions.

'Choices, then,' I said. 'Three choices.'

'I can't wait to hear.'

'Obviously, we've got to get together as soon as possible . . .'

'Richard,' she interrupted, 'with whom did you dine?'

The careful formality warned me. There's only one course in those circumstances. 'Rosemary Trew.'

'Have I met her?'

70

'Not yet. She's Edwin Carter's niece. We met in the afternoon. There was something she wanted to get off her chest.'

'Her bra, perhaps?'

I was silent. Amelia never makes that sort of feeble joke.

'Sorry, Richard, I'm not really myself.'

'You're tired, you had an accident . . .'

'But there's no need to condescend. I just hope you grilled her and discovered what you wanted to know.'

'I know she wasn't wearing a bra.' It took real courage to say that. She recognised it, saw beyond it. 'Dear Richard,' she said. 'So very observant.'

'I was saying – three choices.'

'Oh yes.'

'Now . . . we can meet at Lichfield – but that would mean another long drive for you.'

'Not just at the moment, I think.'

'No, of course not. The second alternative – choice – is for you to drive back here, while I go over to Lichfield and back. It's only about eighty miles away. But you already know how far it would be for you.'

'Richard . . .'

'And the third would be for me to drive to Lichfield and do what I need to, then on to Devon, and you could just sit there and rest till I get home. That'd be best, I think.'

'Richard . . .'

'I shouldn't be long in Lichfield. I'd be with you this evening.'

'I did rather want to see our mill again,' she said gently.

'We must certainly do that.' Frankly, I'd forgotten about it.

'And perhaps you'd introduce me to that . . . Rosemary Trew, was it?' She knew darned well. 'You mean you *want* to drive back here?'

'In my own time. I'm getting to like this car. But . . . there *is* something.'

'Yes?'

'Don't you think this is all becoming rather expensive? This car alone . . .' I could almost hear her shrug. 'Nobody's going to reimburse us.'

For that, too, I hadn't given a thought. 'Llew's death . . .' I began.

'Which could have been an accident,' she said briskly, having clearly given it some thought.

'I've been knocked out.'

'That's happened before. Treat it as experience.'

'And there could've been a miscarriage of justice.'

'You're no longer a policeman.'

How could I explain to her that I would never cease to be? I'd been trained into a cult, with the simple precept that right is right, and wrong is wrong. Nobody had used those words; they would have sounded too pretentious. But the knowledge and understanding had seeped into my soul. Oh, I know . . . nowadays this simplistic philosophy has become blurred and degraded, but we still live in a tight society, in which, if simple moral right becomes no longer an accepted precept, we can look forward to a very precarious future indeed. I was only one man, and couldn't do much towards it. But I knew I had to try to right even the smallest wrong I came across.

I couldn't have said this to Amelia, because it was something private to me alone. Besides, it would've sounded too smug.

So she could not be expected to understand, she was tired, and we were spending money we couldn't afford. She was quite correct, I was no longer a policeman, so what the hell was I doing . . .

'Sorry,' I said. 'I tend to forget, and you're quite right. Tell you what . . . I'll pack our things and settle up here, and drive home. We can give the mill some more thought . . . but for the rest . . . it's really none of my business.'

'We really can't afford the expense.' There was now a hint of apology in her voice.

'I wasn't thinking straight.'

'With what they're asking for the mill, we'd have difficulty as it is.'

'And I really liked it,' I reminded her.

She was biting her lower lip, I could sense that. At last: 'But I'd have loved to see it again.'

'Probably it's damp in the winter . . .'

'Richard, you can't just drop your case now. I'll tell you what we'll do. I'll drive back, and you hold the room there. You can go to Lichfield and do what you've got to do, and drive back, and perhaps we can meet again this evening.'

I grinned at Cindy, whose tail quivered at the end. 'That's what I'd prefer,' I admitted.

'And take care,' she said.

'I'll do that.' I retrieved a thought. 'Oh – and Amelia . . .'

'Yes?'

'Have you checked on the front step?'

'What . . .'

'To check whether the letters are still under the stone.'

'Idiot.' She laughed, and hung up.

Always end on a cheerful note. It helps things along.

I said to Cindy: 'How d'you feel about another drive?'

She seemed to approve, I put some more ointment on her ear, and we went down to the car.

8

I found him in the Close, where I thought he would be. They look after their own, and wouldn't forget an organist, even if only a deputy. It was Sunday. Working day for the Cathedral. I'd walked twice round it before deciding which of the haunting little side entries to investigate.

The three spires towered over me awesomely. I explored, wandered down narrowed passages flanked by tight little ancient cottages, knocked on a few doors and enquired, and eventually found him.

'Are you Duncan Carter?' I asked, although, for some reason I could not have explained, I knew he was. He was certainly the right age, which would be forty-nine.

'Yes.'

'May I come in and speak to you?'

'Not if you're from another newspaper.'

'I'm not.'

He was tall and slim, and carried himself with a strange elegant diffidence – something to do with the tilt of his head – yet there was humour in his large, placid eyes. It was a contained humour. Perhaps he treasured it, as it must have been deeply enshrined to have weathered ten years in prison. The clothes he was wearing, casual and therefore loose, were nevertheless hanging on him in an indication that he'd lost weight. They'd been in store, waiting. His hair was blond, lank, falling across his forehead. One hand persistently reached up and dashed it aside. The lips were full. They might easily have assumed a sulky line.

'Then who are you? Surely not the piano tuner, on a Sunday?' He said it with a drawl that was close to a sneer. They'd probably taught him that inside.

'Can you tell me,' I countered, 'whether you've had a recent visit from an ex-policeman called Hughes – Llew Hughes?'

His eyes were wary. 'And if I have?'

'I'm another one. Mr Hughes is dead. He sort of asked me to pick up and carry on.'

He'd been lounging against the door frame, and now thrust himself upright. 'You'd better come in, hadn't you?' He made a gesture, indicating a door to the right of the narrow, natural-stone hall.

I preceded him into the room. When he'd followed me and closed the door, we'd pretty well absorbed all the spare space.

'This was my place,' he said, 'before it happened. This room was where I worked. Now Frank Leigh's got the position – deputy organist and choirmaster – but he's letting me stay with him. For now. The future's uncertain. As you can see, there isn't much room.'

Beams pressed down on us and walls seemed to bulge inwards. The room, even empty, would have been small. The single window was tiny, the door through which we'd entered was narrow and low. One wall was an open-shelved bookcase, tossed and piled untidily with music and books on music, manuscript paper, a guitar that had found its way in. There was a tiny table, a small upright chair, and standing in the centre proudly, its keyboard towards the window, was a full-sized concert grand piano.

How they'd got it in I couldn't imagine. They'd have had to strip it down to the last key and string. He edged round, sat on the stool, and gestured to the upright chair. I perched myself on it, and from there could see he had manuscript paper sheets on the music stand.

'You look younger than him,' he commented, cocking his head. 'Perhaps you can tell me what's going on. I couldn't understand a word he said.'

'Perhaps because he was over-cautious,' I suggested.

'Well . . .' He glanced away, then back, trying a weak smile.

I had to remember that he'd just done ten years in prison. He'd have had to acquire a protective cynicism in order to survive. I didn't know what he'd been like when he was arrested. Certainly, if he'd led a cloistered life, shut in this very room with his piano and emerging only to walk the few yards into the Cathedral and mount to the organ loft, he'd not have encountered the rough and harrowing side of life.

If he'd been like that, going into prison an innocent man, the shock to his system would have been immense. I had to continue on that assumption, handling gently a personality that had become used to ungentle hands.

I shifted uncomfortably on the chair. 'You were working?' I nodded towards the piano keyboard. 'Sorry if I interrupted you.'

He shrugged. His smile was now attractive. 'A melody. A tune. Nothing much.'

'You can still play? I mean, you haven't forgotten . . . lost your touch?'

'No, no. Hands are fine.' To illustrate, he thundered out a few fistfuls of chords.

'Tried the organ, have you?'

He laughed. 'Lord, no. Any day now, though. I'm not authorised, really, but Frank's going to sneak me in. *Then* you'll hear something. I'll set the spires rocking . . .'

His eyes were sparkling with enthusiasm, until he caught my smile.

'What's funny?'

'I was simply pleased – for you.'

'No need to be.' He shook his head and dashed the hair from his eyes. 'Really, you know, I don't need your pity. God . . . haven't I had enough! They come round . . . came, at first . . . all friendly and welcoming, but you could see it in their eyes. Pity. It's all that's allowing me to stay here. Pity. I'll be glad when I can get away.'

Then he flicked another little smile at me, apologising.

'It doesn't seem to me that you need any,' I said. 'Quite frankly, in your situation I'd have gone mad.'

He eyed me suspiciously. 'Is that what you think happened? I've gone off my head?'

'Far from it. I just thought – the transition, from here to there. Quite a shock, that would be. Especially if you were innocent.'

'Don't start that.'

'What?'

'It's over, done with. I'm out. Oh yes, on parole. Don't imagine I'm a free man, far from it. But I'm out, and I can at least . . .' He played a little dreamy tune with one hand, then stared up at me with mischief in his eyes. 'I can even tell you to leave, and you'd have to go. Now . . . that's freedom for you.'

'But you haven't done that.'

'Because I'm waiting to see what it's all about.'

'So it wasn't such a shock after all?'

'What wasn't?'

'Serving a sentence. I'd have expected you to be complaining. Bitterly. Make an issue of it, for sympathy.'

'I explained. No pity.'

'Sympathy's different. It implies understanding. I can understand, because I sent a lot of people to prison, and knew a lot who'd come out. Always whining, they were. Always claiming they hadn't done it.'

'What in heaven's name are you getting at?'

'I'm wondering whether a knowledge of guilt makes it more acceptable.'

He returned his attention to the keyboard, fingering an intricacy that sounded like Bach. He was communing with a friend.

'I'd rather say', he told me, finishing with a flourish, 'that a knowledge of innocence allows you to treat it as an irrelevance. Besides . . .' He smiled disarmingly. 'Besides, I didn't have it at all bad, considering. It was an open prison. Probably they reckoned I was harmless. They let me use the piano in the canteen whenever I liked, and tune it. It was terrible when I got there. And I got a male voice choir going. They allowed me to compose, too. Oh yes, I write music. Not much good at anything else, but that I can do. Do you realise what that can mean, to somebody like me, Mr . . .'

'Patton. Richard Patton.'

'Mean to me. I've never been one to get out and about, and I suppose, looking back on it, I wasn't much good at looking after myself. They took all that off my hands, all the background day-to-day worries. They gave me a bed and my meals and a piano, and I didn't have to go out in the rain. D'you know, I think the screws envied me.'

He laughed openly, emphasising it with great, crashing chords that rocked my chair. I could feel the sound tingling my skin.

'I wrote an opera, Mr Patton, while I was there. Two string quartets, a piano sonata, a symphony – no, two symphonies. And this . . .'

He launched into a lugubrious yet hauntingly amusing march theme. It mocked itself, mocked its rhythm.

'D'you know what that is?' he demanded.

I shook my head. I'd never heard it before.

'I call it "The March of the Screws". It's from a musical I'm working on. Set in a prison. I'm having great fun with it. It's plotted against the background of a mass break-out, only it's the screws who are trying to get out, not the prisoners.'

'An all-male cast, then? It wouldn't succeed in the West End.'

'Ah, but that's the point. Three wardresses get drafted there by mistake. And a replacement doctor who turns out to be a woman, young, curvy. You know. Listen.'

Again his fingers spoke for him. A dance, a roisterous, driving dance in a hoppity rhythm – five-four time would it be? – then breaking and tumbling across other rhythms, echoes of waltzes and minuets, of bouncy, throaty blues and hard, harsh rock.

He could barely see me through his hair when he looked up, laughing now in uncontained enjoyment.

'That's the ballet,' he explained. 'Second act. In the prison hospital, the first time the new doctor appears. All the prisoners jump from their beds, plastered and bandaged, and the whole stage is full of tumbling convicts, over and under and round the beds, and she in the middle, tossed from one to the other . . . of course, you'd need a proper ballet troupe . . .' He blinked at me. 'You don't like it?'

'I can't wait to see it.'

'I'm going to ask Rosemary Trew to put it on.'

Then he sobered abruptly. The mention of her name had brought him face to face with the reason for my visit.

I waited, but he didn't say any more. He was an emotional and sensitive man who had always found it necessary to withdraw from all contact with cruel reality. Then they'd tossed him in, and he'd been confined with the harshness of reality at its worst. So he'd retreated even further within himself, the shell thickening and contracting. I wondered whether I dared to crack it. His musical mockery of his experiences was evidence of the distress he'd hidden from.

'She seems very well,' I told him. 'Full of life, confident, a successful woman. She was rehearsing a play.' To his blank stare, I explained: 'Well, you didn't ask.'

He had the grace to blush.

'You haven't been to see her?' I asked, knowing he hadn't.

'There *are* certain restrictions.'

'And she hasn't been here?'

For a moment he eyed me uncertainly, then he dashed the hair aside and took the expression with it. And he relaxed.

'Rosemary has her own life. What did you want to see me for? More questions? Isn't *anybody* going to let me forget it?'

'Will you tell me about that evening – when your uncle died.'

'I've been over this . . .'

'I know. A hundred times. But once more – please.'

He shrugged, the shoulder remaining motionless but his head jerking sideways. 'I went to Uncle Edwin's party. No, that's not strictly correct – I was there for a week, and he decided to throw a party. His flop frolic, he called it. Good old Uncle Edwin, barmy to the last.'

'Is that how you see him, insane?'

'Barmy's a different word. Around here it means gently eccentric. Mind you, gently isn't a word I'd choose for him. He could be wild when he liked. Crazy wild. But anyway, I was there for the party.'

'These visits – did you do that often?'

'Two or three times a year. Call 'em script conferences, if you like.'

'He conferred with you?'

'Will you let me tell it!' He waited for my gesture. I made a mental note to pick up on it later. He went on: 'I was there. Five or six other people came along. Me, I'm not one for parties, and in any event, I'd been trying to get a word with Uncle Edwin all that day.'

'You hadn't found time, during the previous days?'

'He was hardly ever there. Back and forth to London. There was a panic on, his latest play failing. You must know all about this.'

'Some. You said you were trying to get a word with him . . .'

'Yes. Of course, he brushed me off. If there was anything he didn't want to talk about, it was money, and that was exactly what I wanted to talk about. Then there was this stupid idea he had about going out for more drinks. Most of them had had enough, anyway, and there seemed to be plenty left. Anyway, he made quite an issue about it. One of the others tried to stop him, joking you know. Pierson, I think. Uncle nearly went at him. So we let him go.'

'Go?' I asked. 'Actually go?'

'His car wouldn't start. It was down there, parked in front of the garages.'

'*His* car, you're talking about? Rosemary's was inside one of the garages, I understand.'

'Yes. The wrong garage, as it turned out. That was my fault. I'd left it there, that afternoon. Why should I care which garage was which?'

'But you knew the doors were radio operated?'

'Oh yes. Like a kid, Uncle Edwin was, with his toys.'

'And you'd parked Rosemary's nose-in, inside the wrong garage?'

'Yes. You know all this,' he said accusingly.

'I'd like to hear it confirmed.'

'I drove into Chirk for some cigarettes. Frankly, I just wanted to get out of the way, Rosemary getting ready for that stupid party, and everything in chaos.'

'Cigarettes, you say? You're not smoking now.'

'I gave it up. Inside.'

'I thought you got a tobacco allowance.'

'We did. I sold mine. I had to pay for my own music paper. It's expensive. Can I go on?'

I nodded, amused at his aggression.

'I wasn't going to switch the cars round for him. To tell you the truth, I'm not much of a driver. Didn't even have a licence, if you must know.'

'I'll bear it in mind, if I need something to fall back on. You'd left the garage door open?'

'I don't know. Well, yes. I remember trying the button on the wall, but it didn't work.'

'But you knew that the radio in your uncle's car would operate that door?'

'Does this matter? Yes, I knew. I'd had it all explained, before. But it wasn't a big thing, whether the door was up or down. Why should I worry, the wretched car was safe. Where did I get to?'

'Your uncle's car wouldn't start.'

'That's it. He came stamping back to the house and told Rosemary that it . . .'

'I thought she'd gone down with him, still trying to persuade him not to go.'

He thought about it, his right hand toying with scales. 'Yes, you're right,' he decided. 'I can see it now. *She* came back for the keys.'

'You used the word stamping.'

'Well . . . *she* was angry. At him and his stubbornness. I'd still got her car keys in my pocket, see. I handed them over. She said something about not knowing what'd got into him, and went back with them.'

'You were where, at that time?'

'On the terrace.'

'And she went down, over the lawn, and round the line of bushes?'

'Yes.'

'And at that time, where were the rest?'

'Heaven knows. All over the place. Somebody was rushing round, trying to get them all together for their childish games.'

'So you were there, alone, on the terrace?'

'I was there,' he said heavily, 'all alone on the terrace.'

'Then Rosemary came back.'

'She came round the rhodos and made a gesture.'

'There's lots of gestures.'

'This was kind of disgust and triumph, all mixed. She waved.'

'Was it dark?'

'Heavens, you do jump about. Yes, I suppose it was dark. The sun'd gone down behind the mountains . . . oh, ages before.'

Detecting his impatience, I spoke placidly. 'Just trying to get the picture. Dark or not, you saw her wave?'

'Yes.'

'Against the background of the car's lights?'

He thought. 'Well, no. There was light from all those windows behind me. Whatever it was, I did see her. And anyway, I wouldn't have seen the car's lights – it was nose-in.'

'True.' I, too, paused for thought. 'She was walking up towards you?'

He nodded. 'At what point – where had she reached – when you heard the car engine start?'

'Lor', you *do* ask some tricky things! How can I remember that?' He shook his head. 'When she came round the bushes, I suppose. Maybe a bit later.'

'But she could see you?'

'I was standing there. Anyway, why else would she have waved? Is this important?'

'I think so. And exactly when did he drive away?'

'Exactly? You're an optimist.'

'When did you hear the engine sound fade?'

'No . . . let me think. She came up to me, and said something about: "He's off." And . . . yes, she said she hoped I'd left enough petrol in. Then she walked off across the terrace. At that time the engine was still running.'

But Rosemary had stated that the engine sound had died away almost at once. Trying not to sound as though it mattered – could be critically important – I said: 'You're sure of that?'

A nerve in the corner of one eye jerked. 'Sure? I suppose so. The engine went on running, and I can remember thinking: what now? It got me wondering if I'd done something wrong – even if he *was* sitting there and watching the petrol gauge, and maybe I *had* left it nearly empty. It's all coming back. Yes . . . I was getting really worried, it'd been so long.'

'How long? Can you remember that?' I couldn't keep the interest out of my voice, and he sensed it. He played three notes, plink, plonk, plunk, and looked across at me again.

'Three minutes, easily. Then the engine faded off, and I *was* relieved, I can tell you.'

'And you were alone at that time?'

'I don't think so. Somebody had come out on to the terrace. Mildred . . . that's Miss Niven, she was just behind me.'

'And did *she* hear the engine sound die away?'

'She must've done, because she said: "Well, he's got off at last." Something like that.'

I had been holding my breath. He could not have known what I was aiming at, but he'd just given himself a very neat alibi for the murder at the earlier time. The snag was that he'd destroyed any alibi Rosemary might have had. I breathed in deeply. 'You mind if I smoke?'

'No. I thought we'd finished.'

'I rather believe we've only just started.'

'You want to hear all about me hanging around, waiting for him to come back?'

'Not particularly. You wouldn't have started this hanging around for quite a while, I suppose?'

He had become bored with it, now that we appeared to have passed the bit that'd interested me. 'Maybe getting on for three-quarters of an hour later I went down, back up, down again. I can't remember how many times. This is making my head ache.'

'But finally, you were standing there in front of the garages, and you heard a faint humming sound stop?'

'You know how it is. I was standing there, in front of the garages, as you say, and the sound changed. I looked round, and all of a sudden I *knew*. You get a nasty, prickling feeling down your back.'

He shuddered. The chord he played softly did the same to me.

'This humming . . . had it been there . . .' I rephrased it. 'Can you say how long it'd been going on?'

'Oh Lord . . .'

'Could it have been there before, when you went down for one of your earlier trips?'

He was silent for so long that I thought he didn't intend to answer. But when his eyes met mine I understood. Distress clouded them.

'Are you telling me', he whispered, 'that I might've, if I'd been smarter . . . could have saved him?'

'I doubt that.'

'But you're saying – you *are* saying, aren't you – that he could've been in that garage a long while.'

'I'm suggesting that.'

His mind made the leap that included our discussion on the time Edwin was supposed to have left. 'You're saying he never even left!' he accused me, angry that he had to face that thought.

'There's evidence supporting that.'

'Then I don't know. I just don't know.' His hair whipped about as he shook his head in despair.

Before he saw all round and through it, I hurried him on. 'You couldn't raise the door?'

'Can't you let me think!'

'The door.'

'I tried the button on the garage wall, but it didn't work. Then I thought of the radio in the other car, but that didn't work, either. So I ran for help, and they all came running down, and somebody managed to lift the door . . .'

'Somebody?'

'Drew Pierson, I think.'

'And you went inside . . .'

'Not me.'

'You knew he was dead?'

'Why d'you have to remind me? What came out – a great waft of heat and fumes and stench! Nobody could've lived in that.'

'So you didn't see the beer and the rest on the rear seat?'

'As though I'd trouble!'

'What if I tell you that I can show that the beer, and probably the rest of the drinks on that rear seat, didn't come from any local pub. The evidence is that your uncle didn't drive away from the garage at all. As he couldn't have closed the doors himself, somebody else did it. He was certainly killed, but not at the time the police believed. What was done to bring it about must've taken place at the time you heard the engine sound fade. What you heard was the door closing down on the car.'

'Dear God, let me think!'

'I've already done the thinking. If he couldn't have operated the door himself, and the beer wasn't fetched by him, then it must have been put there to make it appear that your uncle had driven away, and later returned. The only reason was to create an alibi.'

'I need a drink.'

'So the beer must've been taken there for *that* purpose . . .' I paused. This was the point that was a bit rocky. Where had the drinks *been*? 'It was booze that must have been available, and quite close.'

He was on his feet, gesturing. 'Will it stop you if you've got a drink in your hand?'

'Possibly.'

He reached behind him for the bottom of the bookshelves, and produced a bottle and two glasses. I might have guessed: a drink to Duncan was sherry.

'It's rather dry,' he said doubtfully, desperately reaching for the norm.

I sipped. 'It's fine.' Then I waited.

'The drinks you're talking about', he said, 'were probably the stuff from the boot.'

'Say that again.'

'I had a flat tyre that day, and had to change the wheel. Heavens, I'd never changed a wheel in my life. But when I opened the boot to look for the spare, there was all this drink. I had to lift it out, 'cause the wheel was underneath. I wondered what it was doing there.'

'Oh,' I said. 'Fancy that.' My mind was racing.

'Never gave it another thought.'

So now I had it. Somebody had hidden the drinks in the boot of the Dolomite. The keys were normally left in the car, otherwise Edwin wouldn't have been so annoyed when Duncan took them away in his pocket. All I had to find was who had done that, borrowed the car, bought the drinks . . .

'Who', I asked, 'could've put it there?'

I'd been speaking to myself, and was therefore surprised at his violent reaction. A look of horror clouded his face, and the sherry in his glass shook so much that it nearly spilled. He tried to say something, seemed to choke, and then managed to say: 'It was Rosemary's car.'

'Wait a minute. That drink happens to have been bought in this area. I didn't tell you that.'

The glass banged down on the piano, spilling and probably ruining the polish. His eyes were wild. 'I'm not having it . . . you're throwing around your accusations . . .'

'I'm making no accusations. For Christ's sake listen. How could she have . . .'

'She was here, a few days before,' he said harshly. 'You've known that all the time. Tried to trap me. She was here – came to pick me up and drive me there. And you knew, damn you.'

'I didn't know,' I said softly. 'Not until you told me.'

9

I wanted to go somewhere else, alone, to think about that. But I wasn't going to be allowed to. I had already spent longer with him than I'd expected, yet there were still a number of things I wanted to ask. I eyed him speculatively. He had his fingers to his forehead, as though he really did have a headache, and his face averted. But before he'd been able to hide his features I'd detected a twist of the lips that for one second conveyed bitter disgust.

When he looked at me again he'd regained his composure. 'I could do with some air. What about you?'

'Whatever you say.'

'A few turns round the Close?'

'I could manage that.'

We eased ourselves out of the room and gained the narrow alleyway, then out to the Close. The Cathedral was echoing to the rise of the organ and the voices of the choir.

'Looks like we're in for some rain,' he said.

'Most likely.'

Neither of us wanted to face the real issue. We paced, side by side, he with his long legs, awkwardly striding. He seemed unaware of his old tattered cardigan.

'I'm surprised you never said anything about it,' I commented after a while. My pipe was going well. 'All that drink on the back seat, I mean. It was the basic reason the police officer assumed Edwin had been out and come back, so it was the reason he charged you.'

'He didn't say that.'

'All the same, when the beer and stuff was mentioned, you ought to have realised it.'

He kicked at a stone pensively. 'How did I know what he was basing his reasons on?'

'At the trial – wasn't it mentioned?'

'Not that I can remember. Everybody seemed to take it for granted that Uncle Edwin had been out and come back. Including me.'

Possibly they would. Unless the defence spotted the point and demanded proof, no evidence relating to the drinks need have been given.

'Look, Mr Patton, I've been thinking . . .'

I didn't want him thinking too deeply. 'Did the prosecution produce any motive?'

They wouldn't have needed to, only as a point strengthening their case. He had to think about that. We paused at the head of Dam Street.

'You can just see Dr Johnson's statue,' he told me.

'Did they?'

'Only money. He owed me money.'

'Hardly a good reason for killing him, I'd have thought. Dead, he couldn't have paid you.'

'The inheritance, too.'

'Oh . . . that . . .'

By the time of the trial, Edwin's estate might not have been probated, and its value, or lack of value, not been assessed.

'I'm surprised the question of motive wasn't challenged,' I said. 'It's flimsy.'

'Ah . . . yes. But there was the other,' he said mysteriously, miserably.

I stopped walking. I forced him to pause and face me.

'What other?'

He made a vague gesture, and one leg bent as he cranked himself into a standing position. 'They get together, these lawyers. My barrister said if he challenged on motive the prosecution would bring in the business of Glenda Grace, and we didn't want that, did we, because it'd blur the issue . . .'

'*What* business of Glenda Grace?' I demanded, never having heard of her.

He tried for dignity, but it was pitiful. 'She was a friend of mine – oh, years ago. Not a close friend, but I liked her. Too young for me, anyway. I was fifteen years older than her.' The agony in his voice was terrible to listen to, especially as the choir was mounting to paeans of joy behind him. She'd been a very close friend indeed. 'It wasn't long, the time that I knew her. Then she was off to London and the bright lights. And inside a year after that she was dead. Accidental death, they called it. I don't want to talk about it.'

'You'll have to, won't you! If the defence didn't like to have it mentioned, and you were involved with her death . . .'

'I wasn't even there!' he said, fiercely for him, and he began to walk away.

I caught up with him. 'Where?'

'The flat. Uncle Edwin's flat in London. This was in the good days, when he was doing well. He had a flat. One of those tower block places with a commissionaire, and fancy balconies. There was a party . . .'

'Nothing else but parties . . .'

'Don't listen, if you don't want to.'

'No,' I said. 'Go on. This young woman – Glenda, was it? Tell me about her. How you met her.'

'At a party . . .'

'Not another blasted party!'

This time it was he who stopped, just in order to show me his bared teeth, his face now gaunt, straining for humour. 'The Bishop wouldn't like you to call it that. It was *his* party. There,' he told me, pointing a finger at the solidly complacent building behind me. 'To celebrate a tapestry we'd received as a bequest. She was there. Heaven knows who'd brought her. We seemed to get along fine, and I met her afterwards, several times. I began to wonder . . . but my earnings were nearly nothing. The house free and a small stipend.'

I was disinclined to stop him. Glenda Grace had been someone special to him. We marched ahead, he lifting his face and telling it to the steeples.

'But we had something in common. At that time I was writing plays, nothing much, but Uncle Edwin was polishing them, and that was what she wanted, to get on the stage. She had a good singing voice. Anyway, I gave her an intro to Uncle Edwin, which was the worst thing I could've done. God, if I could take it all back! But you can see what happened – she went to London, and I lost her. I never saw her again.'

'But you followed her career with interest?' I asked.

'Career!' he said with disgust. 'Some career! I should've known better. Uncle Edwin was a playwright – what influence had *he* got? But he could have been kind, sent her back to me, told her . . . but no. Not him. He handed her over to Clyde Greenslade, of all people. That slimy swine.'

For him, that was strong language. I recalled that Greenslade had been one of Edwin's guests on the night he died.

'It wasn't a good move?'

'D'you know what business Greenslade did? Uncle Edwin knew, but *still* he sent her to him. Greenslade did blue movies.'

Oh Lordy me! Porn. I paused to tap out my pipe on my heel.

'Didn't she realise that?'

'She was about as bad as me. Another world.'

'In which case, she'd turn and run.'

'She was beautiful. A kind of youth and innocence . . . just what Greenslade could use. God knows how he persuaded her. All I know is that she was on drugs when she died. Perhaps he told her his stinking films were a stepping-stone to greater things. I wasn't there. I should've gone to see her, but London scares me. I blame myself . . . Greenslade got her started, and she never finished. When she died – at Uncle Edwin's flat – they said she'd been on uppers and downers, whatever those ghastly things are, and speed and cocaine. They said she'd been incapable after a few drinks, and had gone out on the balcony, feeling sick. And fell off! Everybody *knew* she'd been killed. God knows why anybody would want to kill her. But somebody pushed her off the balcony, and I was *here* at the time. They told me the exact time. I was in the Cathedral, playing the organ.'

He seemed to choke, and then he was silent.

'Let's go back,' I said, and like a lost little boy he turned obediently and shuffled along beside me.

'And did you suspect your uncle?' I asked, having given it twenty paces. 'Of killing her,' I amplified.

He turned to me, aghast. 'Of course not.'

'So why didn't your barrister want it to be mentioned?'

'I blamed my uncle for sending her to such a creature as Greenslade.'

'And for that, they thought, you could have killed him?'

'They thought! I was told it wouldn't help me, if it was brought out in court.'

The prosecution, I decided, must have been confident in their case, that they didn't need to emphasise motive.

'Greenslade was at your uncle's other party,' I reminded him, 'on the night he died.'

'Oh yes,' he said, his voice smeared with contempt. 'But by that time he'd gone all legitimate. The big screen, on general release. Perhaps, if she hadn't died, poor Glenda would've made it, too.'

'So . . . if you still cherished any animosity towards anybody over her death, it would surely have been Greenslade. If she fell – or even if she threw herself from the balcony – he was the one most directly to blame.'

'But she didn't,' he said simply. 'She was pushed.'

I didn't pursue it. He hadn't been there. He hadn't, perhaps thankfully, seen what she'd become. It occurred to me that maybe this Glenda Grace (surely an assumed name) hadn't been so innocent as Duncan chose to believe. No young woman, of any sort of moral values, could have been persuaded to work for Clyde Greenslade. I decided, as I say, not to pursue it. Let him cherish his memories.

I followed him back into the house. This involved a grope along the passage, up two steps round a corner, down a step, and into the rear room, which was combined with the kitchen. It was equally cluttered, but with a happy inconsequence and a view to comfort. He sat me in an easy chair, and went to brew tea.

'And yet,' I said, as he placed down the tray, 'there was the money your uncle owed you. The money they produced as a motive.'

He raised his eyebrows. 'If you're convinced I didn't do it, why worry about my motives for doing it?'

'Tell me what money he owed you.'

'Oh . . . for the scripts.'

I recalled he'd mentioned a script conference. 'Explain.'

He sat on a low stool opposite the little table, knees spread and probing like twin spires. 'It was years and years ago . . . when I was trying to write plays. Uncle Edwin was in television then, selling his plays, and he took a couple of mine to show around. Hopeless, of course, but later, when he got going on the stage, he said he might be able to adapt my plays. They were too long for television, you see. Too long for an unknown, anyway. So that's what he did. Adapted my plays. He was the one who knew all about the technique. Me, I could do dialogue. He polished them, and got them produced.'

'Under his own name?'

'Well, he'd done the work, and it was his name that was known.'

'And he paid you?'

'From time to time. When the money came in.'

'This handout – how much would it be?'

'I can't see that's any of your business.'

'Of course not. Just nosy.'

He suddenly grinned, his chin jutting. 'Hard-faced with it, too. Usually a couple of hundred, say. Sometimes more.'

'Every month?'

'You're joking. Two or three times a year. But it was something. I could tell myself I was a professional writer.'

'Which you were.' I suppose, I added to myself.

'And he owed you some?'

'He'd promised me a couple of hundred – but of course he'd had two big flops.'

'Of course.'

We sipped tea and tried to avoid each other's eyes. I found myself less happy with all his information than I'd been when I arrived. Now he'd produced a motive that could be much stronger than money, and he'd admitted he knew the booze was handily in the boot of the Dolomite. I had thought the alibi he had for the time his uncle was supposed to have left was sound, but now I was even doubtful of that. The alibi, if you came to tying it down, would have to be for the exact moment the button on the radio in his uncle's car was pushed. And *that* time was still not satisfactorily confirmed. I could only hope he wouldn't ask . . .

'Mr Patton,' he said, and I knew he was about to. 'I've read about this sort of thing. They were always talking about it in the prison. A pardon.' He was very tentative.

'Yes?' I asked.

'If you can prove I didn't do it – isn't that what I'll get?'

I tried not to sigh. 'What I've got so far is nothing more than evidence that your uncle didn't drive away. It isn't absolute. Some other explanation could well be produced.'

'But all the same . . .'

'It's not strong enough, yet. To tie it down, I'd have to show that the drinks have a positive meaning, not simply pointing away from you, but pointing towards somebody else. And I can assure you, once somebody's been tried, sentenced, and served a term, the authorities are going to be very chary of charging somebody else.'

I was rather proud of that. It might not have been legally solid, but it said it, and simply enough for him to understand. He licked his lips. I wasn't happy with the expression in his eyes.

'But assuming I get it, this pardon, wouldn't I be able to claim damages?'

'It's usual.'

'I mean . . . how much?'

'I couldn't say. Somebody has to assess the value of ten years' loss of freedom. Based on your loss of earnings, I'd say, but there's more to it than that.'

He grimaced. 'And I bet the miserable devils'd knock off the value of my board and lodging inside.'

I said solemnly: 'And the wages of the screws.'

'They wouldn't!' Then he laughed, but it was a miserable affair. 'It's not a time for joking.'

'It's not a time for counting your damages, either.'

'But . . . there was my inheritance, too. I lost all that.'

'My information is that it wasn't worth much. But that would be taken into account – its probable worth to you.'

He gave that some consideration, biting his lip, darting small, questing glances at me. 'I suppose . . . they wouldn't give it back to me?'

He'd never had much, never really enjoyed financial freedom. Ten years before, that might not have worried him, but his term inside had hardened him, and brought him more squarely face to face with reality. So I couldn't blame him for hoping, for the avaricious gleam in his eye. I spoke as casually as I could.

'How could they? You wouldn't want them to take it back from Rosemary?'

He thought again. I poured us both another cup of tea. There was pain in his eyes when he looked up.

'But you said . . . Mr Patton, didn't you say: whoever killed my uncle must have known the booze was there in the car. Didn't you? And Rosemary must've known.' Then, reading my expression, he put his head down and plunged on. 'So that, if it was proved that she killed him, then they'd take the inheritance off her too, and it'd come back to me.'

His face was glistening. I looked down at my cup, not wishing to assess what that statement had cost him.

'You mean, that's how you'd like me to prove it?'

'I didn't say that.'

All hell raged behind his eyes. The resentment – the fury – of his unearned sentence demanded retribution. That Rosemary stood there, in the way of it, was his agony. I tried to salve it with gentle words.

'Well . . . you'd have to consult a solicitor about it. It'd be a very interesting legal point. But . . . what she's got now is not her inheritance, it's what she's made from it. Perhaps we'd better leave it for now . . .'

He saw his hopes fading. I hadn't even been optimistic on his expectations from a pardon. 'Then why did you come here?' he burst out, his cup rattling dangerously in its saucer. 'You raise my hopes . . .'

'Of a possible pardon.'

'. . . and now you chop them down.'

I spoke blandly. His anger was not at me, it was at himself, for having revealed something unpleasant he'd not previously accepted. 'To put right a miscarriage of justice.'

I'd said the wrong thing. 'You coppers, you're all disgusting. Oh, I heard all about you lot. Fascist, all of you. You pick up people's lives and toss them around. They're nothing to you. It all has to look good on paper.'

I put down my cup and got to my feet.

'Oh, don't leave,' he said angrily. 'Let me get one bit of pleasure out of it, and exercise my nice new freedom.' He stood up and looked pathetically dignified. 'I'm asking you to leave this house.'

'Very well. If you say so.'

'I do.'

He dogged my heels to the front door. I turned back, just before the door slammed.

'You'll probably make quite a lot out of the Sunday papers,' I assured him.

Then I walked back to my car.

Me and my brave, brash words! Right is right and wrong is wrong. What a platitudinous load of codswallop! Who was I to decide what was right and what wrong? The conceit of it! I'd plunged into this, my chest beating with proud morality, and all I'd managed to do was raise trouble that was clearly going to spread far and wide.

All I had to show for it on the gain side, so far, was a scorched terrier, who was waiting to be let out. My thoughts were tart, and I was glad she was there to neutralise them.

I took her for a short walk, which became a long one. With my basic motivations undermined, I was in a mood to throw in my hand, but I'd prodded a tiger into life, and it was for me to tame him. We walked back to the car and I produced the water I'd brought in a flask, opened the small tin of dogmeat, and watched as she wolfed it down.

We drove back to Welshpool.

It had taken longer than I'd expected. It took Amelia less time than I'd calculated. The result was that I entered our room unsuspectingly, and there she was, all big eyes and her hair not really under control. Nor her lower lip.

'Richard!'

Then she was in my arms, Cindy having to make a wild leap for safety. You'd have thought we'd just met at the North Pole, our deprivation locking us together, her hands at the back of my neck. She'd lost weight, I swear, the ease with which I could swing her off her feet. But in extenuation, I have to mention that this was the first time we'd been apart.

When we'd recovered our breaths, I said: 'Had a good trip?'

She was heading for a mirror, patting her hair. 'So, so. I thought you'd be back first.'

'It took longer than I'd expected. Duncan Carter turns out to be a strange man, and now I don't know where I am.'

'Are you going to change?' she asked. 'It'll soon be time to go down to dinner.'

'I thought I'd have a bath, and another shave.' Why did I feel so soiled?

'You can tell me all about it afterwards. And how's Cindy doing?'

No need to answer that. Cindy was explaining for herself.

After dinner we went strolling round the town. It was a fine evening. The rain she'd encountered had not travelled north. I walked beside her, Cindy between us, and I couldn't help feeling a sense of unreality. It was as though Llew Hughes had not died, as though Edwin had not, nor Glenda Grace, so many years ago – what would it be? Twelve?

'I thought', she said quietly, 'that we could run along and have another look at the mill in the morning.'

She was reaching for a sense of security. We still had not found anywhere to live that was ours, but I hadn't thought this was troubling her. Only now, with the tiniest hint of insecurity in the form of Rosemary Trew spurring her, was she allowing it to show.

'The thing that's worrying me is damp,' I admitted, as though I'd been thinking of nothing else for days. 'An old stone building, and built for working in, not living in.'

She jerked at my arm. 'But people *have* lived in it. And it's been beautifully converted.'

I'd have used the adverb 'quaintly', but I had to agree. 'That's very true. We'll go first thing after breakfast. By the way, did you part with your car?'

'Oh yes, they collected it. Wait until you see the bill, Richard.'

I grunted. Wait, I thought, until you hear what I've got to tell you.

It didn't get told that night. Well . . . all that separation – what can you expect? Was I going to punch the pillow into shape, draw her towards me, and say: 'There are three murders now?' So I think I'll just jump to the morning.

Did I give you the impression that the mill was isolated? If so, wrongly. It's windmills that have to be on the tops of hills. Water-mills are lower, where the river-flow has gained purpose. This one was at a point where a tributary met a larger one, and here the small hamlet of Tyn-y-bont was situated. We would not be alone. At the point where the two waters met there was a bridge, on the far side of it a farm, and beyond that a row of cottages, probably tied at one time to the farm. We would at least have neighbours, though nowhere to shop, nowhere to post a letter. We would, however, always be within reach of fresh milk and eggs. It's not all sheep in Wales, you know.

The building seemed huge when we got close to it, as it was built high on the bank of the hurtling stream. Always, we'd have its rush and rustle. The wheel, though, had been motionless for years. Its paddles were partly rotted away, though the basic construction was still there. So was the race, a mere trickle at that time. There were small sluice gates to direct the water from the stream and back again. It must have been a long time since the millrace had been in use.

We were standing in what would be the living room, looking out of the narrow window and down to the bridge. Beside us was the millstone. The original owner, who'd masterminded the conversion, had gone to great lengths to retain the lower millstone, and had surfaced it to make a table top. It was so large that I felt like King Arthur. The original square shaft, a foot across, thrust up through the floor. Below was a store room, but down there (I'd explored) it was weird and rather frightening, with all that power waiting to be unleashed, the side shaft thrusting outwards to the waterwheel, and the great, wooden-toothed gearing to transmit it upwards. A wedge had been placed between the teeth to lock it. In a water-mill, it's the lower stone that revolves, not the upper. The principle of this gave me a queer feeling that we could be sitting at a meal one day, and suddenly find the table rotating.

But I must admit, there was no evidence of damp on that calm August morning. The walls were two feet of native stone, the roof huge slabs of Welsh slate, an inch thick. The timbering inside was preserved, and every beam had been cleverly used for a utility purpose. I liked the place. Yes, I liked it.

There was no need to express this to each other. Our fingers touched, and we knew.

We went out to sit on the bank. Cindy went to paddle in the stream.

'She won't fall in the millrace, I hope,' said Amelia.

'I shouldn't think so. Anyway, the water's less than a foot deep.'

She was silent. I felt she was waiting for something. I said: 'Llew gave me the main clue, in his letters. That beer on the back seat of the car.'

She stretched out her legs, and closed her eyes to the sun. I told her the lot, my thoughts on it, the difficulties that had been raised, and Duncan's worrying attitude.

'Is this really any of your concern, Richard?' she murmured.

'Only if Llew was murdered. In that case, I think, I'd have to go on.'

'But it could've been an accident.'

'That's Grayson's theory,' I admitted, 'and I can't contest it.'

'Well then . . .'

'But I've stirred up a source of trouble.' She said nothing. I glanced at her. 'That Duncan, he's got an idea in his head, and I put it there. The next thing you know he'll be throwing accusations around wildly.'

'In which direction?'

'You know what I mean, my dear. Rosemary's.'

'And that wouldn't suit you?'

'I wouldn't be pleased that I'd brought it about.'

'Hmm!' she said.

I plucked a blade of grass and chewed on it. 'And anyway, it's far from clear. It's all right to say that I can show that Duncan could be innocent . . .'

'*That* was carefully worded.'

'Exactly. Because it isn't positive enough. And Duncan's left with the idea that he's as good as got his hands on a free pardon.'

'And hasn't he?'

She was sounding all too casual for my liking. She knew I didn't want to let it go, and she had to know how deeply I felt the necessity to hang on.

'Just look at it,' I told her. 'The stuff on the back seat indicates that Edwin didn't leave at all. Whoever killed him must have put it there, in order to create the impression that Edwin did leave, and return later. In that event it could've been done by anybody there that evening, except Duncan.'

'Even Rosemary?'

'She too, it now appears.'

'Especially as the drinks were in the boot of *her* car.'

'Especially that. But this is the snag. If somebody used that boot for that purpose, it had to be somebody who knew it was available . . .'

'Naturally.'

'And had planned to use it.'

'That seems to follow.'

'So . . . does that mean they also planned that Edwin would *want* to go out for extra drinks? If he didn't, the plan wouldn't work. But it was Edwin who insisted on going out. How could he have been manoeuvred into that? How could it have been expected that he'd use the Dolomite, which had the drinks conveniently in its boot, and which just happened to be parked, so damned conveniently, in a garage whose door could be closed only from the other car outside? It's just too much.'

'Does it irritate you, Richard?'

'And you can't even say that this was a murderer seizing on the chances as they were presented, because they were just too convenient for belief.'

'But is this *your* problem?'

'It's stupid Richard Patton who's blundered in and given Duncan hopes of a pardon. It's me who'll be asked for proof – and me who'll have to come up with answers.'

'Have to?'

Cindy had raced up and was pulling at my sleeve, as she'd pulled at my trouser cuff. She reminded me I'd forgotten the main reason.

'Have to,' I said.

She got to her feet, smoothing herself down. 'Let's go and see whether that estate agent will drop his figure,' she suggested. 'Then you can decide how you're going to go about it.'

10

Putting on my formal voice, I said: 'I wondered whether I could come along and have another word with you.'

Rosemary's tone was light. 'Do you have to ask, Richard?'

I had my back to the room, staring at nothing particular in the street. Behind me, Amelia was idly turning the pages of a magazine.

'What I have to say won't be casual chit-chat,' I said.

'So formal?'

'Have you heard anything from Duncan?'

She was silent. I counted off the seconds. Ten. At last she spoke.

'He hasn't been in touch. But it sounds as though you've seen him.'

'Yes. I need to talk to you before *he* does.'

'We shall be rehearsing all evening,' she said. 'I hope to get a straight run-through. But if there are any breaks, we could talk. So do come along.'

'Thank you,' I said. And hung up. I'd wished to convey that matters were getting serious, but I was aware that I'd sounded ungracious.

I turned to Amelia. 'Care to watch a rehearsal?'

'If you want me with you.'

'Of course I . . .' I grinned at her. 'Did I sound sufficiently stern?'

'She'll be shaking with fear,' she assured me. 'Yes, it all sounds quite interesting.'

Very enigmatical, that was. I suggested we should have an early meal, and go along afterwards, and Amelia made no objection. We ate, we got in the car, we drove away. There was a feeling of constraint between us.

'There it is now,' I said, as the house came into view.

'It looks a bit dreary. What's it like inside?'

'I've only seen the big room they use for rehearsals, and that's a bit bare.' I drove past the knoll. 'Those are the two garages in question.'

I parked where I had before, and we walked up to the terrace. It was still full light, but the sun was dying behind a heavy belt of cloud. Rain later, I thought.

Inside, it was dark enough to necessitate lights. We stood at the same open door, apparently the only one of the bank of tall windows that would open. I saw now why they used studio lights. They could be manoeuvred, giving an approximation to a stage under full illumination, although there was still no furniture. The outer edges of the room were in heavy shadow, and, as there were only three people on the set – Drew Pierson, Mildred Niven, and the girl I'd seen kissing the young man – I had to assume that quite a few people were hidden in the shadows.

As we watched, the scene came to an end, with Pierson saying, presumably in his senior policeman role: 'By heaven, I can't wait to get back with a search warrant.' This with a very suggestive eye on the girl.

It was apparently a laugh line. There were laughs from the shadows, surely polite, as they'd know it inside out, and a patter of applause.

Rosemary walked into the concentration of light. 'That was just fine, but don't overdo the leer, Drew. I think we'll have a break, now. Harry . . .' She looked round. 'Lights please.'

A background reserve of lights sprang on, and the whole room was ablaze. Rosemary turned. She saw us standing there. For one moment her expression was blank, then she whirled around and called out: 'Tea will be along. Sandwiches. Drinks for you drunkards.'

When she turned back to us she'd recovered. She came across, smiling and relaxed, her hand extended.

'Richard, I'm pleased you could get here.' She turned to Amelia, just a hint of uncertainty in the lift of her eyebrows.

'This is my wife. Amelia. Rosemary Trew, my dear.'

I had spent some considerable time with Rosemary, and Amelia's name had not been mentioned. They were both aware of it, and I could feel that they were. But there were smiles heading in all directions. I was not sufficiently educated to interpret them, nor sufficiently adroit to intercept one.

'You told me you wanted a word,' said Rosemary, turning to me. 'We've got a few minutes . . .' A tilt of the head.

'I might need more.'

She gave a mock grimace. 'Has this got to be alone?'

I included Amelia in my gesture. 'Not necessarily.'

'I'll be quite happy here,' said Amelia placidly, robbing the words of any special meaning.

'Will he bully me?'

'Sure to,' said my wife.

Then Mildred Niven swept across the floor with magnificent timing, extending both hands and claiming Amelia as though they were lifelong friends. 'Such boring business! You're his wife? How very lucky you are . . .' She raised one eyebrow archly in my direction.

In this way I found myself alone with Rosemary in the library. I call it that only because of the smell of musty leather bindings, which had permeated the walls. But there were now only empty shelves, along with two leather, studded armchairs, a table, and an atmosphere of chill indifference to anybody's opinion of its lack of welcome. What a fall from grace, to this pathetic reminder of forgotten peace!

'You've seen him?' she asked, as soon as we were inside the door.

She was walking across the room in order to put on a standard lamp. She turned, and gestured to one of the chairs. I shook my head, declining, and fumbled with my pipe. I felt nervous, uncertain of which way to direct the conversation.

'Yes. He's well. He spoke of you with . . . affection.' Had this been true? I was being kind, but it seemed to confuse her.

She was tense, moving her hands erratically, and spoke with impatience. 'Duncan was always such a fool! Not the slightest idea of anything involving life and human relationships.' This, presumably, in rejection or denigration of Duncan's speaking of her with affection. I regretted the exaggeration. 'Has it . . . the prison . . . hardened him?'

'He seems to have come out of it well. Perhaps there was a touch of cynicism.' I lit my pipe. Anything to cover the smell of those departed books. 'I don't know how he was before, but he seems very concerned now about money.'

'I could help him there.'

'I don't think he needs help. There's a certain . . . materialism . . .'

We stopped, looking at each other. She made a gesture, tried a smile. 'Why're we talking like this?' she asked, almost pleading.

She was taut, her own emotions twanging away, but I had to ignore them. I pretended not to understand.

'There's so much to ask you, and so little time, if you're to get on with your work.'

'Oh . . .' A gesture of disillusionment. '. . . ask away, then.'

Either Rosemary or Duncan had told lies, and the fact that I couldn't decide which was irritating me. To unsettle her, and to force myself on to the attack, I plunged in from an indirect angle.

'Why did you deliberately give Duncan an alibi?'

She was silent for the four seconds it took her blush to ripen, and be plucked free. Her hair shook – we were back with the rubber band, a red one. 'Did I?' Her chin was raised. 'But I thought he was the only person without one.'

'That was for the later time. I mean for the earlier one.'

'I don't know . . .' Now the knot of hair was dancing wildly. '*What* earlier one? Don't be difficult, Richard, please.'

'You walked up from the garages, after having taken the keys for your Dolomite to your Uncle Edwin. You met Duncan on the terrace, and gave him a solid alibi for the time your uncle was thought to have driven away.'

Her eyes were blank as her mind fought to accept the idea. 'Thought?' she breathed.

'He gave me a quite detailed account of what happened, but you said, in your statement . . .'

Her hand reached to stop me. 'My statement . . .'

I wasn't intending to be stopped. 'Your statement that you were together, or at least within sight of each other, when the sound of the Dolomite's engine died away. Duncan said . . .'

'You've read my statement?' Her eyes flared.

'. . . in his very circumstantial account, that you'd left him before the engine sound died away.'

'Why're you talking like this?' she said angrily.

'In your statement . . .'

'Damn the statement!' she shouted. 'What the hell're you saying? Uncle Edwin came back . . .'

'Did he?'

'Why are you so cold?'

'Duncan said you'd walked away along the terrace, and it was a good three minutes later that the engine sound died.'

For a moment she looked full into my eyes with a pain that almost unhinged me, then she turned away and took a few paces. To her back, I could allow myself to relax my expression. But I had to be silent, otherwise I'd have been crying out apologies, and heaven knows what that would've done.

When she turned, I was lighting my pipe again. She was quite calm. She even attempted a coyness that was too young for her.

'I don't understand this, Richard. But I suppose you're trying to frighten me.'

'Not frighten.'

'All right. Distress me. Why should Duncan have lied about me? We were friends . . . so close.'

'In your statement . . .'

'Richard . . .' Her hand went to her eyes for a moment. 'In that statement, it didn't matter about the time the engine sound died. I might not have been careful . . . accurate. Why does it matter now?'

I shook my head at her. 'I think you know why. I'm terribly worried that you do know why, that's why I'm being so abrupt with you. I think that your Uncle Edwin was killed *then*, when the sound of the engine died away. Or at least, what was done to kill him was done then. And I have to wonder whether your statement was not, as you say, casually made, but very carefully. Because it gave Duncan an alibi for that time.'

'This is quite ridiculous.'

'No. It is not. The drinks in the back of the car indicate he didn't drive away. They were not bought locally, and they were available. I believe you realised that the time of that garage door closing, when everybody thought the car was driving away, was critical.'

She was very still for a moment, then with an angry gesture she reached up and tore the rubber band from her hair, using it as something to occupy her fingers, stretching it so fiercely that I was sure it would snap. At the same time her hair danced furiously as her shaking head rejected what I'd been saying.

'How could I possibly have thought that?' she demanded angrily. '*Everybody* believed – I still believe – that Uncle Edwin drove away.'

She stopped. I was smiling at her. It cost a lot, that smile.

'But Rosemary, you knew he'd not driven away, because the drinks on the back seat of your car were not bought by him that night, they were bought *by you*, in Lichfield, when you went there to collect Duncan.'

Her breath was drawn in with a gasp, and she was quite white, until anger sent a rush of blood upwards from her neck.

'That's a lie!'

'I don't believe so.'

'Then go and do your believing somewhere else. I'm not going to listen to this.'

'You couldn't have anticipated that Duncan would be charged with the murder. But you wanted to give him an alibi, to play safe. He had the best motive – the inheritance, for what it was worth. But the alibi you gave him was for the wrong time, as it seemed then. He was charged, but for the murder time of much later, when your uncle was believed to have returned.'

She gestured violently – her anger, her bemusement. 'What are you trying to do, damn you?' There were tears in her voice. 'Why would I want to give Duncan an alibi, for heaven's sake?'

'Because of the hints I've received. Only small things, expressions, tones of voice, evasions. I think you two were much closer than you're both pretending.'

She managed to smile. 'And what if we were?' It became a grimace, reverted to a smile.

'It might alter the situation.'

'You're a fool, Richard. Do you know that? Yes, we were very close, but that was long before. It all broke up, oh, at least three years before Uncle Edwin died.'

'What happened?'

'Glenda Grace. That's what happened.'

So we'd come to the other subject I'd wanted to discuss, and with no effort from me. We'd also moved away from the question of the alibi. I wondered whether she'd realised that I'd not been talking about her alibi for Duncan, but his for her. If so, she'd steered me away from it very neatly.

'You knew Glenda Grace?'

'She got her claws . . .' Then she flinched, as though I'd slapped her. Or she had. She shook her head violently. The thought so agitated her that she was no longer able to stand still, and she began pacing, only a few steps one way, a few steps back, almost as though she felt herself restricted by her own taped, white lines.

'It sounds as though you knew her before she even met Duncan,' I suggested.

She stopped pacing and turned to stare at me with mute appeal, her eyes bright, strongly side-lit by the lamp.

'I knew her', she said, 'when she was young and happy, just a schoolgirl. When there was nothing vicious and dirty in her life. But things happen to young girls, things beyond control. Perhaps she was on drugs, even so early. She looked like an angel, Richard, so innocent – those big eyes . . .'

'What are you trying to tell me?' I asked gently.

She flung herself into one of the leather chairs. 'She was my daughter, Richard. You can't expect me to tell you everything, at a first meeting. We were what they now call a one-parent family, while I was struggling to get on the stage, or write . . . don't for God's sake interrupt. Don't tell me I neglected her. We couldn't have been closer. Two sisters, that's how I saw us. Perhaps that was wrong.' She put the back of her hand against her mouth, and turned her shoulder to me.

I waited. I went to look out of the uncurtained window. A spatter of rain hit it. She was speaking again

'Whatever I did, it must've been terribly wrong. One day I realised she genuinely hated me, through and through. She wanted to leave home . . . home, that was a scruffy little flat in London . . . and we had a flaming row. Only then – Richard . . . to see that smooth, beautiful face distorted, and hear those obscenities! I couldn't answer her, couldn't say a word. She walked out, next to nothing in her hands, and out of my life. She was sixteen.'

This was information I'd wanted, or thought I'd needed, but I hadn't been prepared to receive it in this way.

'I'll get you a drink,' I offered.

'No!' she shouted. 'Let me say it. That . . . that was the time I lost heart. The novel, it was useless. Uncle Edwin offered me the job here. So I came. It was like a haven. You can understand why I love this house, every brick, even this smelly old musty room, if you want to know. Oh yes, I saw you twitch your nose.'

'He knew?' I asked. 'Is that why your uncle offered?'

'It came out of the blue. I hadn't seen him for . . . oh, twenty years. When I was at college. I don't think he knew about Glenda. But he might have done. He never mentioned her. Glenda Grace! My God, that was her professional name, and you can just guess what that profession was.'

'I'm glad, anyway, that you've been happy here.'

Then she smiled. The years ran away. This woman was at least fifty, and for the past few minutes had looked sixty. But her face now glowed with warmth.

'Edwin could not have been more thoughtful and kind. And of course, there was Duncan. It was here I met him again . . . we hadn't seen each other since we were children. Then it'd been when our families met – I'm his second cousin, you know. He's three or so years younger than me, but that didn't seem to matter. Have you noticed . . . Duncan's sort of timeless? So serious and unsmiling about his music . . .'

She hadn't heard his plans for a musical play.

'. . . like a university professor, and at the same time he's always been a complete innocent. When we were little I used to bully him terribly. At eleven, a seven-year-old is a natural target for everything. And dear Duncan took it all with – well, eagerness. He's never lost that. He expected me to take him in hand and order his life, and I suppose, as best I could with him being so far away in Lichfield, I did that. There are other cathedrals, you know, other organs. But he wouldn't move, just couldn't work up the energy. I suppose if it'd come to it, I'd have thrown it all up here, and gone to him.'

'And left this house?'

She considered that seriously. 'One thing I can thank her for, I suppose.'

'I beg your pardon?'

'Glenda. I met her again before I'd made up my mind. I'd gone over to Lichfield – it's not too far out of the way, coming here from London – to see Duncan. Richard, I don't see that this is of any interest to you.'

'Another time, perhaps?'

She rose from the chair, even at that time gracefully, and came up to me. Her eyes searched mine. 'You realise why I'm telling you all this?' she asked, touching my arm.

I took that as a genuine question. 'So that I'll understand about Duncan, and why he could not have killed his uncle.'

She slapped my lapel. 'Wrong again. Sometimes, you can be quite stupid, Richard.'

'Can't help it. What were you saying?'

She walked away from me. 'Oh . . . Duncan and me. I was intending to tell him, that day, that I was going to leave here and go to live with him. You understand – wait for any move from Duncan, and I'd wait for ever.'

'Yes. I've met him.'

'But he had to take me to the Bishop's party. Said he was committed. And there she was. Glenda. In that setting – for a few seconds I didn't recognise her. Ridiculous, because she hadn't changed, so beautiful and so innocent, and behind that pretty little doll's face of hers . . . She saw who I was with. It was enough. The fact that it was my arm through Duncan's told her all she needed to know, and he was as good as lost. In the first minute I knew it, Richard. I don't think he said another word to me the whole evening.'

I cleared my throat. Her eyes came round to me. Pain in them. I said: 'Why was she there? I can't reconcile . . .'

'She'd come with Clyde Greenslade.'

'The porn king!'

The laugh she gave was hideous. 'You're as innocent as Duncan, I'll swear. That was what he did – certainly – and that was what *she* did. My Glenda. But the shades of intention are very slim, Richard. A change in the angle of a spotlight, a soft-focus lens, a fractionally different camera angle . . . and it becomes art. Art imitating life, if that's your taste. And Clyde – you *must* meet him – was always an expert at promoting his own image. Charities. Anonymous donations that're leaked to the press. Gifts to the Church. He'd presented a tapestry he'd got his dirty hands on . . . something about the history of Lichfield.'

She had been speaking with hollow bitterness. Only the words 'dirty hands' revealed her feelings fully.

'Lord, but we did have a row,' she said, and her lips twitched to a smile. 'As far as anybody could have a row with Duncan. He just stood there. How *could* I tell him she was my daughter? And the words I used . . . he just did not understand. Of course, once she saw she'd ruined everything for me, dear Glenda went back to London.'

'With an introduction to Uncle Edwin, Duncan told me.'

'That was a laugh. She went back to Greenslade and his art movies.'

'So your uncle never knew about it, this trouble you had with Duncan?'

'He knew,' she said quietly.

'He found out she was your daughter?'

'No. Not that. Oh Richard, I don't like talking about this. I should never have said . . .'

'I'm sorry, but I must know.'

I was faced with the problem that her uncle's murder had left me with a large selection of suspects, and no motive for it. The death of Glenda Grace held all the emotional possibilities to provoke a motive. I had to find the link.

She was standing by the window, with the lash of rain on the panes behind her, me by the empty fireplace. The door to the dining room opened, and Drew put in his shaggy grey head.

'Rosemary, we're ready.'

'For God's sake, get out!' she flared at him.

His face shocked, he withdrew.

'It's gone on long enough,' I said, not wishing to witness her distress any more.

'You might as well hear the lot,' she said, not containing her disgust, arms hugging themselves across her breasts. 'I had a sort of breakdown. Duncan, I'm sure he'd have . . . kind of come back, if I'd tried. But . . . his distress! She'd just marched out of his life, offered him some sort of vague ecstasy, then snatched it away. I couldn't offer that. I had some sort of a breakdown. I had to explain, to Uncle Edwin. He loved me, you know, Richard, in his strange way. All he said was . . .' She tried to laugh, but it was strangely pathetic. 'He said that at least Glenda had *his* thanks, because I'd come back to him. A year later, she was dead.'

She said this with finality, indicating that it was the end. But it wasn't. Gently, I prodded her on.

'That was at another of those wretched parties. Were you there?'

'Of course I was there!' she cried, in contempt at my poor use of logic. 'It was Uncle Edwin's flat. I lived there, when he was in London. And *she* came. Richard, I was sick. I mean that. Literally sick.'

'Oh?'

'She was with Drew Pierson. Dear Drew – on his arm, and with that mocking look in her eyes. I could have killed her.'

She covered her face with her hands. I hated to take it further.

'The impression is that somebody did,' I murmured.

Above her fingers her eyes pleaded.

'I know . . .' I held up a hand. 'She fell. She was drunk. Or she was on drugs. Nevertheless, there's been a suggestion that she was . . . helped on her way.'

'Somebody . . .' She swallowed, and tried again. 'Somebody,' she whispered, 'seemed to think she was killed.'

'There,' I said. 'What did I say?' I cocked my head. 'You'd heard?'

She shook her head. 'I got a note. It said: "I saw you do it. Be at . . ." What does it matter where I was supposed to go?'

'And did you? Go,' I explained.

'As though I would!' She was scornful. 'Why're you looking at me like that?'

'And nothing happened?'

'What? Oh, I see. Of course not.'

'Then they didn't see you do it.' I spread my hands, grinning.

'D'you know, Richard, you could've been a pleasant man, if it wasn't for your training. I've got to get out there. We'll never get through it tonight.'

By some miracle, she'd put on her professional face. As she put her hand on the doorknob I said:

'You didn't tell me . . . *did* you hear your uncle's car drive away?'

She turned, her eyes hard. 'Damn you, Richard.'

'Duncan says you weren't with him when the engine sound died away.'

'Then it must be true,' she snapped.

'I'm terribly afraid he might be banking on that.'

It held her. Straight-backed, she stood facing the door. 'He's coming here?' Her voice was uncertain again.

'I wouldn't be at all surprised.'

She opened the door, went through, closed it behind her. I heard her voice raised.

'All right, everybody. Let's run through the next scene. That's you, Mildred, and . . .'

Her voice faded as she walked away. I was left staring at the door, miserable, uncertain, and despising myself.

11

We didn't get away from there before midnight. Amelia was fascinated by the rehearsals, and only weariness prevented her from staying to the end. I tried to utilise the opportunity, but I could do so only in snatches, and then in a tense whisper in the shadows at the side.

Amelia didn't ask me what had happened in the library. Perhaps she failed to realise that Rosemary had changed. It was the change that disrupted the smooth flow of the play. She was acid and critical, pouncing in every minute or two to interrupt. I was surprised that the cast didn't seem to mind. They were worried, though, I could see that.

I found Mervyn Latimer in the farthest corner at a card table, a tiny desk lamp clamped to its edge. He was the set designer, and his name was on the guest list of Edwin's last party. I sat opposite him. He was working grimly over a batch of designs and sketches.

He barely glanced up at me, and seemed uninterested in my place in the scheme of things. Latimer was a small man, thin and mean-looking, and his eyes pecked from side to side, scanning the designs through huge spectacles with metal rims. His only comment as I settled on to a flimsy chair was:

'She wants another settee in. *Now* she tells me.' His voice was bitter.

'Must be murder,' I agreed, 'working for a woman.'

He spared me another upward glance, wolfish, his teeth showing in a fevered grin.

'She wants it, she gets it.'

'Worked with her before, have you?'

'Known her for years,' he admitted, mumbling it through a pencil stuck between his teeth. 'Wonderful director. Goddamn it, *where* am I goin' to put the bookcase?'

He was the sort of man who complains in order to emphasise the difficulties, and thus burnish the triumph when he conquers them.

'I understand you worked for her uncle, too.'

No reply. He rescued the pencil and scribbled a note across a corner. Then he slapped it down and sat back.

'I know who you are. They warned me.' He produced a battered pack of cigarettes. 'Smoke?' I showed him my pipe. He nodded, and lit up, cupping the match. 'The law,' he said, nodding again. 'Don't you chaps ever get tired? You got your man, so why not forget it?'

He hissed smoke through his teeth. They were brown. He hooked one arm over the back of the chair.

'I'm not the law,' I explained. 'And I'm not convinced the right man was sentenced.'

'Hmm!' He took the cigarette out of his mouth and stared at it. 'I wasn't, at the time. But nobody asked my opinion.'

'Anybody in mind?'

'Oh mate, give over.'

'You were here, at the party, so you knew everybody.'

'That's it, you see. They were all his friends, and my friends too.'

'Friends, for a failure party? That always struck me as strange.'

'Somebody', he said, 'has been giving you wrong impressions.' He tapped ash on to the green baize, swept it away, and ingrained it deeper. 'Edwin wasn't beaten. He knew he'd got the material. His plays. Valuable properties, those plays. It was all a matter of finance. Why d'you think Clyde Greenslade was there? Don't let anybody fool you they were friends. Not since that kid Glenda died, they weren't . . .'

'About her . . .'

But he was into his full flow, all this conducted in a low tone, so as not to disturb the action on the floor. 'It was finance, you see. Clyde'd got money. And good old Drew Pierson, he'd got money. Edwin knew he could get his finance, if he'd only let somebody else do the directing for the next play. *That* was what we were all there for. To persuade Edwin. It was the jam on our bread and butter we were thinking about.'

'I see.'

'Which', he said, picking a shred of tobacco from his tongue, 'was why Edwin's performance was so strange. Even for him. All he wanted was to succeed as a director. Mad for it. Drooling at the chops. Couldn't he see, either way he wasn't going to direct another play! So why . . . and you can explain this . . . why the hell wouldn't he *think* about it? Why couldn't we get him set down still for a minute, to talk?'

'I'm sure I don't know.'

'Going out for more booze! We wanted to get down to business. But he'd gotta go out for more damned booze. Jesus!'

'Nobody could persuade him?'

'Somebody tried. Yeah, it was Drew, and they nearly had a fight over it.'

'So I heard.'

'You don't fight a potential backer.'

'Not if you know what you're doing,' I agreed solemnly.

'I've gotta get on with this.'

In a second he'd switched me off, and his drawings held all his attention.

'And yet . . .' I waited. No attention. I plunged on. 'And yet, you people, suppose to be worried about him dashing off, you set to and played party games.'

He sat back again. 'Are you going to let me get on with this?'

'In a minute. You played party games . . .'

'Games! Who're we talking about? Me – and I'm knocking seventy, sonny – and Mildred, well . . . you've seen her, and Drew Pierson, old whitehead over there, and Clyde Greenslade, as humourless a bladder of lard as you've ever seen, and Harry Martin, that fellow there in the jeans and sweat shirt. He was the only one young enough for party games. We played Scrabble and got a bridge four going . . . Just try concentrating when the centre of it all is off in the night.'

I ticked them off in my mind. He'd mentioned five, and needed six. 'And Rosemary?'

'She tried to organise things. All nice and quiet, it was, until Duncan came rushing in, shouting about the garage and Edwin, and waving that radio in his hand.'

'Shouting what?'

'As though I can remember! Yeah, perhaps I can. About not being able to get the door to go up. That radio . . .'

'And you all dashed down there?'

'Of course, straight over the terrace. Somebody managed to get the door up. I think it was Drew. And . . . well, you know what we found.'

'Yes, I know.' I stared across at the brightly lit area of the floor. The young couple were enduring a telling-off by Mildred Niven, in her best *grande-dame* voice, and Rosemary was standing with her feet paddling in the verge of the light, every nerve stressed as she mentally urged the dialogue onwards.

'Edwin's parties had a tendency towards tragedy,' I murmured.

'Ha!' he said. 'Guessed you wouldn't miss that. Glenda Grace.'

'You were there? At that party too?'

'Most certainly. They'd used my sets.'

'So you know what happened?'

'Nobody knows what happened.'

He didn't seem inclined to enlarge on that, so I ventured on a hunch, to provoke him.

'Somebody seems to. I heard there were threatening notes . . .'

I hadn't taken my eyes from Rosemary during the last exchange. Perhaps she sensed my attention. In any event, she suddenly broke up a tearful response from the young woman, and marched over to where Latimer and I were seated.

'If you two want to talk, why don't you do it elsewhere?' she demanded forcefully.

I raised my eyebrows at her, but couldn't draw a smile. 'Really!' she said, then she marched back.

What had intrigued me was that, during this brief interlude, the actors had reacted complacently, and simply stood there, except that the tears had ceased to flow and Mildred had bent towards the young actress to say something that brought a short laugh. On Rosemary's return they fell straight back into character, Mildred resumed her outraged dignity stance, and the young woman's shoulders and body sagged into the misery of her tears.

And . . . *did* we want to talk? I glanced at Latimer. He jerked his head towards the nearest door. My mention of blackmail notes had hit him.

We were in a corridor, wide and bare and emulsion-painted. At the far end was a door with an inset design of coloured glass. The front door? There was a mirror on the wall just inside it, and an umbrella stand.

'What d'you know about those letters?' Latimer demanded, propping one shoulder against the wall.

'I'd heard.'

'You mean . . .' He clutched my sleeve. '. . . somebody else had one?'

I wasn't going to be drawn, simply bent away from him to tap out my pipe. 'I take it *you* did?'

'Mad. Crazy. Me! I ask you.'

'What did it say?'

'That they'd seen me push her off the balcony. *Nobody* saw her go.'

'Well then. What else did it say?'

'I was supposed to take money in a carrier bag and wait on a park seat . . . oh, some time or other.'

'How long after her death was this?'

'Oh, two months. A bit more.'

'Much money, was it?' I asked, not too interested, and making that plain.

'A thousand. Who could ever . . .'

'So what did you do?'

'Tore the damn letter up and tried to forget it.'

But not with success. 'Then what happened?'

'Nothing.' He stubbed his latest cigarette against the wall.

'So that's all right.'

'How can it ever be all right? Somebody was throwing accusations around! And how could anybody have seen what happened on that balcony? There was a huge curtain. Velvet. Dark green. Floor to ceiling, with a cord-operated pull.'

His designer's eye would have recorded that detail. I patted him on the shoulder. 'Then I wouldn't worry about it.'

'Who's worrying? That was years ago.' He tried to look casual. 'And the inquest said it was an accident, anyway.'

He gave an agitated jerk of his head, ruining the image. 'But you could tell – that damned copper in charge – he thought something wasn't on the up-and-up.'

'Did he say that?'

'She was stoned out of her mind, you know. They found cocaine . . . well, you know how it is.'

'No. I don't, as it happens.'

'She could've done anything. That bitch. Any way she could hurt anybody . . .'

He stopped. She'd hurt him in some way. He mashed a fresh cigarette in his hand and threw it away.

I told him I'd heard about her. My dislike for her was growing steadily. Could such a fiend have been Rosemary's daughter? I bared my teeth at him, hoping he'd take it for a smile.

'I know what you mean. She'd be the last person to hurt herself.'

'Sure. Well. It follows.'

'So it follows she didn't, perhaps, commit suicide. But there's still accident . . . and that's what the coroner's court decided, as you said.'

The thought didn't seem to comfort him, and he seemed about to take it further, but the door along the corridor opened.

'Ah, there you are, Mervyn,' Rosemary said, all smiles and as sweet as pie. 'I've changed my mind about that settee. It'd clutter the stage.'

'*Now* she tells me.' But this time he said it fondly. She had shattered the mood, and recalled him to his work. He prodded me in the ribs. 'Wouldn't have your job for a fortune,' he said. Then he toddled back into the dining room.

I wondered what strange idea he had as to what I was doing, and went to try that front door.

It opened on to a covered half-circle of steps down to a gravelled parking area. Out there it was dark, completely. The lights behind me in the hall barely penetrated the pall of rain, which had now made up its mind and was coming down steadily. The light indicated five vague shapes. I was interested only in hatchbacks, but not all that interested. I would not have been able to recognise the one I'd seen on the night of Llew's fire, anyway.

Away out there a car's headlights spiked through the rain, rising and falling, sometimes flashing straight into my eyes. I watched the cones reaching closer, until it was certain they were coming to the house. I waited. A small vehicle bucked up the drive, parked the other side of the cars, and the lights went out. Dimly I could make out its shape, a square box of vehicle, like a van.

He weaved through the cars, making his way towards the light behind me, an incongruous figure in slacks and a jacket, but wearing an official police cape and a flat cap.

'Is that you, Mr Patton?'

I knew the voice. It was Constable Davies, off-duty, but utilising official property. That was his police van, in which he'd just driven up.

'Constable. You're out late.' He came closer, the grin on his face almost of embarrassment. 'And I'd guess off your patch.'

'Still my territory, sir, but I'm rarely up here.' He mounted the steps into the porch, paused to shake off his cap, and dropped the cape around his feet like a woman stepping out of a skirt. 'This is lucky, I must say. I wanted to see you alone, and here you are.'

There was an air of indecision about him, although it would have taken a firm decision to undertake the drive.

'Better come along in. I might even find you a cup of tea.'

'I'd prefer not, sir, if you don't mind. To both.'

'One thing that irritates me,' I told him, 'and which I'd like you to cure, and that's this business of "sir" all the time. Either Mr Patton, or Richard. All right?'

He gave a sideways smile. 'I'll try Mr Patton for size, if you don't mind.'

'Good. Now . . . Mr Davies . . . why not inside?'

'I wanted to see you alone.'

'The corridor's empty.'

'All the same . . .' He stared at the cap in his left hand before replacing it on his head. 'If you don't mind, here will do. I don't want us to be seen together.'

It restricted our area of movement. I tried three paces one way, three the other. 'All very mysterious,' I said. 'This is private?'

'In some ways.'

'Hmm!' I sucked at the stem of my pipe. 'Since I saw you last, I've obtained a lot of information. Things have changed. How d'you know you can trust me?'

'I've got to trust somebody,' he burst out, then he became embarrassed and looked away. 'No, I mean . . .'

'Even me.'

'Especially you, sir. Mr Patton.'

'Suppose you tell me.'

Still he hesitated. He stared out at the rain. 'I hear your wife got back all right.'

'Tired,' I said. 'But pleased with herself. You', I accused him, 'have been keeping an eye on us.'

'I was up at his place yesterday. Ewr Felen. Poking around the ashes.'

'Ah yes?' Let him do it his own way, I thought.

'His car's still in that shed he used.'

'It was well clear of the fire.'

'I had a look inside the shed.'

'I gathered that.'

'There's a gallon can of petrol in there.'

'I suppose – isolated like that – he'd keep a reserve.'

'Yes, he kept a reserve. Mr Patton,' he burst out, 'he'd been warned, you know. He used to keep a gallon can in the outhouse, attached to the main building. We warned him about it – the danger. Mr Grayson warned him, and asked me to check on it. Check if he'd done anything about shifting it.'

He stopped, as though waiting for me to say something. I searched around for something appropriate. 'And you forgot?'

A pause. Then an emphatic shake of the head. The overhead porch light caught in his dark eyes. 'Not really. It'd only been two days. It wasn't that.' He faced me squarely. 'And anyway, he'd done it. Switched the petrol to his shed. Because it's there.'

'And how d'you know it was the same can?' I asked with interest.

'Well . . . look at it. He wouldn't have had two cans, one in each place. He wouldn't have bought a second, and kept it with the car, and left the other in the outhouse. No . . . it's logic. He was warned, and he shifted his can of petrol from the outhouse to the shed.'

It had come out in a burst of lilting rhetoric, his reasoned argument.

'And so?' I asked quietly.

'So the fire wasn't an accident.' He shook his head again, as though discarding rain from his hair. 'But there was that smell of petrol . . .'

'I see,' I said casually, seeing more than he realised but not committing myself. 'So you came all this way to check your reasoning . . .' I tried to get my pipe going, but a breeze snatched away the flame. '. . . before going to tell Mr Grayson.'

'Mr Grayson knows.'

'Sure?'

'He told me the car was all right. As there aren't any windows, he must've opened the shed door. The can was there, just inside. I kicked it. He couldn't have missed it.' He was gesturing vehemently. 'And the inquest's on Thursday,' he said in a hollow voice.

'The last thing I heard, Mr Grayson was intending to go for accidental death.'

'Still is.'

'I can see your difficulty. You think you ought to give that information at the inquest – you, as the officer first on the scene of the fire. And it wouldn't be a good idea to clash head-on with your Chief Inspector, not in court. I can understand that.'

He was looking at me with disappointment. 'It wasn't that.'

I tapped him on the shoulder with my pipe. 'No need to worry about it. I'll give that evidence. I'll even go a run to Ewr Felen and have a look at it, then I won't be lying. Come to think about it, I'd rather like the chance . . .'

'It wasn't that,' he said again, his voice dead, controlling his anger.

'Wasn't it?' I asked innocently.

'I can give my own evidence, thank you.' His dignity was immature, but it would improve with practice. I said nothing. 'The can of petrol in the shed means he was killed,' he went on. 'Mr Hughes was making enquiries, and somebody killed him. You're making the same enquiries, so things could become difficult for you, Mr Patton.'

'I'm aware of that, laddie. I can look after myself.'

'I'm sure you can.' His former embarrassment returned. He screwed a toe into the slimy surface of the porch. 'I was thinking about your wife.'

'Thank you.'

'I wasn't too happy when she came back,' he said, as though his lips were stiff. 'From home,' he amplified. 'Which I understand to be a long way away.'

'It pleased me,' I told him. 'And it's two hundred miles. I was glad to have her with me, where I can keep an eye on her.'

'Just thought I'd mention it.'

'That's very good of you.'

'And just thought I'd let you know I'll be around. In case, you might say.' He gulped. 'Sir.'

It had taken him some measure of resolution to drive there and tell me this, even more to suggest that I might not be able to look after the welfare of my own wife.

I grinned at him. 'By heaven,' I said, 'but you're going to have a hard time of it in the force, Mr Davies. So formal and so delicate! They'll eat you alive, either the villains or your own superiors. But you've made me feel a damn sight better. I'll be able to see you on the horizon, and know you're there. I'm grateful.'

He managed a wry smile. 'You were ahead of me, all the way,' he accused.

'Most of it. I was simply wondering whether you were going to warn me off.'

He laughed. 'You, sir!'

'We'll have to find time for a drink,' I said, as he turned away. 'If you'll forget the sir.'

He fastened his cape at the neck, perched his hat on his head at a jaunty angle, and marched off into the rain. You'd have thought he'd climbed a mighty peak.

I watched until there was no sign of his lights in the night, then I went back inside to see what they were doing.

The rehearsal now seemed to be going well. Rosemary was making no interruptions, and I got the impression that we were heading for a curtain climax. I edged round in the shadows until I located Amelia in a corner, sitting with Cindy asleep on her lap, and completely immersed in it. I sat beside her, saying nothing. The act came to an end, though apparently the end of the second act, not the play. Another act to come.

Rosemary, who'd been out of my sight at the far side of the room, walked into the light and said:

'That was fine. I didn't interrupt, it was all sweeping along splendidly. Break, everybody. Coffee and buns, and we'll go straight into the third act.'

There were groans. 'It's bloody late, Rosemary.'

'While we're in the swing of it.'

There was no denying her. The complaints were purely formal. Rosemary had decided.

She came over to us, smiling, all the tension between the two of us now swept away.

'We're going to finish very late, I'm afraid. But stay on if you like.'

Amelia glanced at me. Around the room, one by one this time, the main lights were coming on.

'I'm rather tired,' she admitted.

I hastened to say we really ought to be going. Outside, the rain continued to pound on the terrace, which was the quickest way to the car.

'If we could borrow an umbrella or two,' I said.

Rosemary looked blank. 'I don't know . . .' She gestured vaguely. 'Umbrellas?'

'There's a stand full of them in the hall.'

'Oh heavens yes. They've been there for years. Of course, help yourself. If . . .' And her eyes glinted wickedly at me. '. . . you'll promise to return them.'

I promised. Amelia busied herself fastening the lead to Cindy's collar, although she'd be carried to the car. I went out into the hall and walked to the umbrella stand by the front door, and chose two, from the shape of their handles.

One of them was still running with rainwater. I slid it back and drew out another. I didn't want anybody to notice that I'd noticed.

12

The Stag, when fitted with its hood, was not the ideal vehicle in the
Welsh mountains at night in the pouring rain. The hardtop was at the
cottage in Devon, so there was no alternative. With two umbrellas we
reached the car without getting too wet, but inside it became clear that
my latest attempt to repair the hood had not been successful. There was
a pool of water on my seat, and I knew that once we got moving the rain
would drive back at us round the edges of the windscreen.

Amelia is always philosophical. 'Can't be helped, Richard. There's a
dry bed to aim for.'

It seemed that her thoughts were mainly on the bed, because I had the
impression that she was quickly asleep. Certainly her head was back
when I glanced sideways.

But she wasn't asleep. We were approaching Chirk when she
suddenly said: 'Isn't Mildred Niven a remarkable woman?'

I agreed that she was. 'For her age.'

'A wonderful memory.'

'It's the practice they get, from remembering their lines.'

'I really meant, her memory for everyday things. D'you know,
Richard, she remembers the evening of Edwin Carter's death . . . oh, as
clear as yesterday.'

I drove through Chirk. At that time, wind-flustered and streaming
with rain, it was a dead town, with only the streetlights alive and well.

'You've been questioning her,' I said, in a tone of amused com-
mendation.

'I'd call it chatting,' she told me. 'It was only natural the subject should
crop up, and as I knew you were busy on other things . . .' She took a
breath there. She too should have been an actress, the timing she
displayed with her pauses. '. . . I thought it would do no harm if I slanted
things the way you'd want them to go. You not being there,' she repeated, in case I hadn't got the point.

'I'm sure you were very clever about it,' I said, hoping, but confident,
that she hadn't been indiscreet. 'And what did you find out?'

Now we were going faster, the trunk road being reasonably clear of
traffic.

'I knew you'd want to confirm the alibi that Duncan gave you.'

Remembering that it involved Mildred Niven, I said: 'It was something I'd intended to get round to.'

'So you're pleased I came along,' she said coolly.

'Delighted. Even more, if we could get round to what you found out.'

'Refresh my memory,' she said, after I'd raced past a dawdling Lotus. 'What exactly did Duncan tell you?'

'He disappointed me by ruining the alibi Rosemary might have given him. He told me she'd left him three or so minutes before he heard the engine sound die away. And three minutes would have been enough, I think. But then he said Mildred was standing at his elbow, and said something about: "Well, he's off at last." '

'I *thought* that was what you told me, but I couldn't be certain, so I couldn't argue with her. *She* said she joined him just as Rosemary walked away along the terrace, and what she said to him was: "Well, *she's* got him off at last." Meaning Rosemary. Then Mildred left Duncan standing there.'

The brakes snatched as I pulled in behind a cruising coach. After I'd got past it through the tyre spray I had time to give a little thought to what she'd said.

'And at that time – when Mildred left him alone on the terrace – the engine was still running?'

'Yes. She meant, you see, that she'd just heard it start.'

'Of course, at her age, her hearing might not have been so good.'

'It was all of ten years ago, Richard, and her hearing's perfect now.'

'A hearing aid? One she wasn't wearing that night?'

She shook her head. The corner of my eye caught movement, but I couldn't afford to look away from the road.

'Will you say it, please.'

'No hearing aid,' she told me. 'Don't you think I looked? Richard, I admired her ear-rings. Simple. No hearing aid.'

'Then . . . her memory,' I tried, feeling desperate.

'We've been through that. Slow down, Richard, we're nearly there.'

'Nearly where?' I asked in disgust. 'I'm absolutely nowhere. Now . . . Duncan's new alibi for an earlier time – that's up the spout. *Anybody* could've done it, and I've got no damn lead at all!'

I pulled into the hotel car-park, switched off engine and lights, and slapped the steering wheel angrily.

'You told me', said Amelia, tapping my knee in admonishment, 'that it had to be whoever knew the drinks were in the boot of the car.'

'And who've I got for that – Duncan again?'

'And Rosemary. She was in Lichfield.'

'She denied she'd bought the stuff.'

'And you believed her?'

She hadn't opened her door, was sitting quietly, and the tone of her voice indicated she'd been waiting for just such an opening. So gentle was the question, so still and contained was her patience.

I spoke softly. 'I didn't believe her. But the time wasn't right to challenge her.'

She opened the door and got out. Cindy went with her. I handed out one of the umbrellas.

'I'll come round and take her,' I said.

'No. It's all right. I'll walk her round, while you get the key.'

The wind seemed to have taken her voice. Her face was averted. I nodded, though she didn't see it, and ran for the porch.

The night porter was getting used to it, so I didn't have to ring. He was there, just inside the door. I raised an eyebrow at him. He said:

'Gentleman to see you, sir.'

The inclination of his head indicated the lounge, in which there was a single light. I asked the porter if he'd tell my wife where I was, and walked through. Detective Chief Inspector Grayson rose smoothly to his feet.

'My,' he said, 'you *are* working hard.'

'Waited long?'

He shrugged. 'I just wanted to set your mind at rest. About Llew's death.'

He was smiling, but the strain was in his eyes. I had a feeling that he was about to put his career on the line, and decided I should say nothing to encourage him. I waited.

'The forensic evidence is in,' he explained. 'The fire was definitely fuelled with petrol, and the seat of it was the outhouse I mentioned.'

I nodded. 'In which, you told me, he used to keep a spare can.'

'Exactly. So there can't be any doubt it was accidental.'

'That'll be your evidence at the inquest?'

He nodded. 'In which event,' he went on stubbornly, 'there can't be any suggestion that his death was related to his memoirs.'

He smiled. It was out, and he'd committed himself. He hadn't been certain he could say it.

'You're suggesting I should go home, after the inquest?'

'Save time and money.'

'But we've got business in this area. A water-mill we're interested in.'

Now he was prepared to be sociable. 'Yes,' he said, 'so I understand. But think twice – there's dry-rot, I've heard.'

'Thanks for the tip.' I half turned away, then back. 'But hadn't you warned Llew about that petrol? I'm sure you said that.'

'Yes, I warned him.'

I held his eyes. There was a slight tint to his cheeks.

'And told Constable Davies to check,' he was forced to add.

'But Llew hadn't moved it?'

'That damned Davies – there'll be a reprimand for him. Two days, and he hadn't been up there.'

'Perhaps he was busy,' I said equably. 'So the can of petrol didn't find its way to the shed, where he kept his car?'

He held out a palm. 'There isn't a can there now.'

I'd turned away to the lobby, he drifting after me. Amelia waited at the reception desk, keys dangling from one hand, two thirds of Cindy dangling from the other. They said polite things to each other, the porter's eyes darting from face to face. Then Grayson headed for the door.

'Thank you for telling me,' I said after him. 'Particularly for staying up so late.'

The door thumped shut behind him. We walked up the stairs, into our room. Amelia, who knows my every mood, put a hand to my arm.

'Easy, Richard,' she said gently. 'No sense in losing your temper.' She stood facing me, reaching up to link her hands behind my head. 'What did he say?'

I told her, relinquishing my tension with a rueful smile.

'That he'd risk so much, just for his pride!' I said. 'A man can make a mistake . . . but he'd go this far? I can't believe it.'

'We'll check in the morning,' she said comfortingly.

'Pardon?'

'For that dry-rot.'

I laughed, and kissed her. 'How would I live without you?'

In practice, that was what we did. We drove again to the mill.

We went, after breakfast, to the estate agent's, to ask whether we could keep the key for another day. 'Or two,' I added, thinking to annoy Grayson. The agent was only too pleased. The mill had clearly been on his books too long.

'I'm sure you people aren't going to steal the millstone,' he said, laughing.

So we went back to the hotel and prepared a picnic meal. This came about because of Rosemary's phone call, which we'd received almost before we were properly awake. She had heard from Duncan.

'He's coming today,' she said, a hint of tension in her voice. 'For lunch.'

'I rather thought he would.'

'Richard, could you . . . please . . . be here?'

Amelia and I had a quick conference, with my hand blanking the phone, and decided on the packed lunch for her at the mill. I told Rosemary yes, I'd be there at Plâs Ceiriog, and that was how I came to be driving Amelia to the mill again, with a folding picnic chair in the boot.

It had been a rough night, but the rain had ceased with the dawn. There were signs that it might brighten up later, but the roads were wet as we headed west. The river was running high and brown.

'This time,' I said, 'we're going to see our stream a little more active.'

She didn't seem to be listening. 'You're going to see he doesn't say anything ridiculous, aren't you, Richard!'

She didn't have to name him. 'Just as a referee.'

No more was said on the subject. I made one more surreptitious examination of the rear-view mirror. He was still there, Davies in his little blue van. I felt relieved. If I hadn't spotted him, I don't think I could have left Amelia alone.

Beneath the narrow hump-backed bridge the two streams of water met and boiled. Our own stream rushed down and past the mill. I took the car up to it, and we got out.

'There,' I said. 'Look at that.'

There had been a steep bank from the mill down to the water's edge. Half of the bank had become absorbed in the tumbling stream. Debris swirled in it, attempting to cling to the bank, but being tossed onwards. The noise was continuous, seeming to involve every joist in the building.

'It's frightening,' she said, but there was awe and excitement in her voice, not fear.

I went to check that the two gates, in and out, to the millrace were firmly closed. There was barely a trickle getting through, as the gates were so made that the force of the stream's increased weight held them even more tightly closed.

Amelia was already inside. Here the stream's voice was barely a murmur, but the hand I put to one of the beams detected the vibration. The millstone sat in the centre of the room, massively, stolidly.

'It's not going to be very cheerful for you,' I said. 'Why not come with me?'

'No, Richard.' It was her calmly decisive voice. 'You know very well – it's a good idea to spend some time in a place before you decide. The weather's brightening. I'll go for a walk, come back for lunch, and you can pick me up later.'

'If you're sure . . .'

She laughed. 'Your face! You'd think I was going to spend the night in a haunted castle. I want to do this. Now please . . . you go off on your own business. I shall be all right.'

I stood at the window, staring out at the stripped and naked hills, down to the bridge. A trickle of smoke drifted from a cottage chimney. Beyond it, I caught just a glimpse of the blue of Davies' van.

'I'll get off then.'

There was an A road the other side of the River Vyrnwy, and once I'd found this I knew where I was. At a little after eleven o'clock I plunged into the cutting through the belt of pines. I was in good time. It was hardly likely that Duncan could reach there before lunch.

Because there was plenty of time to spare, I pulled the car to a halt as I passed Drew Pierson, got out, and waited for him. It was an un-scheduled meeting, but there were one or two points I thought he could clear up.

He was marching along smartly on the grass verge of the driveway, swinging an ash stick in his right hand, but appearing not to need its assistance. He was dressed as though walking down Oxford Street, in slacks and a smart, short fawn coat and a tweed trilby. His shoes were stout walking brogues. Seeing that I'd stopped and was waiting for him, he waved the stick in greeting and called out:

'Lovely morning.'

The sun had cleared from behind the clouds, and was drawing wisps of mist from the wet ground. I agreed. But the grass was still sufficiently saturated to have soaked his shoes.

Pierson seemed cheerful and fresh, and was breathing easily.

'I always try to do two or three miles every morning,' he told me, coming up, propping his behind on the fist holding the walking stick, and striking a dramatic pose. 'Join me?'

'That depends on how far you've already done.'

'A mile or so.'

'Then I will. Couldn't face three miles, though.'

We fell into step, side by side.

'What?' he said. 'A great, fit chap like you?' He pointed with the stick, straight down into the valley. 'I like to reach that stream there.'

The only great, fit chap around there was himself. He'd scale out at eighteen stone, I decided. If his stride was anything to go by, not one pound of it was a drawback.

'Have to keep fit,' he explained. 'It's tiring, on the stage. You wouldn't believe. And every second is concentration.'

We were using the rudiments of a path, probably trodden by sheep, as it was narrow and wound without any obvious reason. It necessitated walking one behind the other, unless I was prepared to plod beside him in the grass. It was crisp and short, but already I could feel the wet seeping through to my feet.

We reached the stream, and stood looking at it. Just another stream, but this one hadn't come far from its source.

'He's coming, you know,' he said suddenly, prodding at a clod of grass with his stick.

'Duncan? Yes. That's why I'm here.'

'You want to question him?' He glanced at me with interest. 'Unless he's changed, you won't get very far.'

'I've already seen him. No, it's not that. I've got an idea there'll be an argument about alibis.'

'No question there, surely. Everybody else was up at the house.'

I had no intention of explaining how the time required for alibis had changed. To steer him away from it, I said: 'What's this I hear about you trying to stop him from leaving? Edwin, I mean.'

'Yes.' He sounded rueful. 'Shall we head back?' But he made no decisive move.

'There was some business you wanted to discuss,' I prompted.

He lifted the stick and squinted along it, as though it were a gun. 'It was all very unsatisfactory. He *wanted* money. He desperately needed it. He'd got me to come here, Greenslade, the others, and the whole point was to discuss the financing of his next play. Or not, as the case might be.'

'There was reluctance?'

'I'd have put up some of the money, possibly Greenslade the rest, but only if Edwin dropped his stupid ideas of wanting to be a director. He wouldn't even sit still and talk. And then we had to have this idea of his to go out and get more drinks. Fantastic! Edwin was the most unpredictable . . .'

'And you tried to stop him?'

'He was my friend. One of my oldest friends. I've known the family . . . oh, for ever, it seems. He wouldn't listen to me. Yes, it almost came to blows.' He paused, turned and looked at me. His hat was tilted roguishly, his eyes glinted. 'How could I hit him? Damn it, I'd have knocked his silly head off.'

'So you had to let him go?'

'He was almost hysterical. Yes, I let him go.'

'And the next thing you knew was Duncan running in and raising the alarm?'

'Yes. We'd better get back, I think.'

This time he put it into effect, turning on his heel and setting off at a good pace. He didn't want to talk about his friend's death.

The difficulty now was that I wanted to talk, and from the stream it was all uphill. His pace never slackened. I had to walk beside him, wet grass or not, and try to retain sufficient breath to speak.

'They tell me it was you who lifted the garage door,' I panted.

'Those ninnies! Gabbling and hysterical, and clustered round the garage, and trying to work that silly radio! Nobody had thought of grabbing hold of the door handle and giving it a good yank.'

But it must have needed a little more than a 'yank', as the linkage had been broken.

'You hadn't got much faith . . .' I breathed in. '. . . in the radio?'

'No time for all that new-fangled nonsense. Isn't that a peregrine up there?'

I couldn't have lifted my head far enough to check. 'Doubtless. I thought', I went on, 'that Edwin told everyone about his wonderful radios.'

'Told me,' he said complacently. 'Didn't listen. Anyway, when it came to it, the damn thing didn't work, did it? One good jerk, *that's* what did it.' He waved the stick, flexed his shoulders, and pounded on.

I had to allow him to draw ahead. The blasted healthy devil probably lifted weights between acts.

He was waiting for me beside my car, welcoming me with a slight smile. He watched me come to a halt, breathing heavily, my legs shaking.

'It's that pipe,' he said kindly. 'Ruins your wind.'

'I'll be all right.'

He might well have left me to recover on my own, but he had to watch me, enjoying it I'm sure.

'Smoking, and going everywhere by car,' he decided.

'Don't tell me you walked here from Chirk.'

'Now don't be ridiculous, dear boy, I've got my little hatchback, but I walk as much as I can.'

There was one question I'd been determined to ask, winded or not. 'Did you ever receive a blackmailing letter?'

I saw at once that I'd hit him hard. It was as though somebody had handed him the wrong cue, and he didn't know how to go on. When he spoke, even his voice had lost some of its polish.

'What do you know about that?'

'Letters relating to the death of Glenda Grace.'

'Who's been talking to you about this?' he demanded, as though I'd probed a deadly secret.

'People. And you were at that party, so I . . .'

'How d'you know about that?' The shock must have been strong, that he'd still be stalling.

'You were there. You were the one who escorted Glenda Grace to that party.'

Then I waited. Ten seconds, then he had it under control.

'If you know who sent it, then tell me. I'll deal with him, so help me.' The stick was now gripped like a club, but the effect was theatrical.

'I don't know who it was. What did yours say?'

His eyes flickered. He was suddenly abashed, even frightened. I had to tell myself I was talking to a very experienced actor. He licked his lips.

'A threat,' he said simply. 'That I'd been seen . . . pushing her off that balcony. That I, Drew Pierson . . .'

'Was there a demand?'

He stared at me owlishly. 'You know this. A demand for money. Oh, I could afford it, but d'you think I'd pay for vicious scandal, with not a word of truth in it?'

'Of course not. You tore it up, and forgot about it.'

'Forgot!' He lifted that magnificent voice to the mountains. 'I shall never forget, nor forgive. Show me this villain, and I'll take a horsewhip to him!'

I knew I'd lost him to his rhetoric. I climbed into the Stag and started the engine. 'If I find him,' I shouted, 'I'll hand him over to you.'

When I glanced in the rear-view mirror he was still at it, head back and declaiming his complaint to the rolling clouds.

This time I took the full length of the drive, so that I drove up to the front door. As I got out and considered the parked vehicles – four of them hatchbacks – I realised that one car was occupied.

A man sat quietly behind the wheel of a battered Citroën 2CV, a ginger-haired man I hadn't seen before. He looked up, attracted by my interest.

'Just a chauffeur,' he said, grinning. He opened the door and stood with me on the gravel. 'Giving my friend a lift.'

He wasn't any more than five feet six inches, a square-shouldered, red-faced young man, less than thirty, clean-shaven and friendly.

'I know who you are,' I said. 'It's Frank . . .' I snapped my fingers to promote memory. 'Frank Leigh.'

'I brought Duncan,' he explained, delighted that I knew his name.
'Oh Lor'.' I prodded his chest. 'How long . . .'
'You just missed him. He went off that way – round the house.'
I had felt I ought to be there when they met. Leaving as quickly as
I could without being rude, I ran up to the front door, galloped down
the hall, and with great care, so that my arrival would not create
embarrassment, I quietly opened the door into the dining room.

13

He had entered from the terrace and stood just inside the door with
indecision. Although now dressed a little more smartly, he had an air of
tattered disarray. His eyes were roaming round the room, though they
had fortunately passed my door. To him, the room would have changed.
It seemed to disconcert him.

Rosemary entered from the far end, a door that could well have led to
the kitchen area. She was wearing an apron, and she herself must have
been under strain. Any other time she would have whipped off the
apron. She was using it to wipe her hands.

'Duncan . . .'

'Hello, Rosie.'

So that was why she'd told me not to use the diminutive.

She was walking towards him. 'You're thinner. Oh, Duncan, what
have they done to you?' Standing in front of him now, twitching his
lapels, her hands hovering about his hair but not touching.

'Rosie,' he said hoarsely, 'you didn't come.'

'To Lichfield? That room? How could I? Let me look at you . . .'
She stood back. Hadn't she looked enough? No, she had to keep
her distance, in case his hands strayed, and the contact should be
made.

But he'd barely moved, only his eyes. His discomfort might well have
arisen from her detailed scrutiny.

'You ought to know . . .' He shuffled unhappily. 'Rosie, you should
know – this isn't my idea.'

'Not your idea to visit me? Now don't say that. I'd have come . . .' She
bit her lip, and was silent.

'That man came to see me,' he explained. 'There was something I
didn't know about.'

'There's so much you don't know about,' she cut in. 'But there's time. Not now, Duncan, I can't discuss it now.'

'That's why I came,' he said stubbornly. He had had to build himself up for this visit, and was afraid of being side-tracked. 'To discuss it.'

'Not to see me?' she challenged, though this time in a light way, as though she was teasing. And yet his answer would mean so much to her.

His hesitation was too protracted. She couldn't stand and face it. She raised her head and cried out: 'Richard, look who's come to see us.'

Us, you notice. Her nerve had failed her, if not her director's vision, that wide-angled encompassment of a full stage. She'd known I was there, and had kept the knowledge in reserve.

As I came forward Duncan seemed to break from a trance. 'That's the man,' he cried. No dissimulation from Duncan. His relief shone out fresh and bright.

'I'm glad you could make it,' I said. 'How're things going?'

Now that he could turn to me he was at no loss for words. 'You walked out on me and left my mind racing round, wondering what was going on and where it left me. I've been worried stiff.'

'It was you who ordered me out of the house,' I reminded him.

'You didn't have to take any notice of me.'

'Oh, but I did. Have you seen a solicitor?'

He stared at the floor and shook his head. 'Heavens no. I'd look a right fool, taking all that to a solicitor.'

'Then I'd suggest you shouldn't be here, if that's all you've come for.'

I intended it as a mild rebuke. I hadn't missed Rosemary's distress, and if he wouldn't do anything about it, then I had to. Or try, anyway.

She came in on cue. 'But we can't stand here talking. Come to my workroom. It's at least comfortable.'

Duncan made a gesture of agreement, but it was reluctant. What the hell had he expected, that she'd fall into his arms and sob out some sort of admission?

She took us out into the hall. Heads disappeared into doorways. One remained in view. 'Rosemary, when can we get going?' It was Mildred.

'A few minutes,' she said absently. 'I'll be in.'

Then Mildred advanced into the hall, and along it. 'But isn't it . . . but of course, it's Duncan. Oh my dear boy, I hardly recognised you. What have they done to you . . . ?'

'Mildred,' said Rosemary firmly, though she had difficulty handling the waver in her voice, 'do you think you could get them started? I'll be in when I can.'

'But of course, my dear.' She was very quick at taking hints. 'Now don't you dare leave until we've had another word.' She patted Duncan maternally on the arm and turned away, calling out names.

'In here,' said Rosemary.

She had called it her workroom. One end of it was equipped as a working office with a long surface the full width of the wall. On it was a chaos of paper, two phones, several dirty mugs, and a word processor. She would be able to print off her own script copies. The other half was a sitting room, with chairs, easy and otherwise, standing where they happened to have landed, low tables scattered in the spaces, a TV set wedged between the tumbled books on the wall shelves. It was a lived-in room, a contented room.

'Sit where you like,' she said.

Duncan did not do so at once. He said grumpily: 'Does *he* have to be here?' Not looking at me. He'd decided I wasn't on his side.

She plumped herself down in one of the chairs. There'd been a little time to accommodate herself to the mood Duncan had introduced, so she was able to speak lightly. 'I think it would be best, don't you? I mean, if we must discuss business . . .'

He conceded, as far as perching one cheek on the arm of another chair. I retired to the background.

'I know what he's here for,' I said, plunging in before Duncan could say anything terrible. 'I was foolish enough to give him a hint that there could be a pardon.'

'Well, that would be . . .'

Duncan interrupted her. 'It seems to have changed a bit. It was more than a hint.'

'. . . splendid,' she managed to finish.

'But I'd have been more pleased if he'd given me time to take it further,' I went on.

'It was more than a hint,' he repeated, clinging to it.

'But – as you've just said yourself – things have changed a bit.'

I had been concentrating on Duncan, watching the hope and disillusionment fighting for possession of his features. I'd offered him a lifeline, but I hadn't yet cut it to length.

But I was aware of Rosemary and her distress. To her, Duncan had changed. She'd reached for warmth, and he seemed to have no time for anyone but himself. This was a harder, more self-contained Duncan. She didn't know what to do with him, what to offer.

He was looking from me to her, back again, as though he feared a trap. 'You're trying to scare me, aren't you!'

Scare? Such a strange word. 'I don't want you to build up hopes.

125

Duncan,' I said, 'we spoke of a possible pardon. For that, the proof has to be very tight. All I had – still have – is a photograph of not too high a quality, that seems to indicate the drinks and the rest were not bought from around here. Seems. On *that* evidence, I'm willing to say that your uncle didn't drive away that night, and that he was killed before he could drive out of the garage. But it's slim. We don't *know* where all that booze came from.'

'We know darned well . . .' he said plaintively, allowing himself to slide over the arm of the chair and slump into its depths.

'No!' I said sharply, warningly.

'It came from Burton . . .' Now he was mumbling into his chin.

'We know the beer crate originated from there. Don't you see, if we only had somebody's evidence that the beer in that crate . . .' I stopped, caught by a thought. I turned to Rosemary. 'What happened to that stuff on the back seat?' I asked. 'What happened to the car – your Dolomite, Rosemary?'

The abrupt change of direction seemed to catch her by surprise. 'Well I . . . can't say. Let me think.'

On this indecision Duncan pounced. 'She knows. Really, she knows.'

She shot him a glance of pain, then turned back to me. 'They took the car away, for checks or something. So I asked the garage to pick it up from the police yard, and . . . well, dispose of it for me. I didn't see it again. Didn't want to.'

Another chance melted away. I wondered whether the booze had still been there when the garage called to collect the car.

'And your uncle's car?'

Her eyes were blank. She didn't want to talk, wanted to do nothing but be silent, and try to understand the misery caused by Duncan's attitude to her.

Perhaps he realised this, realised too that he'd been ungracious. He leaned forward, hair obscuring his eyes but not enough to hide a shy smile, and said:

'It doesn't matter, Rosie. Don't let it worry you.'

She stammered, flushing slightly. 'With Richard . . .' Her smile at me was radiant, but intended for Duncan. 'With Richard, you'll see . . . find . . . everything m-matters.' She shook her head. 'But I remember now. I asked the garage to dispose of that, too. It wouldn't go, you see. I couldn't get it to start.'

Not sufficient reason for disposing of it, surely. 'They came for it? Did they say what was the matter with it?'

126

Duncan flicked a glance of disapproval at me. 'As though it matters. Leave her alone.'

'I'm not good at cars,' she admitted. 'An arm or something, they said. Going round. I'd associate the word with going round.'

'Rotor arm?'

'That was it,' she said in triumph. 'Fallen off or got lost.'

'That *would* stop it running,' I agreed solemnly. But a rotor arm lives under a distributor cap, and it can't get out. Not on its own. I changed the subject quickly.

'All right. So what we're left with is a photograph, and none too clear. From it, it might be argued that your uncle could not have driven away to get the drinks, and from that we can make the assumption that the person who killed your uncle must have known the booze was available, and deliberately used it to create an alibi. But . . .'

I allowed a pause to build up there. Rosemary nodded. She appreciated the technique. I was deciding that it was time to deflate Duncan's pretentions.

'But . . .' I said, '*you* knew it was there, Duncan. No, no!' I held up my hand. 'Let me finish. The murderer would not have used this trick unless he had an alibi laid on for the later time, when your uncle would be assumed to have returned.'

'And Duncan didn't,' said Rosemary happily. 'Doesn't that prove he didn't do it?'

'Ah yes!' I wagged my head like a wise old judge. 'But we have to think of the effect of this on the legal mind. They're not going to be convinced by inverted reasoning like that. With the law, it's never a matter of what legal precept a particular question doesn't fit, it's what it does. The positive, you see. And if we look at it again, and consider alibis for the earlier time, when Edwin was believed to have driven away, well . . . I'm afraid you're out of luck, Duncan.'

His head came up. His eyes were startled. 'What's this? You know I was on the terrace. Rosie walked up from the garages . . .'

He stopped. This he'd been keeping in reserve. He glanced at her, and licked his lips. And appealed to me with every fibre of his body.

I shook my head at him in sorrow. 'The snag is, you see, that you haven't got an alibi for that earlier time either.'

He half heaved himself to his feet. 'But you told me . . .'

'No,' I said sharply. '*You* told me. You said you were talking to Mildred Niven when the sound of the engine died away.'

'What're you trying to do!'

'And that is not so. She left you. You said yourself that the engine sound went on for a long while. Don't you see, with *that* evidence, you don't stand a chance.'

'I don't believe this. I just don't believe it.' He appealed to Rosemary, waving his arms wildly.

She smiled at him fondly, but it was to me she spoke. 'Stop teasing him, Richard.'

Teasing! What the devil did she think was going on? 'I am trying', I said heavily, 'to get across to him that he can't expect a pardon until I can prove who *did* do it.'

'All right,' he said wildly. 'Then do that.'

'I'm working on it.'

Things were not happening as he'd planned. He pushed off from the chair arms and bounced to his feet. 'Ten more minutes and he'll have me back inside. Is the man insane?'

'Listen to him, Duncan,' she appealed.

'He promised . . . damn it all, I was looking forward to something . . . He said damages, if I got the pardon. Don't you think I lost enough? No need to worry, they'll look after me at Lichfield. The Bishop was very kind – oh, very. The sheep that was lost. I don't want handouts. The sinner that repenteth. I don't repent anything. I didn't do anything. I want what is mine – my rights.'

Rosemary was coming to her feet. In a second she'd have him in her arms, this sheep of hers that'd strayed. I could see it coming off. Duncan couldn't. He could see nothing beyond the barrier raised by ten years of lost life. He was frantic that the new-found bud of promise was not to bloom.

'Not a handout,' he said, calming a little. 'Damages, they call it. Every minute of those ten years weighed and allocated. Not for me, thank you. Just what's mine. What about . . .'

'Heh!' I said.

'. . . my inheritance, Rosie – what about that?'

She was very still. One hand hovered. It had been reaching towards him. Then it paused, and slowly changed direction, up towards her face so that she could stare at it.

'You wouldn't have wanted that,' she said tonelessly to her palm.

'I'm entitled . . .'

'Now just hold on,' I interrupted, my voice rising.

And it was Rosemary who flared at me. 'No, let him say it! Let's hear what he's really come for.'

'I'm sure it's not like that.'

'Then let *him* tell me what it's like,' she said, and she turned her face to him, chin lifted, offering herself to whatever slap he might produce.

'It's no good telling me it was worth nothing,' he said stubbornly, not looking directly at her. 'It might've been worth a lot to me. I could've sold the house . . .'

'Sold the house!' Her voice rose, just short of hysterical amusement. 'Who'd buy this old dump, stuck out here in the wilds? All it was good for was death duties. Don't you dare try to stop me, Richard. No money, an old house, debts. You can have *that* with all my love, Duncan.' She hadn't meant to use the word 'love'. Her voice became entangled in a sob. Then she raised her head again. 'No. Not the house. I'd fight you for the house.'

'Now, now,' I put in. 'Let's have none of that. You're not in court.'

She turned her back on him, not willing to have him witness her distress. It was all right for me to be shocked by the stress on her face, by the wet eyes and the hair that now managed to break free of the rubber band.

I groped frantically for my pipe. 'It's inconceivable,' I said, 'that even with a pardon you'd be given your inheritance back, Duncan. I told you – see a solicitor. You'd get an assessment to allow for its value. Possibly.'

This I said to Rosemary's face. She was dumbly asking me something, but I couldn't interpret it.

'Oh, I see,' he said, disgust in his voice. 'It's all changed since you came to Lichfield. You've got together, you two. Worked something out.'

'Drop it!' I said flatly, watching his eyes, which were suddenly frantic.

'No!' he shouted. 'I'm not going to drop it. All you can talk about is alibis, but I notice it was *mine* you were taking to pieces. But what about Rosie's alibi? She left me, on the terrace. Walked away, into the dark, and the engine went on for a good three minutes. How about *that*, Rosie?'

Her lips were moving, but no words were formed. Eyes huge, fingers reaching towards her face.

We were both silent. It seemed to disconcert him. For a moment he reached out, as though to seize her shoulder and turn her to face him. That he couldn't do it angered him.

'It had to be somebody who knew the drinks were in the boot,' he cried, literally nearly cried, the tears being in his eyes too. His voice softened. 'It was your car, Rosie. You came to Lichfield to pick me up.' Now he was appealing.

She moaned, shaking her head. With a visible effort she slowly turned to face him.

'I came to Lichfield, Duncan, to get some time with you, alone. We hadn't met like that for two years. Remember?' Her voice held no emotion at all. 'Since . . . since Glenda. I hoped that things could be forgotten, that you'd give me one hint . . . Oh Lord, but you're so stupid. There was not a word from you . . . not one warm word. Can you believe I'd be buying crates of beer and planning Uncle Edwin's death – with *that* on my mind?'

In that moment, Duncan could have transformed his life, and hers. He could have done what she was pleading for him to do, simply have taken her in his arms. And she'd have given him the world, if he'd only realised. She'd have shared everything she'd built up from that paltry inheritance, she'd even have put on his musical, as a wedding present. If only he'd seen that.

But he was a simpleton, unwise in the ways of women, unaware . . . and he ruined it.

'You could have bought the stuff on the way to pick me up,' he said simply.

'Right!' she screamed, her temper breaking abruptly. 'If that's your attitude, you can have your damned inheritance.' Her arm came up, hand ready. I thought she was about to slap that ridiculous half-smile of stubborn hesitancy from his face. But no. She was merely thrusting him aside, heading for the big old safe in the corner.

It had an ordinary keyhole, an ordinary iron key, and was probably never locked. All she had to do was grip one hand on the top edge of the door, and with one emphatic heave fling it open. Inside, there was nothing but a pile of manuscript, foolscap size.

'There's your damned inheritance,' she cried. 'That's all I ever had. His plays. See what *you* can get out of them. You can . . . I don't . . .'

We were within a hair's breadth of a torrent of tears. She was choking. He could still have rescued things. She was, to my mind, waiting for that one word . . .

'You can't deny the stuff was in your car,' he said.

'I didn't *know*!' she screamed. 'Oh, get out of my way.'

This last was to me, and she caught at my arm, as though to thrust me aside. But for a second I could feel she needed the support. It took only that second, then she had the door open, and I heard her mumble, 'Got things to do.'

Her step along the corridor was firm.

Duncan turned to me in appeal. 'Well, you can't deny it, can you?'

I couldn't. That was the trouble. A vague idea had been hovering in my mind, but it kept coming against that one hurdle. The booze in the boot. Who had put it there, and who had known it was there? It was true that the area covered by the Burton Upon Trent breweries could be large, but so far I hadn't come across a single hint that anyone except Duncan and Rosemary had had any business in the Midlands at that time. And *any* source of supply would have been satisfactory, for the purpose of creating that alibi. I felt that Rosemary was lying on that issue. I couldn't understand why, and knew I would not know unless and until she admitted it, and told me.

Standing there, I realised with a pang that I could well have prevented their meeting from heading where it had. But I'd hoped to provoke Rosemary into an admission. I'd failed. Every damned thing I did seemed to be failing.

'Well . . .' he said, looking round distractedly, but not, I noticed, at the open safe.

'You could run after her,' I suggested, 'and tell her she's still wearing her apron.'

He stared at me. 'I don't think you're right in the head.'

So I did it, walked after her to tell her, and there she was, in the centre of the dining room floor and taking charge in a distracted way, her right elbow raised and her fingers to her brow, peering beneath her hand, and trying to control the pain behind her eyes. She wasn't troubling about the apron, so why should I? I wandered over to the door on to the terrace.

Her eye caught my movement, and she turned. 'Don't go, Richard, please.' I nodded, and walked on. All I wanted was air. Her voice had sounded distraught.

The clouds were heavy, but seemed to be retreating, leaving a crisp, washed blue behind them. My clouds were gathering. I walked round the terrace and out to the cars, wondering whether I had a spare tin of tobacco in the Stag. My pace broke. I halted.

Duncan was now sitting beside his friend in the car. They were talking together excitedly, Leigh gesticulating in emphasis. Probably he was telling Duncan not to allow her to get away with anything. This was how it would probably have appeared to him. He was giving support, as one would expect from a friend. I suppressed the cynical thought that he might consider there could be something in it for him.

Then Duncan got out of the car and slammed the door decisively. They made signs of friendship to each other, and Leigh drove away.

Duncan turned and saw me standing there, swept his hair from his eyes, and spoke defiantly.

'I've decided to stay.'

'Rosemary will be pleased.'

'You know she must've bought the . . .'

I didn't let him finish. 'How far d'you intend to push her? You'd have no legal right to the blasted inheritance, even if you got her to put it in writing: "I killed my Uncle Edwin." Get legal advice, why don't you! Don't jump in head first.'

He kicked a stone moodily into the shrubbery. 'If only she'd say!'

'Say what, you fool, that she still cares enough about you to want to go back to where you were before?'

'Cares! She? How could she care, if she let me go to prison, and she knowing . . .'

'You don't know that,' I said firmly.

I could perhaps have put more feeling into it if I had not been convinced, myself, that she'd bought the drinks and hidden them in the boot.

We rounded the corner on to the terrace. From the open window there rang out the resonant voice of Drew Pierson.

'Now don't you go breaking things up,' I said warningly.

'They're rehearsing,' he told me, making it sound sacred.

'That seems to be so.'

We stood in the open doorway. Rosemary was six feet in front of us, script in her hand, watching Drew and Mildred in their important dialogue in act two.

She:	You'd expect me to intervene?
He:	Any lady would have broken it up.
She:	This lady withdrew quietly.
He:	But not too far.
She:	I had no wish to be seen. Only to hear.
He:	A lady would not lend her ears to private conversation.
She:	I have always regretted my ears. They protrude. So unladylike.

'Those are my words!' Duncan whispered.

I glanced sideways at him. He was abruptly tense, poised. As I watched, his face relaxed into a smile.

'But those are *my* words!' he cried in delight. 'He left them in.'

The two actors were silent. Rosemary turned. 'Do you *have* to interrupt?'

He was waving his arms wildly. 'My words. Uncle Edwin left them in.'

'What did you say?'

Duncan was overcome by embarrassment. Nobody moved. Eyes were centred on him. 'Sorry, Rosie. But Uncle Edwin gave me the impression he barely kept a thing in . . . and now, I walk in here, and every word I hear is mine. Do you know – can you possibly imagine – what it's like to hear your own words spoken?'

'All right, Duncan,' she said heavily. 'So those were your words. Now let's get on with it. Drew? Can we go back to: "A lady would not lend her ears to private conversation"?'

They proceeded. The scene progressed, and Duncan, beside me, was gradually becoming close to bursting with tension. When he turned to me, plucking at my jacket sleeve, his eyes were shining wildly.

'But . . . it's still mine! Oh Lord . . . Rosie . . . it's mine!'

'Oh, for pity's sake!' Rosemary cut it short by waving her script. Then she threw it at Duncan in pettish anger. 'Read it, and be quiet. Let's get on, for God's sake!'

Duncan scooped it up and riffled through it. Nobody went on. Everybody watched him. Rosemary flapped her arms in exasperation, but there was a sudden, bright intensity about her. The room was so silent that the turning pages were a rage in themselves.

'Fair's Fair,' Duncan whispered. 'Oh, I can't believe it. It's mine. My words. Look – this scene. Twenty years, and it's all coming back.'

Rosemary moved in close. 'Are you telling me that *you* wrote that dialogue, Duncan? All of it?'

He was dazed. When he looked up he could not have been seeing her. 'As far as I've seen. Rosie . . . I . . . sorry.'

She took three more seconds to realise what that could mean, two to decide how to handle it. Then she turned away and called out: 'Break, everybody. I'll let you know.'

She turned back, reached out her right hand, and took his left one.

'You just come with me, Duncan. Let me show you something.'

Dazed, elated, and yet with a simmering anger about him, he allowed himself to be led away.

14

Nobody said I shouldn't follow so I did, though more slowly. In the corridor Rosemary broke into a run, galloping away with Duncan still attached and stumbling after her. I reached the door just as she released him in order to plunge both hands into the safe and produce play after play and slap them down on the working surface. Then she stood back, panting from a severely restrained excitement, and said:

'Look at them. Go on. Take a look.'

Each script consisted of an inch-thick wad of very dog-eared foolscap-sized paper. From where I was standing the words on the pages were very nearly undecipherable, being handwritten in black ink, but with minor amendments in blue ball-point. The title *Fair's Fair* was at the head of the first sheet of one of them.

Duncan spoke with awe. 'But these are the originals. He kept them.'

'Look at the writing,' she said in a tiny voice, and whilst he did so she put her hands to her face, fingers spread, horribly distorting the shape of her eyes.

'I don't need to. This . . . these . . . were what I sent him.'

'The black ink?'

'My fountain pen . . .'

'But Duncan . . .' She whipped down her hands. 'The black, that *is* the plays. The biggest part of them. Don't you see what that means?'

He looked round at me in bewilderment. 'I don't . . . I mean . . . I can't understand why he kept them.'

'Duncan!' she cried wildly, and she flung her arms round his neck, almost dancing him off his feet. 'You idiot – they're yours. Always have been. Still are.' She set him back to the full stretch of her arms. 'Oh . . . don't you understand? You wrote the original words, so they're *your* copyright. You *own* them. Yours. Duncan . . . you utter fool.'

She was laughing, half crying, and he could still not comprehend. But I did. She was happy and excited because this was something she could offer him, as his own, to have and to hold, if it were not to be herself . . . and maybe now he'd cease to pressure her.

The excitement was beginning to get to him, but behind it was the awareness that somehow he'd been cheated. When he turned to me the movement seemed to be a rejection of Rosemary's pleasure, but he appealed to me as though I might be an authority on the subject.

'What's it all mean, Mr Patton?'

'As far as I know,' I said, 'it means that when you wrote those words you established a copyright, and as the major part of the plays is still your work, then you still own the copyright. It means . . . oh, for example, you can go out there and tell those people that you're putting a stop to the production.'

Rosemary slapped my arm. 'Stop putting ideas into his head, Richard, please.' Yet she was uneasy.

'Or you can demand a fee for the use of *Fair's Fair*. Or any of the plays, *ad infinitum*, wherever any of them is produced, anywhere. As far as I know.'

'Rosie,' he said, a hint of accusation in his voice, 'it can't be true.'

'You two', I said, 'will have to get together and negotiate.'

'Hah!' he said.

'But tell me something,' I asked. 'How can you possibly not have known?'

He glanced at Rosemary, who already had her arm linked in his in a proprietorial way, and was smiling with genuine happiness. 'How could I know? I sent plays to Uncle Edwin. He said he could adapt them, and he paid me for them. I just assumed he'd . . . well, bought them. The rotten devil.'

'You didn't sign a contract, assigning the copyrights?'

'There was nothing on paper.'

'Only the plays.' Rosemary giggled at that.

'Yes, the plays,' he agreed.

'But,' I said, 'surely you went to see them performed.'

This appeared to be a preposterous suggestion. 'Me? Go to London? You don't know how I hate that place. All those people . . . no thanks. I didn't trouble, once he'd taken them over.'

Another facet of Edwin's character was emerging. I was beginning to wonder whether I wanted his murderer to be discovered.

'It's a great pity,' I said. 'One trip to the West End, and the whole picture would've changed.'

'And now it has,' said Rosemary. 'Duncan, you and I must get together. There's so much to be decided. But for now . . . we're opening in six weeks at Coventry. So come and watch your play being rehearsed.'

She was carrying him along with her mood, delighted that she had this to offer him. Perhaps my suspicions of her reasons for this had been false. Not the greatest actress could have flooded her eyes with genuine tears of delight as she seized his arm and took him away into his new world.

As they walked into the hall they were totally immersed in each other. Yet neither had fully absorbed the significance. The change for both was going to be tremendous.

Slowly I followed them. Rosemary was making a little speech to explain that Duncan was now going to become intimately involved. Nobody seemed unduly impressed. To them, the play was the thing.

I thought it time I left. No lunch had come my way, and if I hurried I might be in time to share Amelia's. I moved across to Rosemary's side and touched her elbow.

'You're leaving, Richard?'

'There's not much I can do now, and I've left my wife at the mill at Tyn-y-bont.'

'But isn't this really splendid!'

I grinned at her. 'It'll mean a lot to him.'

'And to me.'

'There's the possible pardon, too, if I can only get my proof.'

'Now you don't think he'll have time to worry about that!'

'I suppose not.'

'Oh . . . I nearly forgot. Clyde Greenslade phoned. He'd heard about what you're trying to do. He's coming tomorrow to see you.'

I hadn't known when, or even whether, I'd return there. 'He wants to see me?'

'Yes. He'll be here in the afternoon.'

'Any idea . . .'

'Now Richard, we must get on. Oh, isn't this exciting?'

I agreed that it was exciting, and by the time I'd reached the door they were well into it again, with Duncan sitting on a folding chair at the side, leaning forward intently with a blissful smile on his face.

Now that I knew the route to the mill I relaxed, and very nearly got lost again. It was a relief to top the rise and glimpse the farm below, the scattered cottages, the bridge.

The police van was parked in the farmyard immediately before I reached the bridge. Davies saw me coming, and signalled. I drew up. He came round to my window.

'Everything all right?' I asked.

'At the mill, yes. But they've been trying to get me on the radio all morning.'

I got out of the car and we walked into the farmyard. 'Don't get yourself into trouble,' I said.

He smiled, his face glowing. 'We've got a lot of useful mountains around here, Mr Patton. They cut off the short-wave signals.'

'Convenient.' But I wasn't happy about the way he was involving himself. 'By the way, that petrol can in the shed – it isn't there any more.'

He considered that. The smile slowly died. 'So it's like that?'

'Seems to be. Perhaps, at the inquest, you'd better not mention it. A constable's word against a chief inspector's! You wouldn't stand a chance.'

'Oh, I don't know.' His eyes were steady. 'I took the precaution of photographing it, including part of the shed, the number plate of the car, and a copy of that day's paper, which I just happened to have with me.'

'Official camera?' I asked.

'My own. Several shots, including a close-up with the macro lens of Mr Hughes' fingerprints – which I decided to develop – all over the can.' He scratched the side of his nose thoughtfully.

I sighed. He looked so rosily pleased with himself. 'You married, Mr Davies?'

'No sir – Mr Patton.'

'Living alone, in digs?'

'Alone . . . in a police house.'

'Then you don't stand to lose much, I suppose.'

'You're not pleased?' he asked anxiously, frowning in bafflement.

'Oh son, you're as bad as Duncan. Mr Grayson's a determined man. It *matters* to him that the Edwin Carter case shouldn't be disturbed. He'll have you out, so fast your head'll swim.'

'He wouldn't dare . . . the Chief Constable . . .'

'Knows where he stands and which direction to look.'

'Then what . . .' He slapped a thigh angrily. 'What d'you want me to do?'

'Do nothing. Say what you're expected to say, and nothing more.'

'And go on doing it,' he cut in angrily. 'Till I retire? If it's going to be like that they can stick it . . .'

'Now hold on.'

'And you're as bad as the rest.'

I poked his chest with my pipe stem. 'Don't get worked up, laddie.'

'Your friend gets killed . . .'

'Watch it!'

He stopped, staring at me with his mouth slightly open. I admit my tone had been brisk. I went on more placidly.

'Let me take the risks, eh? You lie low – and behave. I can look after myself, but you're vulnerable.'

He stood very straight and very stiff. 'And your wife, sir, isn't she vulnerable?' He was having the nerve to reprimand me for forgetting! 'With your permission – *without* it, if you like – I'll continue to watch out.'

Shaking my head at him I said: 'As long as they let you – all right. And I'll be grateful. I'm already in your debt.'

His easy smile was almost in gratitude. I slapped his shoulder.

'See you around.'

I drove up to the mill. Though I was disturbed, I did my best, in the short distance, to assume a cheerful aspect.

She was standing outside, waiting for me. 'I saw you coming.'

Grinning, I got out of the car. 'Had a nice day?'

'Too short. Cindy and I . . .' She was jumping up at my legs. '. . . have walked miles.'

'And eaten all the sandwiches, I bet.'

'Haven't you had any lunch?'

'Things at the house got a bit hectic. I'll tell you later.'

'I think there's a sandwich and a whole flask of coffee.'

We went inside. She had her meal laid out on the huge millstone, looking puny on its vast surface. As I ate, the thermos top in my left hand, I stood at the window looking out over the bridge. Amelia chattered away happily behind me, and I must admit I recorded barely a word of it. The rush of the stream outside was strangely comforting.

I gathered that they'd walked upstream to discover its source. They had walked down to the bridge and over it, and down the wider tributary for a mile. Amelia had enquired at the farm, and discovered that it would be possible to obtain fresh milk and free-range eggs, and even fresh pork, though, having been introduced to the piglets, she'd rather gone off pork.

'And you'll never guess who I met,' she said. 'That pleasant Constable Davies . . . isn't that his name?'

I turned. 'Life seems to be full of coincidences.'

'He'd apparently called at the farm on a case. Sheep rustling, he told me. Do they rustle sheep, Richard?' she asked innocently.

'I'd say he was pulling your leg, my dear.'

'Whatever it was, it's taken him a long while. He's only just leaving. Look.'

I turned back. She was correct. He was driving off in his van. From her eyes, I'd seen that she knew why Davies was there. But she didn't pursue it.

The love affair, Amelia and the mill, had progressed. She had roamed it throughout, up the staircase that was close to being a ladder, to examine the bedrooms. 'Only two, Richard, but a lovely bathroom – all modern fittings. And the kitchen, Richard, you haven't seen the kitchen.'

I went to see the kitchen, probably the old grain store and now a long, narrow room, well fitted out, cork-tiled floor, beams festooned with hooks and hangers.

But, because Grayson had taken away the petrol can, the inquest was going to bring in accidental death.

She had spent a few hours with it, working her mind into a mood of sympathy with the mill and its surroundings. I have to admit that the mood eluded me. Yes, I liked it. Yes, I'd be perfectly happy to commit myself to buying it, but my mind wasn't on it.

Amelia knew. I could never hide anything from her. We got our stuff together, and fitted ourselves into the car.

She gave me time to work my way back to a main road, then she said lightly: 'Aren't you going to tell me, Richard?'

I told her what had happened at the house, trying for all the nuances of feeling, so that she'd know what I'd been after and how I'd tried to reach it.

'You're quite convinced it was Rosemary who bought the drinks?' she asked, when I was finally talked dry.

'Who else could it have been? Anybody could have bought stuff for the party, and probably did. From all over the country. But that particular batch of drinks would have to be very close at hand. I mean, a murderer wouldn't want to be seen running across the lawn with a crate of beer. And that batch *was* handy, as though it'd been intended to be handy. Duncan saw it in the boot of Rosemary's car. There's every reason to believe it was bought in the area where Rosemary is known to have been, when she drove over to collect Duncan. How could it possibly have been anyone but Rosemary who bought it, and therefore knew it was available? The murderer had to know . . . oh hell!'

She was silent for a few moments as I crashed the gears going from third to second. Then she said: 'You like her, don't you?'

I have a tendency to like people I admire. 'I admire her,' I said.

She gave a small chuckle. 'You're a gullible fool.' And then, because I glanced sideways in protest: 'It must have been most unpleasant for you.'

I had to speak in extenuation. 'I knew I wasn't going to get anywhere unless I could get her to admit it. With Duncan looking for something to repay him for his missing ten years, I thought I only had to let him put on some pressure. Quite frankly, I was relieved when we discovered he'd legally owned the rights to those plays all the time. As she put it herself: he's going to be too busy to worry about pardons.'

'You *say* you're relieved, but it seems you've reached a dead end.'

'Greenslade's coming to see me tomorrow.'

'You think he'll be any help?'

'No.'

'Then you can't go on.'

'It's beginning to look like that.'

We said no more about it on the journey. It seemed strange to be arriving back at the hotel so early. We would have plenty of time to prepare for dinner, time for my appetite to develop. This I helped along by pacing the room for a few minutes, until Amelia began to seem restless with my failure to relax. I was faced by a gap, with no pointers beckoning me beyond it.

I took Cindy out for a walk. My mind ran over and over what I had uncovered, and the only pattern into which the facts would fit made no sense. A niggling thought at the back of my mind persisted in reminding me that there was something I had intended to check. I was the far side of town when I remembered what it was.

Cindy's little legs were twinkling away as I paced rapidly back to the hotel. From time to time she glanced up, as much as to say: What's the hurry, mate?

'Richard . . .'

'Where did I put that manilla envelope?'

'It's over there. But Richard, Mr Davies phoned.' At my blank expression she explained. 'Constable Davies. Twice,' she said.

As though I wasn't already feeling uneasy! I glanced at the phone. It remained silent.

Sitting on the bed, I up-ended the envelope and sorted out the contents. I'd been a bit of a fool, assuming that Llew Hughes had spotted no more than the single point of the drinks. He'd been very disturbed. There had been, surely, more. I guessed where to start, and remembered there had been such a thing as a list. And there it was:

Contents of pockets of deceased: Edwin Carter.
1. Penknife – one blade broken.
2. Handkerchief (trouser pocket) white.
3. Handkerchief (breast pocket) blue.
4. Ball-point pen, blue.
5. Comb.
6. Forty-three pence in coins.
7. Set of ignition keys (to own car).
8. Wallet containing £14 in notes, a photograph of himself, driving licence, four postage stamps.
9. Rotor arm.
10. Spectacle case containing reading glasses.

The phone rang. I pounced on it, but my mind was shouting: Rotor arm?

'Patton,' I said.

'I'm glad you're back, sir,' Davies said. 'You ought to know . . .'

'What's happened?' I'd detected the agitation in his voice.

'I'm at the station house, my place. I've had a break-in.'

I had to get hold of that fact and examine it. 'You don't mean break, do you Constable?'

'Nothing broken, no. I've checked. No locks forced, no windows broken. But somebody's been here.'

He didn't have to explain to me. There would be duplicate keys to every station house, held at headquarters.

'And taken what?' I asked, guessing the answer.

'My camera had been opened and the cassette taken out. It was *the* film, Mr Patton.'

'The film was taken away? Not simply exposed to light?'

'Taken.'

His waiting seemed breathless, but I had to give it considered thought. Neither of us had to say who'd been responsible, it was just a matter of how it left the situation.

'There's a whole day,' I said at last. 'Wednesday tomorrow, and the inquest on Thursday. There's not much we can do about it now, but it's obvious that your superior is set on an accidental death verdict. I don't think we're now in a position to oppose that, so my suggestion is that we let things happen . . .'

I had deliberately taken that line, speaking as evenly as I could so that Davies would be calmed, and perhaps act sensibly. Some hope!

'You're not going to let him get away with it!' he interrupted angrily.

'I know you've lost a film. Treat it as experience. Now you'll know how people feel when they've been burgled. Next time you go out on a case . . .'

'Well – I never expected to hear . . . He's pushing us around – all right, don't say it, he's got a right to push me around. But don't *you* care? That was your friend who was killed . . .'

'I wish you wouldn't keep reminding me of that.'

'By God, but you're the limit.'

I sensed what was about to happen. 'Don't hang up!' I snapped. Waited a second. 'Are you still there, Davies?'

'I'm still here.'

'Then think about it. What does the inquest verdict matter, anyway? It doesn't stop me from going ahead. The one it affects is Grayson, worrying whether a murder verdict might reveal that Mr Hughes wasn't happy with the Edwin Carter investigation. I don't care how much he worries. Do you?' I demanded.

'Of course I damn well care.'

'Ah yes, but what you were looking forward to was doing a grand act at the inquest with your evidence, and getting your name in the papers.'

'That's a lie!'

'Then prove it. Go to that inquest and give your evidence – how you arrived on the scene. And nothing more.'

'You tricked me into that.'

'Put it down to my vast experience.'

'But you'll go on with it?'

Anything to cool him off and prevent him from doing something stupid. 'Of course I shall.'

He hung up, still ruffled, but, I felt, tamed.

'You weren't very kind to him,' Amelia said reprovingly.

'He's going to get hurt. That damned Grayson! And Davies had to phone just as I was annoyed with myself!' I rubbed my hands over my face. 'I should have trusted Llew,' I explained. 'There had to be more than just the drinks not being local, but I didn't *look*, damn it. Do you know what Edwin Carter had in his pocket? A rotor arm! And I missed it.'

'Does it matter, though?'

'Matter! D'you know what a rotor arm is? It's a thing that goes round when the engine's running and distributes the sparks to the plugs. Without it, the engine won't start.'

'Oh!' she said, putting her hand to her mouth.

'Exactly. Now link that with Edwin's behaviour that evening. He was due to talk money business, but he was agitating to get out. When Drew Pierson tried to restrain him there was nearly a fight. Then what did he do? He made a fuss about using Rosemary's car, because his own car wouldn't start. Of course it wouldn't – he'd taken the rotor arm out. But why should he do that? Because it meant he had to use her car. Why that? Because *he* was the person who knew the drinks were in the boot, and knew he could use them to pretend he'd driven into England to get them. And why should he do that? Only because he intended to drive a similar distance in another direction. You see what that has to mean?'

Her lips were clamped firmly shut. She shook her head. Politeness, I'm sure, just to encourage me.

'He was going through all the actions of a man about to set off and create an alibi. And because he was so tense and worked up about it, it had to be an alibi for something pretty drastic. You know what I think? Edwin Carter was setting out to commit a murder.'

'But he didn't even get started.'

'Exactly. Now d'you see why I couldn't handle Davies gently. I'm mad at myself. It's all backwards, and I didn't see it. It was Edwin who was killed, and I can't understand it.'

I thumped the table in emphasis. Cindy ran and hid under the bed.

Amelia tilted her head, smiling gently. 'You'd better put a tie on, I think, and then you can give it some food.'

After a minute I managed a grin. We went down to dinner.

15

We spent part of the following morning trying to persuade the estate agent to reduce the asking price by £1000, and left it that he'd contact his client and mention our offer, and in the meantime, if we'd care to give it further consideration, and perhaps drive round there again . . .

Apart from meeting Clyde Greenslade that afternoon, I had little to do. I suggested that Amelia should tag along and watch some more rehearsals, but she seemed to have lost interest in activities involving Rosemary, so there was nothing for it but for her to stay at the hotel or spend another afternoon at the mill.

'The mill,' she decided.

'The weather's not very promising.'

'You said I ought to see it at its worst.'

So that was what we decided to do after lunch. I would leave her at the mill and drive on to Plâs Ceiriog, returning in time to get back to the hotel for dinner.

When we drove away the clouds were massing over the mountains ahead. 'I'm not sure it's a good idea,' I said. But she said she could change her mind when we arrived there. The first rain pattered on the windscreen. I drove a little faster, not wishing either of us to get wet when we were driving away from dry clothes. The light was becoming poor, and I put on dipped heads.

'It's going to be dreadful for you,' I said.

'Don't keep saying that, Richard,' she protested. 'You're trying to put me off.'

'As though I would.'

'Then please don't keep telling me how miserable I'm going to be.'

We had left the folding chair at the mill, so she'd have that. She would also, I was grateful to see, have Davies. I'd spotted him when he, too, had had to put on his lights. To him, probably, this would seem like a pleasant day. Wales has a tendency to be like that, especially the region we were now in. The west winds drive in from the Atlantic, sucking up moisture as they go, and when they reach the Welsh mountains they rise, cool in the higher atmosphere, and dump it all in the valleys behind.

When I drove up to the mill the rain was already hammering on to the hood. We ran for it, and burst into the mill, to find that it was so dark we could barely see. The two windows to that large and high living room were far too small, but Amelia took it in her stride.

'If there's a thunderstorm,' she said, 'it'll look wonderful from here.'

'I don't think you'll be that lucky.'

There being no services connected, I cast around in my mind and remembered the battery lamp in the Stag's boot. 'Hold on a sec,' I said, and dashed out. There it was, though whether the batteries would be dead I didn't know. 'Here . . . look . . .'

I set it on one of the beams across the corner of the room. The batteries were all right, but, with the vast and lumbersome shadows absorbing it, the circle of light was paltry. Even, it seemed, it was deceptive, shadows that had been innocent taking on movement and personality.

'I think I'd prefer it off.' Amelia laughed, but shakily.

Cindy remained close to her ankles.

'That blasted Greenslade,' I said. 'I've a good mind not to go.'

'If he's driving all the way from London, it would hardly be polite not to meet him.'

'Then come along with me.'

'No, Richard.' She was sternly dismissive, looking tiny in front of the darkened window. 'I'll stay here. You shouldn't be long, anyway.'

I spread my hands in defeat, went across and kissed her, and promised to hurry.

It's all very well to promise, but even before I reached the bridge the wipers were struggling to clear the screen, and the visibility was terrible. I stopped the car for a moment, and looked back. The mill loomed against the dark hills, looking forlorn without lighting, empty and dead. Then a curtain of rain cut it off, and I drove on, even at that moment hesitating whether to turn back for her. And face her scorn? No – I drove on.

In the farm there were lighted windows. As I passed the farmyard Davies flashed his lights and I flicked on my main beams in acknowledgement. She was not alone, I told myself. I left the main beams on. Only in their confines did the world seem alive. It was daylight, but the valleys and the mountains leaned their dark weight towards me. There was no movement except the steady slash of the rain.

At Plâs Ceiriog it seemed to be easing. I drove round to the front, and parked as close to the porch as possible before making a dive to the front door. I was parked behind a white Rolls, complete with matching chauffeur. So Greenslade had arrived.

'You're wet through,' said Rosemary, meeting me in the corridor.

It was only then that I remembered the two umbrellas in the car. 'It doesn't matter. I shan't be staying long.'

This was a changed Rosemary, a younger woman with light in her eyes and a softer, more feminine stance. She touched my arm, as though we shared a secret.

'I hoped you'd stay. Just for a short while, Richard.'

'He's here, isn't he?'

'I shall be making an announcement,' she told me. '*We* shall, Duncan and I, but of course he said I had to do the talking. And you'll be interested, I'm sure, in the way we've sorted things out.'

'Greenslade . . .'

'We were talking half the night. What we were going to do and how. The copyright thing is going to be very difficult to sort out, and we decided the legal complications would take too long.'

Her eyes were shining up at me. It was difficult for her to stop talking, so that when she did the silence drew more attention than a shout. I said gravely:

'Legal matters always do.'

'And there'll be enough argument over the pardon business.'

Now she had my full attention. I'd perhaps been wrong to believe he'd be side-tracked from it; she had been wrong to suggest that he would.

'We'll need your help over that, Richard.' Now it was *their* pardon.

'Any way I can be of assistance,' I promised, wildly perhaps, but I was wet and beginning to feel cold in that draughty corridor. I wondered how they could possibly pursue the question of the pardon, if she intended to continue to deny she had bought the drinks that were in the Dolomite's boot.

'And we'll need to discuss *that* some time,' she said, nodding, fixing me with a very suggestive look. 'There's something I must tell you. But not now,' she went on hurriedly, interpreting my expression. 'You run along and see Clyde, and then come to the dining room for the announcement.'

The announcement! She gave it the importance of a PM's statement to the House.

'Don't expect me to advise you on the law of contracts,' I said.

She slapped my arm. 'Silly. Clyde's in my workroom. Run along, now.'

'What announcement?'

'The simplest contract of them all,' she said mysteriously.

She whisked her way along the corridor so briskly that my belated 'Congratulations' was murmured to a closed door.

I didn't have time to work out how that affected the situation. Clyde Greenslade was waiting. More important, Amelia was. I headed for the workroom.

He had been described as a bladder of lard. There had been mention of porn – soft, medium or hard-boiled. An impression was implanted in my mind of loose wet lips and lascivious eyes, a suggestive, perhaps lisping voice. Greenslade was therefore a surprise. Yes, he was huge. I'd expected to find him collapsed, limply subsiding into one of the easy chairs, but there was not one chair that would have accommodated him.

He stood in front of the bookcase, six feet three inches of solid bone and muscle, fat only towards the hips, like a pear with his head perched on the thin end. No neck. A shock of dark hair, so ridiculously precise that it had to be a wig. So he was vain. His eyes, level and daunting, certainly indicated no modesty. The fist, clamped round a glass of something clear and bubbling, would have swallowed and mashed mine, if I'd let him have it. But he gave no indication of wishing to shake hands, merely nodded to one of the chairs in invitation.

'Patton, is it?'

I nodded back, ignoring the seat as being a distinct disadvantage.

'And you'll be Greenslade.'

Then I waited. He was a hard businessman. It wouldn't matter to him whether he produced carburettors or lace handkerchiefs, or dirty films. So he would get straight down to business. His eyes narrowed as he considered my silence. I went on waiting.

'Mr Patton,' he said at last, 'I hear you're investigating the death of Edwin Carter.'

I inclined my head. 'You have good spies.'

'I can't afford not to. Can I assume you're making progress?'

'Some.'

He sighed at my lack of response. 'What's your interest in it?'

'A man could've been wrongly sentenced.'

'Your genuine interest.'

'A friend has died.'

146

He raised his glass, eyed it with distaste, and took a large swallow. 'I'm assuming', he decided, 'that you're either being deliberately evasive, or you're stupid. Who's paying you?'

If money wasn't involved, he didn't understand what was going on. And it annoyed him. How could he be in control of something he didn't understand? I smiled at the thought, and he didn't like that, either.

'What's *your* interest, Mr Greenslade? I don't see what's in it for you . . . financially.'

'What the hell does that matter? Whatever they're paying, I'll double.'

This was beginning to sound interesting. I glanced at my watch. Twice nothing was still nothing.

'I didn't want to spend much time on this,' I said. 'I realise you've come a long way. I appreciate that. But I did have the hope that you'd have some information for me. If not – well, I think I'll be off.'

He smiled. I'll swear he smiled. In any event, something happened to his right eye, which could have been a tick or a twinkle. 'You don't know about me, do you, Mr Patton?' He said this with a hint of surprise. 'I make films. I make other things too, but mainly films. It's my money in there, and I feel a certain amount of protective interest in it. I don't like to lose any of it. In fact, I hate the thought. There's a film production coming up, a light comedy. I've already sunk a lot in preliminaries, and on the rights for the original play. Of course, everybody'll tell you that stage plays don't transfer to the screen, but with this I've got ideas. A way to move it around, outdoors, get rid of the static feeling. Have you got the slightest idea what I'm saying, for God's sake?'

'I think so. You're going to tell me you're using one of Edwin Carter's plays.'

'Well . . . ten out of ten. So you can understand – I can't afford any ugly publicity.'

'I had the idea . . .' I took out my pipe and looked round for an ashtray. '. . . that any publicity is good publicity.'

'Don't light that thing in here,' he said, genuine anxiety in his voice. 'I suffer from asthma.'

As he would, perhaps, carrying all that weight around. I put the pipe away, reluctantly.

'You know nothing about publicity,' he told me. 'For a sportsman who plays dirty, uses foul language and worse manners, bad publicity's good for the image. But I'm into family entertainment. Bad publicity could kill me.'

'A change of style,' I murmured.

'We progress.' He was not offended.

But it wasn't publicity he was afraid of. That was merely to blind me to the truth.

'You know who killed Edwin, don't you,' I suggested.

He said nothing.

'And who killed Glenda Grace.'

This provoked a response, not the one I hoped. 'She's got nothing to do with this.'

'I notice you don't deny she was killed.'

'Deny it?' He seemed to inflate, drawing himself up to an even more impressive height and width. 'Are you accusing me?'

'People do seem to get touchy when I mention her,' I said placidly. 'I was suggesting that you know she was killed. *You* wouldn't have killed her. She was your property. She had value to you . . . unless, of course, she was ready for discarding.'

He blew out breath with a rasping sound of contempt, his lips vibrating. 'Hell, but you're ignorant. Somebody's been talking, and God knows what they've told you. That she was beautiful? Of course. That she had a doll's face, completely unexpressive? Oh, I'm sure they said that. But she was an actress and a born comedy genius. Don't raise your eyebrows at me! I know what you're thinking, and it took me a while to realise. Did Buster Keaton ever smile, ever convey anything? No. But you can't deny he was a comic genius.'

'Slapstick,' I murmured.

'And Glenda, with that face of hers, she'd only got to raise an eyebrow and it said everything. Move her chin, and you *knew*. I was beginning to see her as a star. And she was mine, on contract. Then somebody killed her.'

'That was what I was asking. You believe she was killed.'

'Drunk, they said!' He stared at his glass. 'Drugs, they said! Tcha! She could handle anything, that girl.'

'Emotions being buried so deeply,' I commented.

'You trying to be funny?'

'Not succeeding. So you argue that it couldn't have been an accident or suicide. Somebody pushed her.'

He stared at me, his lip curling in contempt.

'Any idea who?' I asked.

'As though that matters now! It's gone. In the past. What the hell're you burbling about?'

'Did you get anything like a threatening letter or blackmail attempt?' I asked. 'After her death,' I amplified. 'Before Edwin died.'

'Now why,' he burst out, 'would anybody think they could blackmail me? I'd have them dealt with.'

'Or sent one? Or more?'

'Now you look here . . .'

I looked. His face was flushed, his eyes angry, and he was not a man I'd care to tangle with.

'Perhaps not,' I conceded. 'She was gone. A property to be discounted, and treated as a tax loss. I thought, you see,' I told him, 'you'd be interested in knowing who'd done it.'

'And pay you for that?' I'd restored his humour. He even managed a laugh, though not a pleasant one. 'It's Edwin's death . . .'

'That's also gone and done with. But it affects your current financial situation, and you're suggesting I should drop my investigations in case of bad publicity! Or whatever,' I went on quickly, before he exploded. 'What were *you* doing on that night, Mr Greenslade?'

'Are you suggesting . . .'

I grinned at him. 'well, that *would* be bad publicity, if the producer was arrested for murder.'

'Goddamn you!'

'Tell me about that evening. You were here. I take it, with your physical difficulties, you weren't rushing around in the night?'

I'd taken it too far. His face was becoming purple. I held up my hand. If he broke into a charge I'd have difficulty in stopping him.

'Very well. Sorry. But I'm asking you to confirm something. Edwin's behaviour that evening – it wasn't in line with what was expected. You'd come here for something else. Not a party. Business, involving money, but Edwin was obsessed with getting in more drinks.'

I'd stretched this out a bit, giving him time to cool down. But I'd hit a nerve.

'The man was insane. It meant everything to him, and he wouldn't get down to business. Going out to top up his bar! Jesus! I told him what I'd got in my car. But would he listen – not him. I'd brought along some stuff. Well, why not? It was a bottle party, wasn't it! So I'd brought a few bottles with me. There it was, on the rear seat . . .'

'Don't tell me you bought it in Lichfield,' I said weakly.

'What the hell's Lichfield? I got it in Richmond. That's Surrey. Are you going to listen? I told him I'd got it in my car. Told him he could have it, but oh no! He was the host, he said. Some host, walking out on us, when there was business to be discussed.'

So I had another confirmation of the theory I'd outlined to Amelia. 'And that was the last you saw of him?'

'Alive, yes. They all ran out. Me . . . a man's got his dignity. I stayed where I was. Not my affair.'

'Of course it was your affair, it was a business deal fallen flat on its face.'

He raised his eyebrows at me. 'Was I going to gallop around, when it was already lost?'

I took out my pipe again, and rammed it back into my pocket. 'But now . . . you're not exactly galloping, but you've come all the way from Richmond . . . on the same errand.'

He moved restlessly, no doubt yearning for the comfort of his Rolls. 'Not the same. The case is dead. I'd like it left that way.'

'I'm sorry. I'll have to be leaving.'

He thrust his hand inside his jacket, and produced a thick, white envelope. I had been wondering, from the bulge, whether he had a gun in there. This was almost as lethal. He tossed it to me.

'If nobody's paying you,' he said, 'perhaps a little spending money . . . Expenses, say. Incurred up to this moment.' He smiled. 'But not beyond.'

It wasn't fastened. I looked inside. They were £50 notes. Two bundles of twenty in each. I fetched them out and counted them, then slid them back. I licked the flap and stuck it down, this giving an impression of finality.

'What would you expect for this?' I asked.

'You know who killed Edwin, don't you?'

I considered my words carefully before I spoke. 'I know. I don't fully understand, but I know.'

'Sounds like a guess,' he said, trying to bend my confidence.

I took the ball-point pen from my top pocket and printed a name on the envelope, then I tossed it back to him. A bad toss. He had to move quickly to field it, but after all, this was money.

'That's who I think it is,' I said. 'If I'm correct, it would be a bribe, and I can't afford to take bribes.' But it would cover expenses, and leave enough over to make certain of the mill. 'If I'm wrong, then I've got no other idea to explore, and I might as well go home anyway. In either event, you can keep it.'

For a long while he stood there with the envelope in his hand, staring at the name, then he slid it into his pocket. The hand emerged, and in the same sweep fell on the phone on the working surface.

'If you'll excuse me, I've got some phoning to do.'

I nodded, and went out into the hall. He was already dialling. Business had to be pursued.

Rosemary pounced on me. 'Richard! You've been so long. We're waiting in there.'

I glanced at my watch, annoyed by how long I'd been.

'Come on, Rosemary, you can manage without me. I've got to go and pick up my wife.'

'But I wanted you to be there. Especially you. It's you who's brought it about.'

I smiled at her. 'I really must go. She's all alone at the mill, and it's getting darker every minute.'

'But . . .' She bit her lip, her expression bouncing from disappointment to excitement. 'Oh, you *are* infuriating.' She leaned towards me to whisper it, as though all the world hadn't already guessed. 'We're going to get married, Duncan and me.'

I kissed her on the cheek. 'And about time, too. Now, I must be off . . .'

'No . . . wait.' Her fingers clawed at my arm. 'There was something else. I've promised myself I'd tell you, but after the anouncement. Something very important.'

It took me back to the Christmases of my childhood, when I'd had to express astonished delight at each present, when I'd already raided the cupboard under the stairs, and knew. I knew now what she was going to tell me, and it didn't matter any more. 'I wonder what that could be.'

'After the announcement. I promise.'

'Tell me now.' My nerves were stretching at this extended word game.

She shook her head, lips firmly pouted. The hair was now restrained by another rubber band. Yellow.

'All right,' I said, my voice rising. 'Phone me. I'll be at the hotel.'

'No. In person. Face to face.'

'For God's sake!' Then I calmed. 'We're face to face now. Or come to the hotel. But now . . . I've got to pick Amelia up at the mill.'

She nodded. Mischief was in her eyes. But I saw only that dark bulk of mill under the black skies, and had difficulty in managing a smile as I turned away.

I stood in the porch. The sky was even more overcast, and I had to wait for a few moments for my eyes to adapt. The porch light wasn't on; it was officially still daylight. The rain roared on the roofs of the cars outside. In the Rolls, the chauffeur had the light on and was reading a paperback. I put down my head to make a dash for it, and two shapes moved in on me, one each side.

They didn't actually put a finger on me, but I sensed that their hands were ready. I saw the outlines of peaked caps, the shapes of shoulder straps.

'Mr Patton?' asked a calm voice.

'Yes?'

'Police, sir. I'd like you to come along with us. The Chief Inspector wants a word.'

16

I didn't have to ask the name of the Chief Inspector. 'Another time,' I said.

'Now, sir. Please.'

'Look, Constable . . .'

'Sergeant, sir.'

'Look, Sergeant, I've got urgent business. Whatever Mr Grayson has to say, it can wait.'

'He didn't put it like that. Not exactly.'

'I don't care how he bloody well put it. I'm driving away from here. And now. You can follow me if you like.'

Now that my eyes were used to it, I could see his face in the shadows, not to recognise an expression, but to observe that it was a round face, a country face. He would obey instructions. To the very word.

'My instructions are, sir, that if you offer any resistance I'm to charge you, and give you an official warning.'

'Charge me!' I controlled my temper. 'What charge?'

'Obstructing a police officer in his enquiries.'

You have to be calm in these circumstances, not say or do anything to make the situation worse. There could be no such valid charge, but, once they'd made it, I could be held for twenty-four hours. Which would obstruct *me* in my enquiries! I couldn't afford twenty-four hours, not even twenty-four minutes.

For a moment I considered making a break for it. A backwards elbow in one direction, a quick turn and a straight right in the other . . . But he read my mind.

'I have a man sitting in your car, sir.'

I had a quick mental image of Amelia waiting in the mill, and the blood ran hot behind my eyes. But then I remembered: Davies was there.

In the end, compliance would be the quickest. 'Very well,' I said tersely.

We walked out into the pounding rain. Nothing of the mountains was visible, though their bulk was a tangible presence. A man was sitting in my driving seat.

'In the official car, Mr Patton, please,' said the Sergeant.

'Nobody's driving my car. I'll follow you.'

He laughed. I knew it was hopeless. I bent to the open door of the Stag. 'You'll need to double de-clutch on third to second,' I told him. 'And it pulls to the left on braking.'

'I'll remember that,' said the young man.

'And if you wreck my car I'll have your teeth out.'

'That too.'

'And the roof leaks. I hope you get soaked.'

He smiled, a friendly smile, showing all the teeth he wanted to keep. 'I've already discovered about the hood, sir.'

We walked over to the official Montego, me into the back with the Sergeant. We drove to Oswestry. I sat there, mentally urging the driver to greater efforts, and working out in detail what I would like to do to Chief Inspector Grayson.

There were no formalities at the station, no pause at the duty desk to sign me in, not even a glance in that direction from the Sergeant. He didn't have to persuade me to hurry. I couldn't wait to get at Grayson.

There was a small room, with two kitchen chairs, one each side of a plain wooden table. Grayson was already seated at one side of it, facing me. He looked up with a smile. He'd be enjoying this. Behind me the door closed. I glanced round. We were alone together. When I turned back, Grayson indicated the other chair.

'Sit down. Smoke if you like.'

So this was to be informal, with no third party to give evidence. I sat down. The impulse was to send him flying out of his chair and march out, but that would be playing into his hands. I wouldn't get far, and he'd have a genuine charge to fling at me.

Above all, I didn't wish to allow him to see that any delay agitated me. He wasn't going to get that satisfaction.

'What the hell's all this?' I demanded.

'We're alone,' he said. 'This is unofficial. Just you and me.' He made it sound as though that was a favour.

'I want to know what you think you're doing.'

His eyes were bright. His fingers, on the table in front of me, were still. No nerves. 'This is for you, Mr Patton. Shall we say I've become concerned about your activities around here.'

'I've got a legitimate reason for being in this area. We're interested in a mill . . .'

'I know about the mill. I just think it's time you made up your mind that it doesn't suit you, and got off home. Devon, isn't it? Far enough.'

'There's unsettled business.'

'I don't think so. I settled it ten years ago.'

I stared at him, at my pipe in my hand, wondering whether to ram it down his throat. 'If that's all you've got to say, I'll be off.'

'Or I could make it official,' he said softly.

'Of all the nonsense . . .'

'I could raise my voice, and have a man in here in two seconds, then I'd charge you, and we'd go on from there.'

'Charge me with what?' I managed to speak quietly. I began to fill my pipe, wishing my hands were as steady as his.

'Obstructing an officer in . . .'

'Your duties involve the death of Llewellyn Hughes.'

'Those are the exact duties I'm referring to,' he said placidly. Then he sat back and waited.

I lit the pipe. I'm quite proud of that. I even managed to direct the smoke towards the ceiling instead of into his face, but while my eyes were following it he'd slipped his hand inside his jacket. When I looked down, he had half a dozen photographs spread on the table.

'One of my hobbies,' he explained. 'I'm an amateur photographer. I developed the film and printed those myself. Take a look, Mr Patton. A close look.'

I took a look. They were exactly as Davies had described them. I couldn't understand why Grayson was showing them to me.

'You're admitting you stole these from Constable Davies' station house?' I asked, looking up. 'So you must have seen him taking them.'

He shook his head, sad at such a suggestion. 'Whatever gave you that idea? No. I took them myself. I can produce them in court, and say that the day before I shot those there was no petrol can in that shed. I would also say that I had reason to believe – you being so emphatic that Llew's death was not an accident – that *you* had planted the can there. I would explain that that was the reason I took the shots, to make a record of the facts.'

'And then you took . . .' I lost the sentence because he'd taken my breath away.

'I would also say that the following day I returned there, and the petrol can had gone, you having thought better of it and realised your fingerprints might be on it.'

'Where's the close-up of the fingerprints?'

'There wasn't one. I didn't think to do that. Silly of me.'

'But you can't . . . you can't be such a fool. It'd be thrown out of court. And you'd have committed perjury.'

For a moment his eyes narrowed, but all the same he managed to smile. 'It needn't get as far as a court.'

'It would if I denied it. If you charged me and I demanded a solicitor, and took it all the way . . .'

I stopped. That smile was still there, a little uncertain perhaps, but he knew he had me. I also realised that he was quite aware that Amelia was at the mill, and that he was keeping me from her. And that it was causing me distress.

'I can't believe you'd go this far,' I said tensely. 'For a paltry case, when you were only an inspector! You're afraid of a challenge to your work.'

'A reversed verdict would go against me.' And he meant it. He didn't mean simply his record, either. He meant himself. He existed on his self-confidence, which carried him on from success to success. But that confidence was insecure. The simple fact that he couldn't allow himself to be challenged meant that he knew it. So that this single, simple early case – the reasoning of which he was very proud – meant a lot to him. Destroy his efforts there, and you'd destroy him, as a person.

I leaned back, snatching a glance at my watch in the process. It was late, late.

'I know your case was false,' I told him. 'Duncan Carter didn't kill his uncle. I know who did, how . . . and possibly why. And you expect *that* to remain buried? Oh come on, Grayson, see sense.'

His smile was hideous. 'Can you prove it?'

'Prove, no. Reason it through, yes.'

'Not good enough. Look, I don't want us to bang our heads together on this. Promise me you'll go home. Tomorrow. Promise me that, and I'll . . .'

'What?' I demanded.

'I'll let you go.'

'*Let* me!' I thrust back my chair with my legs, and bent over him. He came wearily to his feet, as though exasperated with my attitude.

'Don't force me into charging you, Mr Patton.'

He knew Amelia was at the mill. He might not have known Davies was there, and he could be assuming she was alone and isolated. He was telling me that he was prepared to shut me away, and have me plead with him to fetch her back to the hotel. I saw all that, and knew it as a deliberate threat.

I turned away to the door, but he'd taken advantage of my few seconds of thought and was already moving in that direction. He stood with his back to it.

'I don't want to call for assistance.'

The rage was like a hot flame through my head, but I could see him clearly. Everything seemed to be taking a long while. The transference of my pipe from right hand to left hand appeared to be infinitely slow. It was giving me time to balance the operation. His eyes were naturally following my left hand, as I was about to leave both hands free.

'Get out of my way,' I said, but even that was very slow, coming out as a growl.

Then I hit him in the stomach with my right fist, watching it move, even having time to guide it. His eyes were still on my left hand in the moment before they rolled up, and the wind gusted out of his open mouth as he collapsed to the floor.

In moments of high adrenalin flow, time becomes distorted. I reached down and swung him away from the door, and was through it, and had closed it behind me in a second. Then I walked steadily towards the entrance.

They watched me leave. They actually watched as I walked past them. Their instructions had been to bring me in, not to keep me there. I cleared my throat. My voice was back to normal. Well . . . nearly.

'I hope you left the keys in.'

The young man who'd driven the Stag smiled and nodded. 'Keys in. Gearbox in one piece.'

I walked out into the throbbing downpour. The Stag was at the kerb. I slid on to a pool of water, turned the key, got gear in and engine going in the same second, and snaked the car out of the streaming gutter and along the black, empty street.

I was heading in the wrong direction, so I took the first left, left again, and continued on until I could cut back to the road I needed. The rain had flushed away pedestrians and most of the cars. In half a mile I saw only one other vehicle, a van heading the opposite way, spray high from his wheels and a rainbow of bouncing mist caught in the streetlights from his roof.

Grayson would know where I was heading. A minute on his radio, and he could have me headed off. I was gambling on the fact that he would not. He wouldn't dare to expose his unofficial activities. But certainly he'd follow me himself. I'd handed him an ideal charge: assaulting a police officer in the performance of his duties. In a police station, too! Oh . . . lovely.

I tried to put Grayson firmly out of my mind. The driving demanded it. As I drove up into the mountains the sky pressed down on me, and within a mile or two I was absorbed by the black clouds. My headlights were brilliant cones in a heavy, grey mist, but as I climbed I realised that the rain was easing. I was involved with its source.

By now the hazards were the effects of the rain. Placid streams that had lined the lanes had burst their banks. I found myself driving, it seemed, along the courses of rivers, never certain where the outer edges of the hard surface might be, but unable to allow the revs to die below a certain level in case the engine stalled. Most of the time I was in second gear, driving hard, forcing on. The car bucked, and I fought the wheel. I held it on the road more by instinct than anything else.

I met no other vehicles, saw no sign of movement at all, only that steady stream of rain driving into the searching cones of my lights.

When I came out at the head of our valley there was nothing to be seen but a swirling bowl of mist below me. I was above the clouds, above the rain. I got up into third, and plunged down into it.

Davies should have seen my approaching beams, as a lightening of the pall. I would have expected him to flash in response, as he would surely realise it was me. As I passed the cottages I could just detect the lights in their windows. I was only fifty yards from the farm entrance, and there had still been no sign from him. The curve in the road panned my headlight beam, which flashed briefly across drooping trees and out-buildings, just flicking over one corner of the police van, and giving me a brief impression of a tattered bundle lying against one of the barns, just inside the yard.

I braked heavily and scrambled out of the car. I'd already driven on a few feet too far, so that my dipped heads were not focused on it. My shadow danced along the wall of the barn.

Davies was lying in the lee of the wall. His cape flared around him, dabbling in the mud. He was face down, hands outstretched, fingers grasping for security. His head was on one side, his peaked cap lying beside it.

I lifted his head carefully. 'Davies!' I crouched so that his head was on my knee. My hand came away sticky. He groaned. I slapped his cheek gently, twice, three times. 'Davies! Come on!' His eyes flickered.

'Rich . . .' he mumbled.

I lowered his face into the mud again and got to my feet. The light from the farm window beckoned. I stumbled across wet cobbles, found the door, and pounded on it.

The old chap who opened up looked startled. There was a shotgun leaning against the wall close to his right hand. He said something aggressive in Welsh. I turned, pointing back.

'Constable Davies is lying by the barn. He's been assaulted. Will you get him inside and look after him?'

He turned his head and shouted: 'Gwyneth!' Then he was elbowing past me, still in shirt-sleeves, rolled beyond the elbow. 'Show me,' he said.

We ran head down together. We bent over Davies. His eyes were open now, and he recognised me.

'Richard . . . sorry . . .'

'I've got to leave you,' I said to him, and to the old man. I turned my head. 'Will you phone for assistance?'

'Don't waste time talking,' he said, and he began to speak to Davies in Welsh, which I had to assume was comforting.

I ran for the Stag and clambered in. Even above its humming engine I could hear the stream fighting its way beneath the bridge. All was a grey, flat image. I took off in second gear, wheels spinning.

The surface of the drive up to the mill had been poor in the dry. Now it was a mush of slate chippings impounded into slimy mud. The Stag slithered and hesitated, sometimes with its nose pointing directly towards our brook, which was brimming its banks. I could no longer hear the engine because of the rush and swirl of the water, and had difficulty controlling the revs. The wheels spun. I juggled with the steering.

It came out of the mist as a dark, angular shape. This side there was only the kitchen window, so that I did not expect to see light. On the final, steeper slope the tyre slip became so bad that I abandoned the car, scrambling along on foot and almost slipping on to my face once or twice.

Parked just beyond the mill was the heavy shape of a car.

I did not pause to investigate. The door of the mill was open an inch or two. I thrust it fully open and ran in, Amelia's name on my lips, but not spoken aloud.

The battery lamp was at her side on the floor, its glow now very meagre. It was sufficient to show me that she was sitting on the picnic chair and facing the millstone, clasping Cindy so closely to her that I was surprised the poor little devil could breathe. She hadn't turned to face me, though she could not have failed to hear my tramping feet. Her eyes were fixed on the millstone. This was the reason she had the lamp in that position. She had to watch the millstone.

She had watched it for too long.

'Amelia!' I whispered.

A tiny jerk of her head indicated she had heard me, but it was the jolt of someone trying to fight clear of a nightmare, and not succeeding.

I was aware of the sound, which had become part of the whole structure. Not the background rumble and roar of the racing water outside, but a harsh, hard sound of constrained power fighting for release, the jolt and groan, the pause, the jolt and groan again.

I followed the direction of her eyes.

The great millstone was moving. With its ponderous dignity of several tons, it moved an inch, two inches, six, then stopped. The throb of impact went down through my toes. Then the groan of release, and the stone rotated back, paused . . . then it began again. A giant hand was laid to it, yet it resisted. The hand persisted. I felt that if something didn't give way the whole mill would be shaken loose, tossed away by the inevitable and unnerving force.

I had to tell myself to look away. I crouched down in front of her, shielding her from the sight of it, and fumbled for her cold hands. It was a mercy I couldn't see her eyes, sufficient that I felt the hypnotic fear that gripped her.

'Amelia, it's Richard. I'm here. Amelia . . . please . . . Amelia, love.'

I was rubbing her hands. She was shuddering, her head moving now, shaking backwards and forwards in rejection.

'You didn't . . . oh, Richard, I just couldn't . . .'

'It's all right. Give yourself a few minutes, then we'll get out of here.' I still couldn't understand why she was so upset.

'But I can't . . .' She gulped. 'Can't go out.'

'Can't?' I asked gently.

She was now so close to tears that I could feel her need for them must be greater than mine for her lucidity. There was a terrible fear for her sanity, and I couldn't stop thinking about the car outside.

'Why can't you?' I asked.

'It . . . it was worse than I expected,' she said, her voice empty. 'The rain. Much worse.'

I nodded. 'No thunder?'

I'd said that to lighten the tension. Her lips flickered in response.

'The noise of the stream outside . . . oh, I got used to that. But then I heard someone driving up, and I thought it was you. Why wasn't it you, Richard? Why, why?'

'I'll tell you, but not now.'

She seemed not to hear that. 'And then . . . then I heard a grating sound and the wheel tried to move. I could feel it trying. Then there was a bang from down below, and the wheel did move. That terrible sound, grating and crunching, and it moved. Slowly, Richard, kind of rumbling, but I wanted it to stop.'

'Of course you would.'

'And then – it did stop, but oh dear Lord, it started *that*. What it's doing now. A jerk, a stop, a sort of breath, another jerk, and I couldn't get away from it. There was nowhere I could go . . .'

'The farm.'

'I didn't dare go outside,' she whispered, and she covered her face with her hands. The next words were mumbled through her fingers. 'Because I knew *something* was stopping it, and I didn't dare to see what it was.'

At last she was sobbing. 'I'll look,' I said. 'I'll look for you, love.'

But, face buried in her hands, she was weeping her way clear of it. On her lap, Cindy whined softly.

After a while I was able to get her to her feet, my arm round her, and I found she was so stiff that her legs would barely support her.

'Get you into the car,' I murmured.

I took the lamp with us, for what good it was. We made it outside. I led her down, sliding and staggering, to the Stag and got her inside, Cindy on her lap again. I tossed the lamp on to the rear seat and reached past her for my torch in the map compartment.

'I'll just be a minute.'

'Hurry, Richard.'

'Got to stop it,' I said.

She knew what I meant. I explored the stream with my torch, flicked its beam down into the millrace.

The sluice gates had been opened. Now the stream was swinging part of its energy into the race, where the bottom third of the wheel was covered. The water crowded and surged to climb over and round the paddles.

It was dangerous to stand there. The bank down to the stream was steep, but there was a fence guarding the millrace. A low fence. I allowed myself to slip down to it. There was prepared access to both the gates, each like a miniature canal lock. I nearly made a mistake. My mind wasn't operating properly, and I very nearly closed the lower gate before I'd closed the upper one.

I now had to scramble up the bank again, when one false step would have thrown me into the stream. Then a trek round the mill and a descent to the upper gate. It took very little effort to close it. The main force of the stream was intended to hold it shut. This meant it would have needed considerable effort to open it.

As it closed, the water level subsided, gurgling and surging against the back-flow from the lower gate. The wheel sighed, then was at peace.

In the light from my torch I watched the water as it receded, black down there, watched as the obstruction was slowly revealed: the trailing legs, the shirt of an indecipherable colour, the hair, still caught back by its yellow rubber band.

Slowly I climbed back, my legs shaking. It seemed a great effort to make the full distance around the mill, and I had to persuade myself of the necessity to slide down and close the lower gate. I did not raise the torch beam to see what effect this had had.

Far away I could hear the wail of a police siren: Davies would send them up here. The mist was surging with blue to the rotation of the car's roof light.

I bent against the door of the Stag.

'I'm sorry, but we shan't be able to leave for a little while. Why don't you come and sit in the other car? It'll be drier, more comfortable.'

'The other car?' Her voice lacked life.

'The BMW.'

'Rosemary's?'

'Yes. I don't think she'd mind.'

17

The key was in the ignition lock so I ran up the engine to get some warmth into the car. Amelia was shivering. I sat beside her, and for a while she didn't speak, asked no questions, seemed stunned. Eventually I said I'd go and see what was happening, but without enthusiasm. Amelia didn't glance at me.

'She was coming to see you, Richard,' she said softly, miserably.

'Yes. To see me.' I thumped the heel of my hand on the steering wheel. 'And the terrible thing is that I knew what she wanted to tell me. If I'd been here . . .'

'Not your fault.' She pressed my arm. 'If she slipped in the dark . . .'

'No!' I cut in. I cleared my throat. 'She was coming to tell me what's been obvious for a long while. Which was that she was the one who'd bought that booze in the boot of her car, and bought it purely and simply because Edwin asked her to. But if she did that . . . Amelia, I've been so damned slow in understanding. Fit that in with Edwin's actions on the evening he died – heavens, we know what *that* meant . . . he was arranging an alibi for himself. The drinks Rosemary bought were the centre-pin of his alibi. But after he died, Rosemary must have understood what he'd been doing . . . must have.'

'You can't assume that,' she murmured, tapping my knuckles reprovingly.

I glanced at the rear-view mirror. Activity was strung out down the approach drive, lights bobbing and vehicles manoeuvring. 'I think I can,' I told her. 'You see, Rosemary herself received one of those threatening letters. As Edwin's secretary, she more than likely opened the one addressed to him. As we were saying, they were bait, to see who reacted. And there was Rosemary, observing what was happening – even helping him – and she saw her uncle reacting like mad. So when he died, she could hardly help but realise that she'd been a party in arranging his alibi, and that he'd intended to eliminate the person who was issuing those threats.'

'And she's said nothing?' Amelia stirred. The dull grey disc of her face turned towards me. 'All these years, Richard, and she's said nothing!'

'Exactly.'

'You *can* be annoying! What do you mean: exactly? And with poor Duncan in prison!'

'I know. She said nothing about what she suspected, and allowed Duncan to go to prison. But don't forget, there'd been that distressing episode with Glenda, and it was Edwin who'd stepped in, just when she needed somebody. So she wasn't at that time desperately concerned about Duncan, and after all they were only suspicions. And she loved Edwin. In effect, they'd come together at a time when they needed each other. She loved Edwin for his inadequacy. She thought his failures as a director weren't terribly important. They'd seem to her to be a reflection of his modesty as a writer. It wasn't modesty – the plays weren't his work – but she didn't know that. Edwin was frantic to succeed in something. He was in despair at the end, and it wouldn't have been at all surprising if he'd really committed suicide.'

'Poor, dear man,' she whispered.

I glanced at her. 'Yes . . . poor Edwin. But you can see how they needed each other, Edwin and Rosemary. Yet . . . and have you thought of this, my dear? . . . the arranging of the alibi and the death of Edwin meant one thing she would have to face. The trap had been set for whoever had killed Glenda Grace, and it was Edwin who'd fallen head first into it. So her beloved Edwin had killed her daughter.'

I heard Amelia draw in a deep breath, but she didn't say anything. I went on quietly.

'He didn't know that, of course. All Edwin would know was that Glenda had already hurt Rosemary deeply, with what had happened over Duncan. Then, at the party at his flat, there was Glenda again, and Rosemary was once more deeply affected. Remember, she was physically sick. That would be too much for Edwin. He wasn't going to allow that piece of rubbish – as he'd consider Glenda to be – to harm his Rosemary. So, he helped her on her way from his balcony. No . . . don't say anything. Let me finish. It means that Rosemary discovered this on the evening Edwin died, and still she said nothing. I said she only suspected who had killed him, but I believe she gradually came to know who and why. Mind you, I think she'd still have remained silent, if it hadn't been for this business with Duncan and the copyright discovery. It changed everything. Her whole life was going to open up with Duncan. She wanted it to start clear of any background worries . . . so she came here to tell me that she was the one who'd bought the booze that was on the back seat of her car.'

Amelia was silent for a full minute. 'I see,' she said at last.

'What do you see?'

'Why you're so angry with yourself.'

'It shows, does it?'

'When you go all quiet, and your voice gets toneless.'

I tried to laugh, but it nearly choked me. 'She came here to tell me that, not realising she'd be telling me who killed Edwin and Llew Hughes. But *that* person realised, followed her here . . .' Her fingers were on my arm. I reached over and rested my hand on hers. 'If I'd been a little brighter, just a bit quicker on the uptake, I could have understood all this, and seen how dangerous it would be for her to tell me, and . . . oh hell, I don't know! That blasted Grayson!'

'He's nothing. He doesn't matter. Don't let him upset you, Richard.'

'He got it all wrong, everything. The time of Edwin's death, the motive, even the means! Think what happened – Edwin spending all evening trying to arrange himself a perfect alibi. He was going to return after a while with beer and spirits on the rear seat of the car, as though he'd driven into England for it, when all the time he intended to drive in the opposite direction. Of course, nobody would be there to meet him.

That wouldn't be necessary. He'd already made it clear he was taking the bait. But he must have been so anxious to get it all correct to the last detail that he switched the stuff from the boot to the back seat *before* he left. And his murderer, watching the garage from the shadows, must have enjoyed a long and happy laugh because an alibi was being created by Edwin, and it was one the murderer could use. A tap on the head, shut the door, and it'd be done. It was going to look as though Edwin had died when he returned, at which time the murderer would be sharing company in the dining room. Heavens, it was lovely!'

'Now you're being bitter, Richard. It's another sign.'

In the dark I turned and grinned at her, at least I uncovered my teeth. 'Yes love, I'm furious. And before I use any of it on you . . .'

'That's likely!'

'. . . I'll just go and tell them we're leaving.'

'Yes,' she agreed. 'Let's get away from here.' She wrapped her arms around her shoulders.

'I'll be a couple of minutes.'

She didn't notice when I reached into the glove compartment, where I knew it would be, and slipped out the control radio for Rosemary's garage door. With this in my pocket, I climbed out of the BMW.

It had stopped raining. The mist was sinking gradually into the ground, and on the edge of the sky the light was reaching beneath the bank of cloud. The effect was of sunrise, though the sun had never risen from that direction. The mill was taking shape, its anonymous menace mellowing into acceptable solidity.

I had taken Cindy with me, partly to allow her a little freedom but mainly so that I could cling to her lead. It gave my left hand something to do. The other hand gripped my pipe. It was desperately important to have both hands occupied.

I found Grayson inside the mill. He was talking to another man, whom I'd never seen, and who was sitting casually on the millstone, one toe reaching the floor, the other swinging idly. He was wearing a dark hat and a short Crombie coat, and by virtue of his quiet confidence I guessed him to be a senior officer, probably Chief Superintendent of the county CID.

They turned and looked at me. The light in there had banished the haunting shadows and came from two portable shaded lamps. It was not bright enough for me to be able to read the expression on the stranger's thin, aesthetic face. I spoke directly to Grayson.

'We're leaving now. My wife's feeling better.' That was in case he cared. He didn't. His reply was harsh and strained.

'You'll leave when I say.'

I listened to my own even voice, admiring the control. 'You know where to find me. We're both very tired, and we haven't eaten for a long while.'

I turned away. His voice snapped out. 'Stay where you are.'

Slowly I twisted back, making shushing noises to Cindy, who was grumbling deep in her little chest. 'Something more?'

'There are charges . . .'

'Nonsense. You're not competent to make valid charges, Grayson. You balled up the Edwin Carter investigation, you've deliberately confused the Llew Hughes murder . . .'

He took two paces towards me. Now I could grin freely, delighted that he was offering me another chance. The stranger's swinging toe halted. He did not raise his voice.

'Grayson!'

Grayson halted. I'd got my confirmation; this was indeed a senior officer. Looking past Grayson's shoulder, I spoke directly to him.

'Do you know the Edwin Carter case?'

'I've read the case papers.'

'Then . . . for your information . . . I'll tell you that I can prove that your investigating officer – Grayson here – made a complete botch of it. Duncan Carter could not have killed his Uncle Edwin. The time of death was assumed incorrectly. Even the wonderful theory of the garage door was invalid. I'm quite prepared to go into full detail. But not now.'

'And this?' A slim hand moved, embracing the mill and its tragedy. There was the flash of a white shirt cuff.

'Rosemary was hoping to see me here, but I was delayed. Ask Grayson about that.' I flashed a grimace at Grayson, who was poised, face set, eyes venomous. 'She was followed here by someone who put Constable Davies out of action before throwing Rosemary into the millrace.'

'The same person who . . .'

'Who killed Edwin Carter, yes.'

'The name?'

'I think I know.'

'Proof?'

'Only theory.'

'Ah!' A thin smile came my way. 'Pity. I'll see you – your hotel – in the morning. Shall we say?'

'In the morning.'

Then I really did move away, and managed two paces towards the door. Feet rapped on the naked floorboards behind me and a fist clamped on my shoulder. I stood very still. A throat was cleared. The fingers relaxed and I swivelled my head to stare into Grayson's wild eyes.

'And ask Mr Grayson', I said, 'how Duncan's fingerprints came to be on the radio that operated the garage door.' I produced it, and waved it under Grayson's nose. 'This one, in fact. Ask him that, when the evidence is that at least half a dozen people handled it after Duncan had tried to open the door with it. Ask Grayson', I said, directly into Grayson's face, 'whether he got Duncan to show him how the radio worked, *after* Grayson had carefully cleaned it. Misinterpreting evidence is one thing. Anybody can do that. But what sort of policeman fakes the evidence?'

There was silence. Nobody moved. I broke it by saying quietly: 'The sort who'd love to shut my mouth by sticking his fist in it?'

The silence was unbroken when I walked out into the damp evening, very proud of my restraint. I could have claimed self-defence.

Amelia saw me coming and hopped out of Rosemary's car. 'You were more than two minutes,' she said accusingly.

'Time well spent. Let's see if we can get the Stag out.'

There were cars and vans parked behind us all the way down the approach track, but I was in no mood to be obstructed. A bit of to-and-froing got me facing down the slope, and I slid and bumped past them, two wheels up the bank most of the time, and coasted down to the farm.

The sun, having risen to chase away the lower edge of the clouds, had tired of the game, and was now sinking behind the mountains. A short day for the sun, a long one for me.

I turned in through the entrance to the farm. The old man must have been at the window, and had the door open before we'd crossed the yard. Amelia questioned nothing.

'How is he?' I asked.

Davies answered himself. They had him sitting at the table, drinking tea. He was still a little grey, but colour crept into his cheeks when he saw us.

'Oh Lord, am I glad . . .'

'I'm all right,' said Amelia quickly, understanding his concern. 'You look terrible, Constable.'

His smile was twisted. 'Call me Owen, ma'am.'

We were invited to sit at the table. The teapot was huge. Between us we drained it twice, that and hand-crafted pork pie followed by slices of spiced cake setting us up, restoring us to normal. I brought Davies up to date with events. His face became set, and I could see he blamed himself for Rosemary's death. I shook my head at him. We both knew who was to blame.

Eventually: 'Are you fit to drive your van?' I asked him.

'Where d'you want me to go?'

'Plâs Ceiriog.'

'Not far. I can manage it.'

We said thanks and goodbye to the farmer and his wife. I knew they would never be our neighbours. Then we drove away, Amelia beside me and Davies ahead in his van. He'd insisted on leading, claiming he knew a short cut, which proved to be tortuous and bumpy. When we reached the drive to Plâs Ceiriog I flashed him not to drive all the way up to it. He allowed me to pass him, and I led the way to the parking patch in front of the garages. We cut engines and lights, and had a conference.

'What've you got in mind?' Owen asked.

I took a few paces to the right and looked up towards the house. The lights were bright, flooding out on to the terrace. 'A sort of reconstruction,' I told him.

Owen's eyes gleamed. 'I've always wanted to be in one of those.'

'They don't always work. Have you got a small screwdriver in your kit?'

'Got everything.' He went to fetch it.

Amelia tugged at my arm. 'What is it you're doing, Richard?'

'A kind of trap. There's a bit in it for you, my dear. How are you as an actress?'

'Quite hopeless.'

'We'll see.'

'But you can't expect me to . . . all those professionals . . . Richard!'

I turned to Owen. 'Got one? Good.'

'You'll have to tell me what to do,' said Amelia weakly.

'It'll be easy,' I assured her.

The garage door went up smoothly when I operated the radio. We went inside, and I put on the lights. As I'd guessed, the wiring ran nakedly up the wall from the external switch, and it took only a second to unconnect it. I ran the Stag inside, cut the engine, and explained.

'I want it just as it was on the night Edwin died. Car inside ticking over, door closed. We'll get Duncan down here – that's your job, Amelia. I want you to walk in – the front door, I think, to make it seem we've just driven up there – and ask if anybody's seen Rosemary.'

'Oh . . . I couldn't. Why me?'

'Or Owen could do it. But it would seem more natural for you to.'

'I suppose so.'

'That's fine then. And when they say no, as they will, and probably tell you she drove away, then you ask Duncan quietly to come down here.'

Her hand went to her mouth. 'Duncan! I'd forgotten.'

'Yes. I'll have to tell him first. It'd be too much of a shock to play the trick on him. Then, when he comes . . . I'll explain what I want.'

'Can I take Cindy?' she asked.

'It'd look natural, yes.'

She bit her lip. 'Now?'

'When you're ready.' I smiled. She squared her shoulders, and marched away up the rest of the drive to the front of the house.

18

The setting was ideal. It was the same time of the year, almost the same time of the evening, with the light about what it would have been then. Owen moved his van back into the deeper shadows, and I waited.

They came down from the terrace, Amelia and Cindy, with Duncan at her shoulder, he gesticulating and talking rapidly, she nodding in apparent agreement but not committing herself. As they rounded the end of the shrubbery he saw me standing in the light from the garage, paused, then came forward quickly.

'What *is* this?' he demanded. 'Where's Rosie?'

But I had to check first with Amelia. 'All right?'

'They're all very worried,' she told me. 'They seemed to know she'd driven away.'

'Anybody say they saw her leave?'

She shook her head. I could see she was close to tears.

Duncan said: 'Will somebody please explain. Why have I been brought down here?' He was trying to hold himself together and maintain a standard of dignity, but he'd sensed something was wrong and I could detect his disintegration in the hunting of his eyes, the wildness of his gestures.

'I wanted to tell you down here,' I said, 'away from the others, because otherwise it could've been too big a shock.' His mouth fell open and he made inarticulate sounds. 'I'm sorry, Duncan, but it's bad news. Rosemary is dead. The millrace . . .'

'She can't . . . no, you're wrong. She can't be dead.'

'I'm afraid there's no mistake. She was drowned in the millrace, and it was no accident. She went there to tell me something which would also have told me who killed your Uncle Edwin, so she was prevented from telling me anything.'

He was trying to get away from it, to be anywhere but there where it was happening, but there was no direction he could take and he shifted back and forth with his shoulders, his feet not responding. 'Oh dear Lord!' he croaked. 'What . . . how . . .' Then the anger caught him. 'Who?' he demanded, and his waving hands closed into fists.

'I think I can show you who,' I told him. 'But I need your help.'

'Help? What can I do . . .'

'A trick. A set-up I'm planning.'

His eyes glazed. It was too soon. He put up his hands and covered his face.

I waited as his shoulders shook, until the hands moved enough for me to see his eyes.

'I want to re-create what happened on the night your uncle died. So I need you, Duncan. When you're ready – when you think you can manage it – I'd like you to run up to the house, just as you did on that evening, and tell them there's somebody shut inside the garage with the engine running. One person will know it can't be Rosemary. The rest will assume it must be. Then we watch what happens.'

He shook his head and turned away, stopped, looked back. 'Up there? In the house? Whoever killed her?'

'I believe so.'

'I'll try,' he said. 'I can't promise.' His face was set in a grim, grey determination.

We watched him walk away up the slightly sloping lawn to the terrace, at which point his legs seemed to gain energy, until he had enough impetus to burst in through the tall window. I heard his voice raised. There was a clatter of response, then they came, pouring over the terrace, Duncan first, the two young people at his heels, a tall man in a cream uniform, who was probably Clyde Greenslade's chauffeur, then Mervyn Latimer (Lights) and Harry Martin (Sets) together, shouting at each other. Drew Pierson maintained his dignity as a possible future knight of the stage, and was not hurrying. Dame Mildred could not, although Clyde Greenslade took her arm. He could have picked her up and run with her, but she was flapping at his fingers, rejecting even his hand at her elbow.

By that time I had started the Stag's engine, walked outside to face the garage, and operated the radio. The door was now down, light knifing round its edges. I turned off the radio's switch and stood with it in my hand, uselessly pressing the operating button.

'What is it?' boomed Pierson from the rear, and Harry Martin grabbed the radio from me.

'Try the button,' shouted Mervyn Latimer. 'The wall button.'

The young couple were the closest to the garage. They operated one button each. The door to the companion garage obediently opened. The one outlined with light did nothing.

'Rosemary!' Dame Mildred screamed. 'Do something! Somebody do something!'

They were grabbing the radio from each other, jabbing at the button, nobody bothering to check whether it was switched on. Duncan shouted: 'I've tried that.'

He hadn't, not this time, but he'd thought himself into the act, and he was recalling what he'd done previously. He jumped up and down. 'It doesn't work.'

Dame Mildred swept her gaze around. 'But why should Rosemary do this?' she demanded. She plucked at my elbow.

'Didn't you know?' I managed to inject anger into my voice. It wasn't difficult. 'She was just about at the end of her tether.' I went across and reached down to tug at the door handle, which was about a foot from the ground. 'Somebody help me, damn it. We've got to get her out of here.'

'What the hell d'you mean?' Drew Pierson thundered. 'End of her tether!'

I straightened, easing my shoulders. 'You try it. You did it last time.'

'Last time?'

'Edwin's death. You lifted the door open.'

'That was ten years ago. What did you mean . . . the end of her tether?'

'Didn't you know? Rosemary had a daughter . . .'

'Rosie!' cried Duncan in agony. He was not acting now.

'You're stronger than me,' I told Pierson. 'You did it before. Grab hold of the handle and lift the door, if you have to break it.'

He stared at me. 'A daughter?' He turned his back to me, and bent to the handle.

I heard comment rustle around the group. 'A daughter? A daughter!'

It was not simply a matter of lifting the weight of the door, the automatic linkage would have to be broken, too. Pierson linked both hands in the handle, one over the other, and spread his legs.

'What's this about a daughter?' asked Greenslade.

'She told me.' My eyes were on Pierson's shoulders. They were locked as he put on the pressure. 'A daughter. You knew her,

Greenslade. I expect you all knew her, those of you who were here when Edwin died. Her name was Glenda Grace.'

Drew Pierson gave a grunt and fell back from the door. 'It won't move.'

'Try again,' I said. 'You managed it last time.'

But his face was red from exertion, his fingers twitching.

'Do something!' Mildred screamed.

'You'll never lift that,' said Greenslade, having taken a look at the other garage door. 'There's a complicated linkage. We'll need crowbars.' He raised his voice. 'Anybody know where there's a crowbar?'

'But Drew did it last time,' I assured him. 'Didn't he?' I asked.

'Yes, Drew,' cried Mildred. 'You did it last time. Don't waste time talking about that little slut Glenda Grace.'

Mervyn Latimer was holding the radio. I'd been watching its movement from hand to hand. I took it from him, turned, and saw that Clyde Greenslade was trying to lift the door. He was bigger than Drew Pierson, stronger in a more passive way, but though his shoulders shook, the door would not move. Inside, the engine ran on, faster now, as it began to over-heat.

'But it's Glenda Grace who's behind it all,' I said, allowing my voice to reach everybody. 'It was her death that brought about everything else since then. Edwin Carter killed her. That's very clear now. He was the only one amongst you all who reacted to those threatening notes. So it was *seen* that he'd killed Glenda. And Edwin died, in this garage here, with the same door closed on his car. I wonder why the radio didn't lift it then. I wonder why Drew can't lift it this time.'

'Older,' gasped Drew.

'I think not. I think that door could not be lifted . . .'

I pressed the on switch of the radio and then the button. The door slid up. There was a fluttering gasp, they all surged forward, then stopped when it was seen that this was not Rosemary's immaculate BMW, but my scruffy Stag. Greenslade shouted something angrily. I walked in and turned off the engine. The fumes nearly choked me. I returned, panting, to the doorway, blinking out at the half-circle of faces now facing me.

Mildred was making 'eek-eek' sounds of distress, with Harry Martin's arm around her shoulders protectively. Mervyn Latimer was trying not to laugh on the release of his tension. The two young people were clinging to each other, her head against his shoulder. Greenslade was tense with fury, deep rumblings coming from his chest. I thought he might be on the verge of running at me. Drew Pierson stood with his face grey, his arms swinging loosely at his sides.

'What the hell's this?' he growled.

'What it isn't is Rosemary,' I said. 'I'm sorry to break the news this way, but she's dead, and a few miles from here. She was killed, because she'd decided to tell me something that couldn't help but lead me to the person who killed her Uncle Edwin. Yes, I'm sure she'd known who it was for a long time, but for some reason she'd decided to remain silent. Until this evening. There must have been a strong reason for her silence . . .' I tried to smile around at them, but it was a stiff grimace.

'A *very* good reason,' I went on, 'because Rosemary knew that her Uncle Edwin had killed her daughter, Glenda Grace.'

Greenslade made a sound of disgust, and turned away. 'Oh . . . come on!'

'Don't misunderstand me. She didn't know until the night Edwin died. She knew then – but so did his murderer.'

'I don't believe this.' Pierson spoke with only a poor imitation of his stage voice, hoarsely, with restrained passion.

'Believe what?' I asked. 'That Edwin killed Glenda Grace, or that she was Rosemary's daughter?'

He made an impatient gesture.

'Well . . . I for one didn't know she was Rosemary's daughter,' said Mildred, tight-lipped. 'Did you, Drew?'

'No!' He said it violently.

'But she told me so,' I said. 'And Edwin killed her. We know that, because of his remarkable reaction to the threatening letter he received. Then Edwin was killed by whoever closed this door on him.' I gestured up to it, where it lay snugly beneath the roof. 'But it wasn't closed with the radio. If that'd been done, Drew wouldn't have been able to lift it by hand. That's been demonstrated. It was closed like this.'

What I did next was based on theory alone. I had noticed that the door, when closing automatically, did so rapidly at first, then more slowly for the last bit. I'd reasoned that it meant the linkage had a strong, but slower, leverage at the bottom end. At the top, as it was at that moment, the linkage would have been at its weakest. I thought. I hoped.

I reached up to the handle on the underside, got both hands on it, and jumped, coming down with all my weight. There was a crack, and the door came down so fast that it almost pressed me into the ground. I struggled from underneath, then lifted it back. Not so easy – that door was heavy.

'Like that,' I said.

'So what?' Greenslade was not impressed. 'Yeah,' said his chauffeur, remembering who paid his wages.

I drew a deep breath. 'I couldn't see why Duncan was unable to lift it by using the radio. But this explains it. The linkage had been broken, that was why, and that was done when the door was shut on Edwin and the car, not when it was opened.'

I looked round, but there was no comment. 'It shows that whoever shut this door didn't use the obvious way of doing it by operating one of the two available radio transmitters. The wall button was out of action, and perhaps that was tried. But the radio in Edwin's car, which was standing right where you all are now, wasn't used. You'd think he didn't even know *how* the radios work. But I was told you all knew that. You were told by Edwin, who was proud of his fancy gadgets. All but one of you, that is.'

'Oh dear me,' said Mildred. She touched his elbow. 'That's you, Drew. He means you. You didn't want to know – remember?'

He shook his head angrily. 'I'm not listening to this.'

'But who', I asked, 'almost came to blows with Edwin, trying to stop him going out that evening – but really testing how important it was to Edwin?'

'This is plain, bloody nonsense,' he roared, his voice back to full strength.

'You haven't been listening, Drew,' I told him. 'I've explained that Rosemary must have known who killed Edwin, because of the motive, which was the death of Glenda. But she remained silent. She loved her uncle, yet she said nothing. Why? There had to be someone who was even more important to her. Just think around, and wonder who that could be. Who else but Glenda's father? They must have been intimate at some time! There could still have been fond memories. Were you still fond of *her*, Drew? After all, you said you'd been a friend of the family since she was a child.'

'Are you saying . . .'

I cut in crisply. 'That you were Glenda's father? Yes, I'm saying that.'

'Damn you!' He was choking, his face livid as he threw himself at me. I caught his wrists, his fingers reaching for my throat, and held him. I couldn't have done it for long, he was berserk, spittle flying in my face, but Greenslade stepped in from behind him and got his arms round Pierson's chest. He was dragged from me, struggling and shouting.

'I wasn't her father! Wasn't!'

'Rosemary must have known. Remember the party at the flat, when Glenda died? Rosemary was sick. She'd seen Glenda there, her daughter, who'd been instrumental in taking Duncan from her, cynically and coldly. Rosemary was sick, and Edwin observed that. But she wasn't sick because Glenda was there. Her reaction was too strong – she was physically sick. And why not, seeing Glenda on *your* arm, Drew? Can't you understand – Rosemary saw you as Glenda's latest lover . . .'

'For God's sake!' Drew gasped. 'I was not . . .' He stopped, staring at me, realising that he was committed.

'Not what?' I asked, and I managed to be gentle. 'Not her lover . . . or not her father?'

Greenslade stood with Drew Pierson clasped against his chest, glaring past Drew's head as though it was my fault.

'I was not her father,' sobbed Drew.

I gave it a couple of seconds. Nobody seemed to be looking at anybody else.

'All right,' I said. 'If that's how you want it. We'll assume that you, although a lifetime friend of the family, were so much out of contact with Rosemary that you didn't know she'd borne your child. We'll accept that. But d'you want people to believe Glenda was your mistress, and that you were committing incest, even unknowingly . . .'

'No!' He shouted, writhing again in Greenslade's arms.

'. . . or would you rather they thought you *knew* she was your daughter, and you were doing no more than escorting her proudly to Edwin's flat for his party?'

I saw Clyde Greenslade bare his teeth. Drew's head was bobbing against his chest.

'Say it!' said Greenslade, his teeth barely parting.

'I knew . . .' Drew whispered. 'Knew I was her father. I was proud. Proud! And Edwin killed her!'

There was a whimper from behind me, then Duncan ran past and began to pound his feeble fists into Drew's uncovered face.

Greenslade's rubbery lips distorted with disgust. He lifted Drew from his feet, twisting him away from Duncan's assault. He was shouting: 'Don't mark his face! Don't mark his face!'

Dear heaven, I thought, did he still believe his prime property, Drew Pierson, would be available for his film?

I heard Owen Davies shout, and he ran forward. I joined him. We struggled with Greenslade, and finally tore Pierson free. Owen was panting. He raised his voice.

'I think we'll all go up to the house.'

Amelia was pressed against me. I took her in my arms, for support. Mine. Around us, they were recovering from the shock, muttering together, shuffling their feet, stealing glances at Drew as he tried to get to his feet and stay there.

'Oh dear,' said Mildred. 'Whatever are we going to do to replace him? Would *you* like to play the part of the policeman, Mr Patton?'

I smiled at her, shaking my head. I'd had enough of that.

Quietly, when nobody was looking, we got into the Stag and drove away.